Tales from the Goldilocks Zone

Edited by Polly McCann

Illustrated by Hayley Patterson

FLYING KETCHUP PRESS ®
KANSAS CITY, MISSOURI

ACKNOWLEDGMENTS

Appreciative acknowledgment of thanks to editorial intern Tiffany Kaye White and graphic design intern Raegan Moran who made this project possible. We couldn't have done it without the editorial assistance of Desiree Middleton. Very special thanks to J.S.H. who designed the call for submissions and came up with the epic title of this book collection.

Cover design by Raegan Moran. Title font is Phosphate

Flying Ketchup Press® is a trademarked small press seeking submissions through Submittable.com to discover and develop new voices in poetry, drama, fiction, and non-fiction with a special emphasis in new short stories. We are a publisher made by and for creatives in the Heartland. Our dream is to salvage lost treasure troves of written and illustrated work– to create worlds of wonder and delight; to share stories. Maybe yours.

Find us at www.flyingketchuppress.com

All inquiries should be addressed to:
Flying Ketchup Press
11608 N. Charlotte Street, Kansas City, MO 64115.

Editor: McCann, Polly Alice
Illustrator: Patterson, Hayley

ISBN-13: 978-1-970151-08-4

DEDICATION

Dedicated to the guy who told us to call it
Tales from the Goldilocks Zone.
Here's to new worlds of wonder and delight.

Table of Contents

Once I found a collection of short stories in an old red cloth binding- forgotten on a shelf. It was during a dark time in my life when I didn't have much hope. Each story was better than the last. Afterwards, I decided that life was full of possibilities and magic and love. I decided I could become a writer, an artist, an adventure. Anything was possible. That's what I hope one of these short stories might do for you. Short stories are to entertain and satisfy. While poetry is about voice, short stories are about choice. They are meant to make readers think and wonder about the character's decisions, reactions and world view. Short stories are great morning, evening and night, and any time in between- and often they become a lifelong friend traveling with you along life's journey.

Polly Alice McCann

AMANDA MICHELLE MOON

writes early in the morning, late at night, and other times when she should be sleeping, usually with a cup of coffee in the basement storage room she converted to an office. Her essays have appeared in Blood and Thunder: Musings on the Art of Medicine, 2nd and Church, and Radiantmag.com, among others. She has written two novels about the true-life unsolved mystery of a pair of Wizard of Oz worn ruby slippers from the perspective first of a fictional criminal, and then of the people affected by the theft. Find out more at www.amandamichellemoon.com.

Eidetic

Amanda Michelle Moon

The black bottle is only two inches tall and an inch around. At first glance, the plug in the top looks like a cork, but is actually a specially made high density chemical composition used for securing memories. I squint, trying to make my eyes see its invisible contents.

The technology was new when Frank and I were married. We bought it for next to nothing by agreeing to fill out a survey a year later.

Is the memory still intact?

Any problems with the memory?

A hand-written label on the bottom of the bottle reads:

September 18.

Sixteen years ago. A special day that would fill most women with worry, I wasn't. I was thirty-three, I'd known plenty of men. Frank was the first I'd ever stayed with long enough to consider marrying. Then it seemed like the only thing to do.

The ceremony was in a city park. We picked a tree to stand under, and my sister had her kids create an aisle from sticks and rocks they'd foraged from the woods. I wore a simple, old-fashioned dress: satin with lace edging at the cuffs and collar. It was white when my grandmother first wore it but had faded to a soft ivory. I liked how it offset my brown hair and the deep caramel color my skin always took on by the end of the summer. The dress was my old and borrowed. My mother gave me a necklace to be my new and blue. "It will match your eyes," she said.

My father wore blue jeans and a red flannel shirt, sleeves rolled up because of the heat, and walked me down the aisle with slow, deliberate steps. No music, but the service was far from quiet.

1

There were birds chirping in the trees, we could hear the screams of kids on the playground at the other end of the park, and the muffled giggles and running from the children our guests had brought.

The scent of honeysuckle and fresh mud flowed around us. The recent rains had overflowed the creek. We were lucky we weren't sinking with each step.

He looked good in the dark gray suit he'd borrowed from a friend. His own light blue work shirt contrasted well with the jacket and navy-blue bowtie I'd never seen before. A nice surprise.

I watched Frank's face as Dad and I paced toward the altar. He had a habit of narrowing his eyes—like he was squinting into the sun—when he became agitated, and that's the way he looked at me now. His entire demeanor screamed get this over with, as he shuffled from one foot to the other.

I didn't blame him. I agreed. But Dad, with his back straight and head high, was oblivious to my feelings and Frank's mood as he stared straight ahead and took stiff, formal steps, ignoring my attempts to speed us up.

Later when asked, Frank would say I'd misread him. He was overwhelmingly happy. So happy he could barely standstill. But no matter how many times I'd relived the day, I never saw happiness on his face. Not once.

It was possible I'd read the situation wrong. Our whole marriage seemed to be one big miscommunication. Impatience was another big theme with us, so I might just as well have been right.

Our marriage. Sixteen years and over. Gone. Dust. Like it never even happened. The only evidence we were ever together was our daughter, Sarah. She didn't understand where Daddy was. Why she woke up one morning last week, and he wasn't there. Why he didn't kiss her goodnight anymore.

And I didn't have the words to explain.

Memory bottling became common in the years after the wedding. I have dozens of bottles with other remembrances. Sarah's favorites to play with are the day I found out I was pregnant and the day of her birth. At first, I was nervous the feelings would fade, lose their potency over time, or eventually just run out. But the salesmen hadn't lied. No matter how many times Sarah uncorked the bottles, the memories were no less powerful, no less real. Every single time they made me cry and Sarah squeal, both with joy.

As it became cheaper, I'd begun preserving ordinary days. Like the pictures we used to take with cell phones, these days when nothing special happened but were so good, so beautiful, I wanted to keep them with me. They sit, displayed like trophies, in a glass case made expressly to hold the vessels. Climate controlled. Special lighting. Protected.

My bottles are red. They come in a variety of shapes and sizes. Ironically, the largest, and most beautiful, hold my nightmares. Terrible images I want to forget.

I volunteered for a scientific study working to remove bad memories from a person's conscious entirely. The idea was to start with bad dreams – take all the bad ones out, leave only the good ones. Ultimately, though, it proved impossible to separate the bad from good; the study was abandoned. A blessing lost its vibrance without remembering pain. Even good dreams held shadows. I received a check in the mail with a letter saying I shouldn't destroy the

nightmares. "You never know what you might learn from them," it read. So I'd left them on the shelf, but high, out of Sarah's reach. She didn't need to experience the monsters that used to haunt me.

All the black bottles are Frank's, and, other than routine cleaning and maintenance, I have never touched them. I was cognizant of the rage that would ensue. His privacy was sacrosanct. He needed to feel like he had things that were his, that he hadn't lost himself entirely in this family, this marriage he'd obviously wanted more than I had.

None of it matters anymore. He' is gone. He won't know. And even if he finds out, who cares? Who could blame me?

With the nails of my first finger and thumb, I pinch the exposed edges of the thin, gray cork and began to pull gently. There is a tiny pop, a hiss, and the cork comes straight up and out in one smooth motion. Shocked, I quickly re-cover the bottle. I don't remember the memories hissing when Sarah played with them long ago.

Maybe I've forgotten. It has been so long since I opened a memory.

I don't understand how the

technology works, or what substance is actually in the bottles. When we'd saved our wedding, we'd gone into a special office downtown. Now they do it online. You put on a special pair of glasses, rest your palms on a tablet, and think about the memory. The next day, a bottle arrives in the mail. No knives, no electrodes, no needles. No long stringy thing being plucked out of your brain. It seems impossible. But, somehow, it works.

Of course, you can only bottle what you can actually remember. They are hoping to improve the technology to recover lost memories and to clarify and correct memories as it preserves them, but in all these years they have made little progress.

I consider going down the hall to ask Sarah about the hiss. Her memory is as reliable as any container, and at nine she has a better understanding of most technology than I do. But to ask would be to bring up Frank. Sarah would want to experience the memory too.

I sit down. The chair, next to what has always been Frank's side of the bed, is nothing special: gray upholstery, low arms, wooden legs. We purchased it at a second-hand store. In our first home it was the only chair in our living room, the one seat we could offer guests besides the ratty couch we'd hauled out of my parent's basement. When Sarah was a baby, I nursed her in this chair. More recently, Frank sat here late into the night when he couldn't sleep, reading or working on his computer. The chair still smells like him. Woody and oily, sweet and clean all at the same time.

I close my eyes, take a deep breath, and uncorked the bottle again.

This time, there is no hissing sound.

I hold the bottle in my right hand and carefully pour a single drop into my left palm. It is nearly invisible and close to being entirely weightless, but it's there, like holding cold air. I curl my fingers, protecting, set the bottle aside, and press my hands together. I rub, spreading the memory like lotion.

The very first time I was able to relive a memory, the feeling frightened me. Being in my body, and aware of my surroundings, but also completely separate from myself. I could move and walk and talk, if I wanted to (I tried once, just to be sure) but I wasn't connected to my body in any emotional way until I left the memory. My mind processed all the surrounding stimuli in the memory, but without registering it. It was exactly how I imagined Buddhist Monks felt when they meditated.

I feel my body sinks further into the chair.

Clear sky, but the scent of rain hung in the air. Exactly as I remember it. But now, there is tension. We had fought. I wanted the wedding moved inside; Frank insisted on an outdoor ceremony. There was a pull between the pride of winning—with the sunshine and the birds, it was an absolutely perfect day—and worry. What if the smell wasn't the rain that had gone but rain that was still coming? What if he was wrong?

I grip the arm of the chair. Something is crushing my chest, shortening my breath. Drowning me. There is a terrible ache in the pit of my stomach like I'm in a car hurtling over hills and around corners. I think I might vomit.

I sit up, gasping, with shaking hands.

The discomfort is immediately gone.

I can breathe normally.

I squeezed my eyes open and shut. Blinking. It is as if I had imagined the entire thing.

Sarah turns on music. I hear the bouncing of her feet on the wooden floor of her room. Dance party. The music should occupy her for hopefully thirty minutes. Uninterrupted time is hard to come by as a single mother, and now I'm wasting it. I'm going to do this; I need to finish.

I lean back and begin rubbing my hands again, slipping back into the memory. Immediately my chest constricts. The pain is back. I gasp, about to sit up again, and realize it isn't my pain. It's part of Frank's consciousness on that day.

The smell of burned coffee. In the corner of the kitchen is the warmer, power light on. The pot is empty. The corners of Frank's starched shirt are poking into the bottom of his freshly shaved chin as he fusses with his bowtie, tying and re-tying until he is so frustrated that he flips down his collar and leaves the ends of the tie hanging around his neck. His head falls forward and there is a wave of relief as he rubs the muscles on the back of his neck with scratchy, callused fingertips.

A low rumble outside the window announces Jack's arrival. His beat-up pickup has no muffler. The exhaust wafts through the open windows as the screen door slams against the side of the house.

"You need a new spring for that door," Jack says.

Frank glares.

Jack holds up his hands. "Sorry. Not today."

Frank flips his collar again and tilts his chin up. "I can't get this damn thing tied."

Jack is wearing a pair of navy-blue slacks, pleated in front, with a brown button-down shirt. The ivory and navy stripes of the shirt offset his tan skin and strawberry blond hair. He is almost a full head shorter than Frank and can reach the tie but pushes Frank's chin further out of the way before he grabs the loose ends. Frank lifts his shoulders to help support his head and Jack's smell fills his nostrils: cigarettes, exhaust, beer and the same bar soap they'd both been using since they were kids.

"You ready?"

Frank understands Jack is asking about the marriage not about the wedding. "Absolutely,"

he says. A sudden pain stabs him in the stomach, taking the air out of his lungs.

"It's not that tight," Jack says, straightening the sides of the now tied tie. He sticks his finger between the knot and Frank's Adam's apple to prove his point.

"No," Frank grunts. He won't show pain, even as he's holding his lurching stomach. "It's fine. Thanks."

"You've got butterflies." Jack claps Frank on the shoulder. It is the closest these brothers ever get to an actual hug. "Let's go."

"Give me a minute, I'll be right out."

The memory becomes fuzzy, almost like a dream, as they all do in the middle. A mixture of smells and thoughts and emotions all jumbled together, simultaneous images of Jack cranking the stereo in his truck and a few leaves falling gently out of the oak tree in the front yard. The small crowd gathered for the ceremony, the scent of someone grilling at the other end of the park, and the sound of Frank's dining room chair scraping on the linoleum floor as he sits down, the scratchy stiffness of the shirt against his chest and arms. The soft satin of my dress under his fingers.

The feel of my hip bones under his thumbs, hands holding my body to his. A whiff of lavender. A taste of mint.

The tangle lasts so long I begin to come to the present, worried this memory is defective and won't continue. I've heard of it happening, but never experienced it myself. Tears threaten corners of my eyes as I rub my hands together again. The memory can't be broken. It's all I have left.

I grab the bottle, pour more than I'm supposed to. Fill my palm, catching a drop just before it lands on my jeans. I wash my hands with the liquid, grasping tighter and rubbing harder than before. When the weight settles over me again it is heavier, pressing me back, pinning me to the chair. I am back in Frank's house, but I'm not watching him anymore. No longer an invisible bystander, I am with him, moving, feeling, being. I am him.

He checks—I check—his—my pockets: ID, credit card, ring. Everything I need. But something is wrong. The emptiness, the pain. It has been coming and going, always growing more intense, for weeks. I know what it is. I've broken the rules, texting my bride-to-be:

I love you. I can't wait to marry you today.

A moment later my phone buzzed with her response.

:-)

A smiley face. It should have been more enthusiastic. At the very least, admonishment for breaking tradition by making contact. I'm not surprised. She has been more excited about being engaged and married than about the actual ceremony. Every time she's assured me, she can't wait for us to be married, there's been a nagging in the back of my mind. The hole opening in the pit of my stomach.

I need her. Like she's a part of my body. I ache with physical pain when we're apart for more than a day or two. I sneeze and cough when she has a cold.

I know she doesn't feel as deeply.

But she does love me.

She does.

Right?

I might be her fallback plan, but it's been five years, and she said she's ready. Being with her is all I've wanted.

Is it enough?

What if another option came along? Would she still choose me?

Do I care?

It's not even really a question.

She hadn't even wanted a real ceremony. A justice of the peace would have been fine, she'd said. A marriage license to make the relationship official, that's all she wanted.

Her promise wasn't for forever, but for now. To file joint taxes and be each other's emergency contact.

Maybe I should call it off.

Walk out to Jack's truck, drive over to the park, tell everyone. Be a man about it.

She wouldn't be surprised. Probably not even disappointed.

I pick up my phone and her face fills the screen. Windblown hair, sunglasses perched on the tip of her nose, shining blue eyes that cut to the right in annoyance. Annoyed with me when I took it, there's a smile playing on the edge of her lips.

My stomach lurches, worse this time, and I barely make it to the toilet before this morning's bacon and eggs are swimming. The heaving stops. I wet a washcloth with cold water and mop sweat from my forehead and cheeks.

I can't call it off.

It doesn't matter if she loves me.

I love her, and she's choosing me. At least for today.

I'll take what I can get.

I am jerked back to reality. I don't know what tore me out of the memory, other than the crushing in my chest. This time, it doesn't lift as I become fully conscious. It becomes worse. My breaths are short, my lungs refuse to inflate.

He knew.

He knew the whole time.

I'd tried to love him, I really had, reasoning he was good for me. Back then I was looking for something better. Maybe I'd never stopped.

It wasn't even about Frank. It was about our town, our life, so repetitious, so exactly what I had been determined to grow up and avoid. My mother said it was normal to wonder what might be "out there" for me. Wherever "out there" was. Frank felt the same. It was an understanding we had.

At least, that's what I thought.

When he left, I wasn't surprised it was over. Just that he'd found a way out before I did.

I cork the bottle and stand to put it back on the shelf. The top is askew. I reposition it, to hold the seal. Someday this will be Sarah's memory, too. When she is older and I can explain it to her.

It's time to move on with my day. With my life.

But my mind won't stop. The thoughts nag: Why did he go through with it? Why did he marry me at all? Why did he stay for sixteen years if he knew all along?

The cork is still crooked. I pull it out. The motion might be involuntary, tilting until a single drop hits the tip of my forefinger. Rubbing it gently with my thumb, I am torn. I cannot lose myself in the past.

But I want to know.

Jack shouts from the truck, "Yo, bro, it's time to go!" then cackles at his own joke.

Frank stands from the table, pushes the chair in. He shuts off the coffee pot and leaves. On the way out the door, he stops to shut off the coffee pot.

In the truck, he lays his suit jacket across his knees to make sure it doesn't touch the dirty floor. Jack revs the engine, pulls away from the curb. He says something, but Frank can't hear and doesn't ask for a repeat.

They ride in silence, heads bobbing simultaneously with the radio, all the way to the park.

"Wait here," Jack says, jumping out his door. He reaches into a cooler in the bed and pulls out two brown bottles. "Want one?"

Frank shakes his head and watches children using the makeshift aisle as a racetrack. Their tiny feet flatten the grass and give the aisle definition. It is perfect. He opens his door and gets out as Jack approaches with the minister.

"We're all set. She'll be here in five minutes," Jack says.

"Congratulations," Father Thomas says, extending his hand.

"Thank you." Frank takes the hand, surprised as always by the older man's grip. Father has to be pushing seventy. He's been leading the parish since long before Frank was born, he'd even baptized him as a baby. Even though Frank never went to church, Father said, "It would be an honor" when Frank asked him to officiate the ceremony.

The crowd is mostly the bride's family: aunts, uncles, cousins...people Frank has met but can't distinctly remember. His own parents died so long ago he barely feels their absence except on days like this.

A little girl peeks at him from behind her mom. He waves. She smiles and hides her face in the woman's skirt. Frank doesn't recognize either of them.

Father Thomas nudges him slightly with his elbow. "It's time," he says.

Frank follows Father Thomas to the altar. The crowd quiets. All but the smallest children are still.

He doesn't see where she came from, but all heads swivel as if on cue and suddenly there she is, on her father's arm, beginning the slow, steady walk down the aisle. It isn't the step-together-step-together march of a formal ceremony, but a deliberate, reliable trek closer and closer to him. The bride holds her head up but keeps her eyes on the ground a few steps in front of her feet. She doesn't meet Frank's eyes.

Frank doesn't care. He is mesmerized, unconsciously rocking from the balls of his feet to the heels, swaying with the breeze. Even knowing what he knows, confirmed by the fact that she won't look up to meet his eyes, he swells with pride. This beautiful, perfect woman is his. Maybe he isn't her first choice, but she is choosing him. For however long he has, he will love her more than life itself.

He refuses to let any doubt or fear register as he repeats his vows with conviction, promising he will make her happy. His love will be enough for the both of them until she finds her own.

The memory fades out, as they do, slowly, leaving me in the present. Frank had known, and he'd married me, anyway. I tried many times over the years to tell him, to explain how I felt. He refused to listen, always interrupting to assure me of his love. It was infuriating. I didn't think he understood.

I gave up after Sarah was born, resigned myself to the life we were building. Even if it wasn't what I wanted, it was a good, happy life. I'd reminded myself to appreciate it.

And, slowly, I had begun to love our life together. So gradual, I didn't realize it while it was happening. One morning, I woke up and reached across the bed for his hip. I chose to be the one to initiate the pull of our bodies together.

The sheets were cold. I opened one eye and saw his side of the bed was empty.

Wrapping myself in a robe to shield against the February cold, I padded to the kitchen where I knew he would be, drinking his morning coffee.

It had been sixteen years.

Today would be the first time I would say "I love you," first.

Not "I love you, too."

Not a response.

A statement.

But the kitchen was empty, the coffee pot cold.

And he was still gone. ✎

"I close my eyes, take a deep breath, and uncorked the bottle again." — Eidetic

AMY BERNSTEIN

writes fiction for the stage and the page. Her work explores
collisions and conflicts between politics and culture, telling
stories of winners and losers in a wide variety of settings. Much
of Amy's work is not realistic, but that does not mean it isn't
real. She aims to portray universal emotional truths in a wide
array of unexpected settings, including a farm where a talking
cow is hellbent on revolution; a bakery where a young woman
turns into a cake; and a suburban backyard transformed by
a sea of tents filled with jobless Americans. Amy writes from
home in concentrated bursts, bracketed by periods of thinking
and plotting, but no writing. And then there are days when she
doesn't think or write but binge-watches TV instead. Responding
to rejection is a constant challenge; Amy's solution is to keep
writing–defiantly. Several of Amy's plays are available on
newplayexchange.org.

Water Always Glints in the Sun

Amy Bernstein

Vera rotates her silent-running, fuel-cell-powered skiff until she's facing B-Harbor Sector One. She comes to a full stop. After fifteen years as a water stabilization specialist, this particular view still triggers a welcome twinge of joyous mystery, especially at night. The Twin Pyramids: the tips of two translucent triangles—one light, one dark–believed to have once been part of a museum for fish. It's a miracle they've survived, after all that's happened here. Hover-lights move in tandem with the rippling water, continually illuminating the glassy pyramids from above, reminiscent of how the North Star guided sailors in ancient times. From out here, what remains of the mainland…of solid soil, is out of view; B-Harbor, the commercial hub of Sector One, is a tangled flow of hydro-highways, streams, and inlets, punctuated by irregularly shaped man-made structures of all sorts—beautiful ruins—whose origins and purposes are long forgotten. The past is an undiscovered country, Vera once read. All we can ever do, she thinks, is reinvent the past through the lens of the present—the only reality we truly know.

And what Vera knows, for sure, is that B-Harbor must be protected at any cost. It's the beating heart of the entire Baltimore Watershed—and the Atlantic Central Coastline's undisputed center of power, commerce, and culture. With so much soil and shoreline lost over the last century—most of Delmarva, all of Annapolis, and so much more, including Hooper's Island, Smith Island, Jane's Island, Kent Island, Pasadena, Centerville, Crisfield, and Dundalk, just for starters—everyone in the mid-coast region has coalesced around Baltimore. Even Washington, D.C., has reverted to the uninhabitable swampland it once was. Nature, it seems, saw fit to restore Baltimore to its former colonial status as a bustling seaport. Vera appreciates the irony, even if the history of its people, their struggles and fates, are murky now.

To the west, she can just make out the shadowy contours and turquoise glow of the Camden Yards Aqua & Education Center. Vera spent countless hours there as a kid, studying hydrology and enviro-engineering with her peers, while also perfecting her backstroke and butterfly in the enormous bowl-shaped pool that Baltimore rightly claims as largest, and best, on the Coastline. Vera could easily draw a map from memory of the rest of B-Harbor: The office and restaurant barges. The apartment towers rising atop extendable hydraulic pilings that remind her of a flock of black-winged stilt birds. And the tourist water-respites— barges tricked out to mimic old-fashioned land-based hotels, dotted with fake trees and grass.

But enough of this. If all goes as planned tonight, Baltimore will still be around in the morning, ready to be appreciated with fresh eyes. Vera forces herself to look away from home and turns the skiff toward the Key Bridge Remnant. Thousands of hover-light beams form neat lanes arrayed across the open water as far as the eye can see. Ordinarily, these lanes are teeming with Sector-bound vessel traffic. But tonight, only essential personnel are permitted out here, and Vera, as the newly appointed Chief of Sector One, is as essential as they come. Tonight, Vera's sleek skiff is the only vessel generating any wake and very little at that. She looks skyward: No stars. When are there ever stars? The hover-lights obscure the sky, laying down a carpet of white light as far as the human eye can see. Vera hasn't seen stars since that long-ago night out at Deep Creek Lake, which is, after all, still a lake, bounded by soil. That glimpse of Orion's Belt was astounding...but enough, she reminds herself again.

"Thea," Vera calls to her AI-Mate. "Set a course for the coordinates where the initial breach is most likely to occur."

"Course set," Thea responds. "Bonner, Coffey, and Steiner are there now."

"Thea," Vera says, her body tensing, because she already knows the answer to her next question. "Has the Council approved my request to put Sector One on high alert?"

"No." Thea responds. "The Council's most recent ruling, setting new speed limits for Class D skiffs, had been issued 46 hours ago."

Damn, Vera thinks. Damn their caution and complacency and trivial obsessions. It's one thing to trust her and the Pod—Bonner, Coffey, and Steiner—to get the job done. But this isn't just any job. And doesn't the public have a right to know, and a right to prepare for an emergency evacuation? Yet all any of us has been told is that the hydro-lanes are closed tonight for routine maintenance. This isn't right. It's my home, too, Vera thinks, and my parents and my brother are just as much at risk. Yet the Council, in its infinite wisdom… Stop, she tells herself. Just stop.

Vera's skiff picks up speed and makes a bee-line for Regional Hydropower Management System 3, roughly 75 nautical miles from B-Harbor Sector One. This morning's data showed a 99.3 percent probability that RHM 3, the largest system of its series in Maryland, most of it looming four kilometers below the surface, is on the verge of breaking down. And if that happens, B-Harbor's carefully integrated hydro-ecosystem will be overwhelmed,

triggering a cascading failure of drinking water, storm water, and wastewater treatment systems. A total disaster. Technology only takes you so far in this world, as Vera and the Pod know well. Ultimately, nature wins. Humans, she thinks grimly, are lucky to come in a distant second. By this time tomorrow, second place had better look a lot like winning.

Vera pulls up alongside the coordinates of RHM 3's surface-level sensor control unit. Bonner, Coffey, and Steiner, dressed in identical bio-wetgear suits, are standing together in a single, bobbing skiff. They could almost be triplets, with their shaved heads—by far, the most practical way to perform water work. All three have the lean, hungry demeanor of people who live on high alert. Ah, the Pod—the ones Vera counts on to read the tides, track the algae blooms and nutrient cycles, monitor the data, and even smell the roiling water with their very own noses. There's still something to be said for the human factor. And for trust: the four of them grew up together on these waters, and together, entered the ranks of top Coastline specialists. Vera could never have been tapped for Chief without their unqualified support.

"Hail to the Chief," Bonner says.

"Hilarious," Vera retorts. "Where's my suit?"

"Uh, Vere, you shouldn't go down," Coffey says.

"Oh, I'm going down," Vera replies. "C'mon. My suit. We're wasting time."

"Think about it, Vera," Steiner says. "You can't implement and manage at the same time."

"Seriously," Bonner counters. "We need you topside, working with Thea on the data as it comes in."

"You know Thea can work with me anywhere," Vera says. "Besides, I cleared all this with the Council. I told them I had to see for myself. They wanted us to send the bots down alone, but I convinced them we need human eyes on this."

"Which is why we are here," Coffey huffs. "When are you gonna start acting like a Chief?"

"When are you three gonna stop treating me like I've sprouted two heads?" Vera snaps.

"What did I tell you?" Steiner says to Bonner and Coffey, as the three exchange a knowing look.

Vera studies them. A small smile plays at the corner of her lips. "OK, OK, I get it," she says. "I hate being sidelined. Why should I miss all the fun?"

"Hey," Steiner says, "you've got a job to do, and so do we."

"We're still the Pod," says Bonner.

"Still joined at the hip, like it or not," Coffey says, rolling his eyes.

"Womb to tomb," Vera says, smiling. There's nobody she'd rather be in the soup with, right now. "But I'm not kidding. Give me a bio-suit."

"No," comes the unison response.

Thea cuts off further debate. "Optimal dive and inspection time begins in four minutes and 16 seconds," the AI-Mate says, for everyone to hear. "Time to RHM 3 failure is now seven hours, 32 minutes, and 11 seconds."

"Thea, what's the current probability of failure?" Vera asks.

"Sensor data shows probable failure has risen to nine-nine-point six."

"It's go time," Vera says. When she was six, she watched a holo-story about a boy who put his finger in a dike—a defensive seawall, she thought, even then—to keep the waters from engulfing the boy's village. That image, of water ready to morph from the stuff of everyday life into a life-threatening weapon, has been with her ever since. And she knows it's why she is where she is this very minute.

The Pod plunges overboard and Vera activates her bio-vest—a highly calibrated sensor-capture garment that keeps her warm on a cold night over open water while filtering all the relevant data she needs to keep on top of the situation as it evolves. She looks out across the lane of hover-lights that vanish from view as they stretch back toward home, toward B-Harbor. Thousands of families in their stilt-raised apartments, relaxed and unaware, are tucking their children into bed, while tourists settle onto artificially turfed patios, sipping cocktails. Vera imagines her younger brother Geoff enveloped by a holo-movie, completely unaware that tonight everything could go wrong. Where are the Council's priorities? Vera wonders, shaking her head.

For the next several hours, she casts politics aside, as she and the Pod, working in tandem with a focus on identifying the cause of the impending breach—whether the problem is structural or a rare network error—and figuring out how to stop it before passing the point of no return. From her skiff on the surface, all is calm: the night is cold and clear, illuminated only by the hover-lights beaming across the water as it slaps the boat. Thea projects a holographic image above the bow, so Vera can follow Bonner, Coffey, and Steiner as they fan out to inspect each centimeter of the hulking RHM 3, its murky bulk looking something like a sunken treasure ship.

"Not to rub it in," Bonner says from below, "but it's a beautiful night down here."

"Which is worrisome," Coffey adds. "What are we missing?"

"Time check?" Steiner asks.

"Two hours, 47 minutes to probable failure," Thea reports.

"Check the heat sensors again," Vera says. Hundreds of temperature sensors cover the titanium-Q exterior of RHM 3 to help stabilize turbidity and other factors that could stress the carefully calibrated ecosystem surrounding B-Harbor, and by extension, all of Sector One.

"I detect no sensor anomalies outside of normal tolerances," Thea reports.

"Visual, tactile, and instrument

inspections reveal nothing out of the ordinary," says Steiner. Bonner traces a question mark in the water. Vera looks up into the night sky, wishing that just one star would poke through. This whole situation makes little sense. If this infrastructure fails—for whatever reason—a flood of pathogens, chemicals, and algal toxins will invade the life support systems at B-Harbor with an overpowering whoosh. And Vera cannot imagine allowing that to happen on her watch; cannot fathom a world without Baltimore, which for centuries has fought off enemies from outside and inside its own borders, always reinventing itself as a stronger, better, more dynamic metropolis each time. Including now.

She has a sudden thought. What if there's nothing wrong with RHM 3? What if the problem lies with Thea? Technology: infallible until it's not. "Thea," she says, "run a self-diagnostic on your own diagnostics."

"Good idea," Coffey replies. "We're running out of ideas."

"And time," Bonner says.

"Thanks, Captain Obvious," Steiner adds. "Seriously, though. We've cross-checked all our calibrations and everything seems to be working."

"You must be tired," Vera says. "Come on back."

"Vera, I think we should stay below until we figure out what's going on," Bonner says.

"Bonner," says Vera. "I'm the one with two heads, remember? I'm not asking."

"OK, tyrant," says Coffey.

"Lord and master," adds Steiner.

"Hah-hah," Vera says.

"Self-diagnostic protocol review completed," Thea reports. "No internal malfunctions found."

That settles it. The Pod resurfaces together and board Vera's skiff. The four of them hug, wordlessly, the bio-suits dripping onto the shallow deck. "Stow your wet gear here, jump back into your skiff, and take a breath," Vera says. "You've done all you can." They nod, their faces drained with exhaustion. The bio-suits' advanced breathing ports let you remain underwater for up to 24 hours, but human energy still has its limits. While the others regroup in their own skiff, Vera quickly and quietly replaces her bio-vest with one of the discarded bio-suits, still wet on the outside, warm on the inside. As she tilts backward into the water with a small splash, she sees the first sliver of pink morning light on the eastern horizon.

"Sector 1 Chief is zero point five kilometers below the surface and descending," Thea reports.

"No, no, no, no," says Coffey.

"She's going to do something rash," Steiner says as he grabs the side of the skiff.

"Not rash, stupid," says Bonner.

"This is like that time she dared us to take our skiffs over the Grand Waterfall, out by Cunningham," Coffey says. "That was really, really stupid."

"And if we hadn't been there..." Steiner adds. The three stand in the bobbing skiff, each deciding just how far Vera will go to find whatever it is they've been searching for all night.

"She doesn't trust you, Thea," says Bonner.

"What about us?" Steiner says. "Why can't she—"

"Thea, show us Sector One's Chief," Coffey says. Thea projects a holo-view of Vera, heading toward RHM 3, propulsion bubbles streaming behind her.

"So friggin' arrogant," Steiner states. "It's not our fault if—"

"Shut up," Bonner snaps.

Vera is now abreast of RHM 3. Right about now, they're telling each other I'm an idiot. Or arrogant. Or both. But deep down, they know that's not it. After all, it's our home.

Vera surveys the area next to RHM 3 that she knows her colleagues—and Thea—have scoured. The answer isn't here. She doesn't think she's smarter. Actually, she suspects she might be more sentimental. About saving B-Harbor. And Baltimore. And all of Sector 1. Or even just Geoff. And they all distrust sentiment. Feelings. Because, their primary shared language is science. But she speaks.

"Where's she going?" Steiner asks.

"Wherever it is, we've already been there," Bonney says.

"Thea," Steiner says. "Thea..." But they don't know what's left to ask, what they — let alone Thea — can say that will protect, or even save, Vera, if it comes to that.

"You know she's gonna do what she's gonna do," Coffey says, rubbing Steiner's shoulders. The Pod stands there, unsure how to help their friend and leader.

"Sector One Chief has arrived at RHM 3," Thea reports. The Pod watches the holo-projection over the bow, the dawn beginning to illuminate the scene.

"Time to failure?" Vera's first words since her descent.

"Thea don't—" Bonner says.

"Thirty minutes and 52 seconds," Thea responds because that's what she does.

Vera scans the enormous, irregular circumference of RHM 3 and feels her ways along its walls, looking for anything, any anomaly, that might solve this puzzle. And then she sees a shadowy darkness, darker than the surrounding water, yet not entirely dark, as if something is moving, creating a deep-water disturbance within a slim crevice between adjoining segments of this life-saving beast. There. It must be there.

Fear does not tempt her as she pokes her arm into the narrow crevice. Dozens of Brief Squids—gelatinous, translucent creatures, with a spray of black specks on their broad little backs, latch onto her arm.

"What's happening?" Bonner asks, peering at the holo-projection. But Vera already knows—or thinks she does. The Brief Squid, a small mollusk, was once bottom-dweller in the lower Chesapeake. But after a century of climate change, the creature's habitat expanded as the waters warmed. And the little squids have thrived. The little monsters love the warmth radiating from the walls of RHM 3, and who could blame them? Vera calmly withdraws her bio-suited arm and regards the squids with respect and even a bit of affection. And then it hits her: the squids have massed on RHM 3 as if it were an electric blanket on a cold winter night, to where they've absorbed, as a group, a significant percentage of the sensor heat, leaving the titanium-Q exposed to the actual elements. And that's the source of confusion right there: RHM 3's surface has become increasingly brittle, but the squids fool the sensors—and Thea—because as little heat-seeking missiles they've remained glued to the wall's surface. So the readings are fine, but all the heat is being siphoned away.

"Vera, we see them," says Coffey. "But—"

"They're beside the point," Bonner jumps in.

"No," Vera says. "They are the point."

"Time to failure is nine minutes and forty-five seconds."

"Vera, what are you—?" Steiner called.

"Trust me on this. I'll be topside in five minutes."

Vera has a plan. Her bio-suit is warmer than the water, and instinct drives the squids. If she can lure enough of them—get them to follow her—the RHM 3 settings should return to normal. Vera slides as much of her body into the crevice as she can, which disturbs the colony of squids hugging RHM 3. That minor disturbance persuades enough of them to migrate to Vera's bio-suit. Quickly—more quickly than she anticipates— the translucent creatures hug every inch of her, in overlapping layers, as if their lives depended on it, as they bloat her body.

Slowly, Vera propels herself out of the crevice. The squids cover her bio-mask, blocking her vision. Her arms and legs are heavy with the weight of so many small creatures. Her plan seems to be working, but it's harder than she expected.

"I get it," Coffey says, as the three of them follow Vera's movements. "Thea, program RHM 3 external sensors to emit a low-voltage charge when anything comes in contact with the titanium-Q."

"Brilliant, Coffey," Vera says. "That's what I'm talkin' about."

"RHM 3 structural integrity is stabilizing," Thea reports.

"Teamwork!" shouts Bonner to the open sea.

"Sector One Chief has just entered Depth Level 4," Thea continues. "Her metabolics are exceeding recommended parameters."

"Wait. She's sinking," Bonner says, alarmed.

"She didn't count on the squids' water weight overwhelming her suit's propulsion," Steiner says.

"We have to do something!" Bonner says.

"You and I will go after her," Steiner says. "Coffey, work with Thea." He moves to the end of their skiff, hoping to jump over to Vera's and grab his bio-suit.

"Your bio-suit propulsion systems are not capable of overtaking Section One Chief at current rate of descent," Thea says.

"Then what do you propose?!" Coffey asks. "Options?!"

"Vera!" Coffey, Bonner, and Steiner shout together. Their words hang a moment in the cold silence, as the pink of morning emerges.

"I'm going over the Grand Waterfall, after all, guys," Vera says, her voice sounding far away.

"Thea, display Vera's life support systems," Steiner says. Thea complies. They stare at the holo-display in growing despair, as if their own lives depend on the readings.

"Oxygen sufficient for 19 hours," Thea reports. "But suit pressurization is failing,.." Thea reports.

"No more failing!" Coffey yells.

"No more complaining," comes the increasingly faint reply from Vera. "Protect B-Hour harbor."

"Thea Options!" Bonner calls out.

"Evaluating recovery scenarios," Thea replies.

"We're not talking about recovery Thea!" Steiner says, his voice rising in pitch. "We're talking about rescue! What's wrong with you!"

"Tell Geoff I love him," Vera whispers. "It's beautiful here. But it's not Baltimore." The clouds as they shape-shift across B-Harbor, are skittered by the wind. The water as it glitters and ripples in sunlight. Knowing that the city will survive to become its next best self, on water or on land, it doesn't matter. "I only wanted to help keep it all going. Just wish I could see what happens next."

Thea pilots both skiffs back to B-Harbor as Bonner, Coffey, and Steiner slouch in stunned silence. The morning sun glints on the water and is reflected off the hard surfaces of the B-Harbor bound vessels crowding toward the docks, now that the Council has re-opened the traffic lanes. By the time the Pod reach the dock, children are being ferried, noisily to their school barges. The tourists are setting off on guided tours of B-Harbor. And Baltimore is back in business, for another day, at least. ✎

REBECCA MAY HOPE

delights in reading and writing the well-crafted phrase. While wordsmithing is its own reward, her weekly writers' group provides the impetus to keep writing and polishing—so she has something to share with her fellow authors. Rebecca couldn't imagine a life without teaching; her middle school, high school, and college students give her a chance to share her passion for words with a new crop of young people each year. When she feels the need to follow Wordsworth's advice ("Up, up, my friend, and quit your books!"), you'll find her playing with or rocking her grandbabies; walking her rambunctious ninety-pound Labradoodle on the nature trails near her home in Champlin, Minnesota; or pampering her softer-than-air Ragdoll cat. Learn more about Rebecca's writing at www.RebeccaMayHope.com.

Time Race

Rebecca May Hope

Sirens wailed in the background when Marcy answered her mother's phone call. Heavy breathing came across first, then, "The boiler in our building just exploded."

Marcy gasped. "Mom! Are you guys okay?"

"The ambulance is here. They're taking someone out."

Her mother broke down sobbing. Her father's voice took over. "We were pulling into the parking lot when—boom! Scared us to death! My eardrums are still ringing from that and your mom's scream, but otherwise, thank God, we're both fine."

Relieved, Marcy collapsed on her sofa. She'd supported her parents' decision to retire to South Carolina, but that meant she couldn't be there for them. After calming them as best she could, she said goodbye and let out a long sigh. Now that the other shoe had dropped, she could relax.

The first shoe had fallen two days ago when, just as she drove past an electric pole, its fuse blew. The bang startled her, and she screamed. In the rearview mirror, she watched a cloud of brownish-black smoke wafting upwards from the pole. She felt the all-too-familiar icy sensation along the back of her neck and across her shoulders.

That frigid feeling accompanied by a bizarre coincidence—why should it explode just as she reached it? — signaled the first half of one of her quirky correlations, as she called them. The second half, she knew from experience, would occur twenty-four to seventy-two hours later. She watched the news for bombings, and her heart beat a little faster when she fueled her car.

A few years ago, while jogging in a nearby park, a balloon got away from a little girl. Marcy hadn't seen it until it blew across her path. The second it touched the tread of her running shoe, it popped, scaring her so much that she rolled onto the grass and twisted her right ankle. The little eight-year-old girl with long black hair called her parents over to help, but Marcy had limped home on her own, the iciness across her shoulders contrasting with her burning ankle. Two days later the right front tire on her car blew out, causing her to end up in the ditch. An older woman, Hmong, again with long black hair, she saw the accident and stopped to help- called a tow truck and waited with Marcy until it arrived. Although she wasn't injured, her Honda Civic required extensive repairs.

It was the closest a quirky correlation had come to threatening her own life. She had learned long ago that the follow-up would be unpredictable—no use guessing what the original incident might portend. It might affect her personally, it might affect a loved one, or it might precede a weighty national or international event.

Things like that had happened to Marcy since grade school—maybe before. In high school, she'd given up trying to share the quirky correlations with anyone. Her friends suspected she was making up tales for attention, so she kept the incidents to herself, recording them in a private journal.

She took out the well-worn notebook and logged the latest correlation.

Part One: Power line fuse exploded when I drove by. Part Two: 57 hours later, the boiler in Mom and Dad's condo complex exploded.

By now she'd amassed pages and pages of anecdotes covering fifteen years of her life.

As she tucked the journal into the drawer of the coffee table, a wave of melancholy washed over her. Two years ago, a month before their wedding date, she'd let Zach read the journal. The sick look of fear on his face when he passed it back to her foreshadowed doom as surely as anything she'd ever recorded. The next day he broke their engagement, suggesting she needed psychiatric help. She'd almost burned the journal after that, but the damage had been done.

She checked her watch as she brushed away a tear. Good— she hadn't missed her favorite reality TV show. She clicked it on, made herself a cup of Egyptian Licorice tea, and curled up with a blanket. At least now she knew she wasn't alone. Every week the program, *It Happened Again but Bigger*, featured quirky correlations involving people from all over the country. When the program premiered a year ago, she'd expected Zach to call to apologize. But he never did.

Now that the program was such a big hit, her friends from high school wouldn't admit they'd spurned her accounts. Some of them had even found a story of their own to tell. Marcy gave them the benefit of the doubt. It was probably a Baader-Meinhof phenomenon—like when you learn a new word and then suddenly see it everywhere. The TV program must have awakened their ability to spot the connected event pairs in their own lives.

Tonight's episode featured a suburban family whose kids were playing in the yard, throwing sticks to a bounding goldendoodle. One stick ricocheted off the dog's teeth and flew toward a toddler-sized playhouse where it lodged neatly into the plastic chimney. Three days later the limb of a tree across the street fell onto the chimney of the neighbor's house. Thankfully, no one was injured.

At the end of the episode, a message flashed on the screen. *It Happened Again but Bigger* would hold interviews in the Minneapolis area next week. They'd make the best stories into episodes.

Marcy arrived for her interview ten minutes early. She'd chosen several dramatic stories to relate besides her tire blow-out—many of them better than any she'd seen on the program. Having one of her correlations broadcast on national TV would vindicate her at last and maybe help heal the wounds years of scorn had caused.

Journal in hand, she entered a second-floor suite in a nondescript professional building. A menagerie of characters filled the waiting room: a Goth girl, several women in sweats, a few flawlessly dressed executives, and a grungy man who whispered to himself. One by one, the receptionist called their numbers and ushered them through a door marked:

PRIVATE

One by one, they left after a minute or two without making eye contact with anyone. With every rejected interviewee who strode or shuffled past, Marcy's jitters intensified.

When she finally stepped through the door, she found

a man and woman seated at a round conference table. Dressed in gray business suits and wearing stern expressions, they didn't look like the Hollywood creative types Marcy had expected. Between them, they exuded as much charm as a single IRS auditor.

"Have a seat," the man said. "Is that your journal?"

Marcy nodded and sat.

"Give us your best story in one-minute flat," the woman said.

Marcy gulped. Only one. She'd practiced telling the one about her sister most, but it required a preface. "It's gross."

Stony-faced, the man gestured for her to continue.

"For years I had a benign cyst on my abdomen near my navel," Marcy began. "It didn't bother me, and it was rather small, so the dermatologist said to leave it alone. But six months ago it got distended and red, so I went in to have it removed. An intern named Dr. Radke was leaning against the wall, observing everything. When the scalpel pierced my skin, the cyst burst." She scrunched her nose in disgust. "The contents squirted out and landed smack dab on the intern's name badge."

The woman remained stoic. "That was Part One?"

"Yes."

"Part Two?" the man intoned. They both stared at her intently.

"Three days later, my sister Hannah went into premature labor and had to have an emergency C-section. The only doctor available was an intern: Dr. Drake."

They squinted.

"Radke, Drake. They're anagrams, get it? And my cyst surgery was like a mini-C-section." She quickly added, "My nephew's fine—so cute! And Hannah made a quick recovery."

The man and woman locked eyes, then rose simultaneously. Assuming she was dismissed, Marcy cringed at how stupid she'd sounded. She should have told the tire blow-out story. She turned to leave, but the man and woman rounded the table, blocking her exit.

"That's exactly what we're looking for," said the man, still not smiling.

"Please, step through here." The woman opened a side door and motioned Marcy through it. "Take a seat, and someone will be with you shortly."

Marcy flinched as the door

clicked shut behind her.

In the windowless gray room, men and women—some younger, some older—sat at round tables. They wore calm but intent expressions as they tapped and swiped the screens of ten-inch tablets. Unlike in the waiting room, these people all looked intelligent, successful, and normal. Two tables were full, but the third was occupied by one man with no tablet. About thirty and good-looking, he rested his chin on his hand, his elbow propped on the table.

Marcy joined him.

"Welcome." His easy smile formed little crinkles at the corners of his steel-blue eyes. He had a stylish close-cropped haircut and wore a silver stud at the top of his left ear. A lilac dress shirt, unbuttoned at the collar, complemented his olive skin.

Still trembling from the terse interview, Marcy asked, "Did they tell you to wait here, too?"

The man shrugged and raised his eyebrows. "They liked your story, I take it."

She bit her lower lip. "I guess?"

"Want to share?"

As she told her story again, more slowly this time, she relaxed. Her companion's friendly interest restored her confidence.

When she finished, he stroked his chin thoughtfully. "Yeah, they'd probably call that a Category 5 pre-echo."

Confused, Marcy tilted her head. "Say what?"

"They grade them. Like hurricanes. Yours is as powerful as they come."

"What did you call it? Pre-what?"

"Pre-echo." He sipped his bottled water. "Sound echoes come after the sound. Time echoes come before the event. They only want strong pre-echoes. So they let most people go."

Marcy tried to quell her quiver of excitement. "So you think they'll produce my story?"

He laughed—a rich but indulgent laugh that suggested she'd made a cute blunder. "Nah."

A flush crept up her face.

"They don't use real pre-echoes for the show."

"But it's reality TV."

"Exactly."

Marcy buried her forehead in her hand, her mind swimming.

She looked up. "Then what's all this about?"

Resting both arms on the table, he leaned toward her. "The sixties had the Space Race. We've got the Time Race."

She studied his expression for sarcasm, but he looked sincere. "Time Race?"

"The show's a net—to draw in pre-echo receivers. Category Fivers like you—they're rare. And they've learned to keep mum. But they're—you are—crucial to winning the Time Race. The show just persuades you to share your stories. With us."

"Us?"

"The government."

Marcy blinked and leaned away. "I thought you were interviewing, like me."

"I'm interviewing right now."

"You're the interviewer?"

"Yep." He offered his hand. "I'm Steven."

Marcy crossed her arms. "Why so sneaky? Are you CIA?"

He let his hand drop to the tabletop. "Our name doesn't matter. That's not important. What is, is for us to master time before the Russians do. Do you want Putin controlling time travel?"

Marcy rolled her eyes and pushed her chair back. "Very funny. Stop messing with me."

"Scout's honor." He flashed a three-fingered pledge, then patted the air with both hands to signal her to stay seated. "Time travel—that's Phase Three. First, we learn to predict the future—then morph it. Then travel in time."

"How? With pre-echoes?"

"You got it." He cocked his index finger. "Pre-echoes are the key—the messages the future sends us. You get messages one to three days in advance." He nodded toward the people at the other tables. "For some of them, it's weeks or months."

Marcy shook her head. "You're wasting your time. You can't predict the future this way. I've tried for twenty years to figure out what my part one coincidences mean. Part two is random—there's no way to guess where it's going."

"Not by yourself." Steven's eyes twinkled, and his lips edged toward a smile. "But by using sophisticated algorithms and compiling data from thousands of correlations, here and in a hundred other cities—we think we can."

"Seriously?" Marcy considered his words. A thrill rose in her chest. For so long she'd wanted to make sense of her dual events. Knowing they meant something after all was soothing yet exhilarating—like licorice root tea coursing through her veins.

"You think if we can predict tragic events, we can stop them?"

A timely warning might have prevented the boiler explosion at her parents' building. Perhaps her sister could have carried her baby to term. The possibilities were endless.

"We can use this technology for good." His brow furrowed. "But imagine if pre-echoes were weaponized. Wars. Terrorism. The death toll would be astronomical. Our enemies would know our every move—and foil us at every turn."

Marcy shivered at the thought. She scanned the room. "Russia's doing this, too?"

He nodded solemnly, then arched his brows. "But our agents over there tell us our TV show finds many more receivers—and better ones—than their secret police find."

Goose flesh rose on Marcy's arms. "Is this military?"

He waved his hand dismissively. "We interface with the Joint Chiefs and many other departments—Commerce, Justice, Homeland Security." He leaned forward and locked eyes with her. "We're this close to cracking the code." He pinched his finger toward his thumb. "But we need better correlations. Category Fivers are essential. You're solid gold. Few people have the opportunity to serve their country—and humanity—like you do. I'd love to have you on my team."

Marcy let his smile warm her. She already felt a connection with him she'd always longed for with Zach. This man would understand, not fear, her uniqueness. She eyed his left hand—no ring. Perhaps he was her true soulmate, and destiny had brought her here.

But an unwelcome twinge of doubt niggled. What did solid gold mean, exactly? Profit? A resource to control and manipulate?

"I know it's a lot to take in." He reached across the table and gently touched her hand. "Do you want something to eat? Coffee?" He nodded toward the counter on the far wall. "Help yourself."

With her head swirling, she crossed the room and scanned the selections. Bananas, granola bars, little bags of chips, applesauce. She glanced back to the table. A man in a gray suit had joined Steven. They both looked at her.

She pretended to study the snacks, but a hundred thoughts bombarded her. The feeling of their eyes on her tickled the hairs on the back of her neck as she rotated the carousel of Keurig pods. Mostly coffee, which she'd never acquired a taste for. At last, she spotted a green-foil label: green tea. It wasn't licorice root, but it would do. She plunked the pod into the machine, positioned her cup, and pressed the button.

A moment later Steven joined her and selected a pod for himself. "My boss says they've run your background check. We'd like to offer you a position. Just a few hours a week to start, but it could work into full time—if you're interested."

Marcy's lips parted in surprise. That was fast. "Doing what?"

He removed his cup from the machine, nodded back at their table, and carried both drinks back. As he set their cups down, the pungent coffee fragrance wafted her way. He must have chosen Jet Fuel.

He blew into his cup and took a drink. "First you'll enter data from your journal into our system." He gestured toward the others. "Like they're doing. But for someone with your abilities, we have more interesting—more challenging—work."

Marcy drank in the praise like a wilted flower. Her current position handling customer complaints for a barely solvent health insurer wasn't rewarding. Simply being appreciated would improve her life instantly. She envisioned herself as a top-secret agent—Steven's sidekick.

He leaned back and crossed his arms, causing the lilac shirt to tighten over his firm chest and biceps. "Sorry, but I can't be more specific 'till you sign your paperwork. Confidentiality and all that."

She tried to ignore his good looks. "Aren't you afraid I'll tell people what I've already seen?" A playful taunt edged her voice. "I haven't signed anything yet."

He shrugged. "You know what it's like to have people doubt your word, maybe even question your sanity. You wouldn't want them to think you're a conspiracy nut, too."

Though his tone was nonthreatening, the remark hit home. There was nobody in her life she could share today's experience with. Hannah hadn't known about the cyst. The sisters had grown closer only when, as Hannah put it, Marcy stopped pretending she could tell the future in hindsight.

Marcy studied the people around her. How fascinating it would be to meet them and hear their stories. They'd welcome her as a—what had he called her? Category Fiver. For the first time in her life, she might fit in.

Suddenly she caught her breath. She hadn't noticed before, but the others wore silver studs in their left ears, too, just like Steven's. She eyed his. "What's with the earrings?"

"Snazzy, right?" He laughed. "They're not mind control. They measure our brain waves and record how they change when we receive a pre-echo." His smile gleamed. "Don't worry, they can't read your thoughts."

Despite his direct eye contact and relaxed demeanor, a warning fluttered in Marcy's stomach. She dropped her eyes. How she wanted to believe him. But she had to think this through.

She reached for her tea, which had stopped steaming, and took a sip. She sputtered. "Whoa!" Vigorously she wiped her mouth with a napkin. "Did you take my tea? This is coffee!"

"Nope." He lifted her cup and sniffed it, then waved his hand before his face. "Smells like Jet Fuel. Not your cup of tea, huh?"

The bitterness tingled on her tongue, but the mistake irritated her even more. How did coffee grounds get into a green tea pod? And why had she ended up with that defective pod? At this exact time? An icy sensation crept down her neck and across her shoulder blades—icier than she'd ever felt before.

She clenched her fists under the table. "Can you point me to the ladies' room?"

He nodded toward a door behind her under an exit sign.

Picking up her purse and journal, she feigned an innocent smile. "Excuse me a minute."

She stepped into a common hallway. After a quick glance back, she bypassed the rest room and headed down the stairs to the foyer. No one followed.

The coffee coincidence had jolted her. The frigid feeling confirmed it as a pre-echo. For the first time ever, she could easily predict Part Two. Like the mislabeled coffee pod, tampering with time was bound to produce unwanted and bitter results. Whether Steven knew it or not, his explanation of the Time Race was mild—and a rude awakening lay ahead.

Without looking back, Marcy strode across the parking lot and hopped into her Civic. She tossed her journal onto the passenger seat. Reflected in her side mirror, a man exited the building and scanned the lot as if looking for someone. No lilac shirt—just a gray business suit.

She shifted the car into reverse, drive then maneuvered onto the street.✎

POLLY ALICE MCCANN

Polly Alice received her BFA in Studio Art from Messiah University near Harrisburg, PA and her MFA from Hamline University in Writing for Children and Young Adults. Her art has been published in US newspapers and magazines and is showing across the US. She is a creative writing instructor with Society of Young Inklings, and a mother of two. An avid poet, writing adjunct, illustrator, and curator- she is the founder and Managing Editor for Flying Ketchup Press where she "curates" galleries of talent inside small sharable packages. She says her favorite thing is to tell stories- other people's, her own- maybe yours.

The Ketchup

Polly Alice

Lane peered up into the rearview mirror. Through the back window the gray. Jeep, she could see highway K rolling out splicing endless farmland and syphons of lush green fir trees of Breezewood Valley. She hardly noticed the blue Pennsylvania hills beyond that, a constant presence. No one was behind her. Odd for this time of day. She sped up a little, just a few miles over the speed limit wouldn't hurt. She chuckled. No one cared about speeding. Everyone did it. But speeding always made her think of Nancy Drew— who never went over the speed limit even when kidnappers were chasing her. Course no one was chasing her. Lane was headed home from an audition. She angled the mirror down briefly to check her makeup. "No surprise," Her mom's hazel-brown eyes stared back at her. Her black hair slightly frizzy this time of day — her lipstick long gone.

Jeez, she had to get home in time for book club. Ironic as she hadn't read the book. When was the last time she'd opened one? When Lane was younger, every week she'd checked out six books out of from the Clinton County library. "Six is the maximum you may check out, young lady," the librarian had said. Lane had turned away quickly so the older woman wouldn't see her tears at the injustice of such a small number.

She pressed the accelerator a bit more. Lane was late. She didn't read the book this month. No problem discussing a book she never read, she'd fake it. It was nonfiction. Anyone could read the chapter headings and fill in the rest. Did anyone read the chapters? It was four now. If she hurried, she'd still have time to clean up and cook dinner before everyone came over.

The road glared with the sun angling downward— earlier this time of year— which made it hard to see around the bend. The trees were turning red and yellow in bursts of unexpected warmth. Zen's radio— she called her car Zen— didn't work, hadn't ever worked since she met her boyfriend, Nick. They met in a short theater course during the January term. The entire three weeks spent on the production of the ancient Greek play called The Birds.

"Wanna go for a ride in my car—after practice?" Nick had asked her in the wings while Lane held tightly to her clipboard and the ropes for several set pieces, mostly clouds, she needed to lower at the right times. Annoyed at the interruption from listening for her cue, she ignored him there in the darkness of the wings.

Nick stood just shy of five foot six inches tall. On stage, a rather handsome dark-haired football player called out to the empty theater, "But you yourself, by the name of the gods, what animal are you?"

Lane shook her head. What would her roommate Shay say if she went out with a sociology major?

"After rehearsal, you mean?" was all Lane could answer while trying to keep the pegboard cloud from knocking into the tall guy's head.

A month later, at the cast party. Lane gave in and gave Nick her number. He wore a blue sweater, tight jeans and leather loafers. She couldn't deal approaching Senior year without a boyfriend. She handed him a drink and smiled. They ended up walking home together. She still remembered the long walks they took often that summer.

On a chilly October night with little stars twinkling in the distance, she'd curled up next to Nick, leaned her head on his shoulder and asked, "What's its name?"

Nick reddened. "What?"

"Your car. Sheesh. Your car's name?"

Nick looked at his bookbag, hoping for an answer and saw his textbook for Religions of Asia, "Zen. Yeah, Dear old Zen— my dad gave him to me. Really close to my dad, practically worship the guy."

"Great name," Lane had answered snuggling close. How nice that he liked his Dad.

* * *

Lane pressed the gas a bit more. She mentally calculated how long it would take to prepare dinner for six. She'd boil the noodles first, not last this time. Ten miles over the speed limit wasn't too much, was it? She needed at least an hour to clean up. Why had she pondered so long over which noodles to buy at Lowery's Grocery— they all tasted the same.

If she had her own car, she could have gone to the store yesterday and not been so crunched for time. This was the first chance she'd had to drive anywhere in weeks. They had bought a vehicle for her with her graduation money from her parents. Against her better judgment, they'd bid on a van at an auction.

"This is a dumb idea, Nick," she'd said as he raised his hand to bid on a large white van that didn't run, and Nick didn't know how to fix things— not even a simple loose board on the back of her dresser when they moved in together. She had the only toolbox among them she discovered, so she hammered the board back on by herself. Nick left the room when he saw the cobwebs on the bottom of the drawer. He hated spiders.

When they towed the enormous hunk of metal home, she'd said, "You bought the van, Nick. You fix it." It just sat there

in the driveway. It broke down on her way to visit her parents. She hadn't seen them since graduation. It broke down on the way to the city, so she'd been hanging out at home all summer. Lane had to take the job at the women's clothing shop in town, Fashion Bee. She turned down the job as prop manager at the theater. "I'm sorry, the commute is just too far right now," she'd answered when they called to hire her.

Most days, she worked at the dress shop, she caught a ride to work with a friend, or walked. It had all turned out for the best, anyway. Terry and Devin, their best friends, lived nearby. They'd moved in right after their graduation party/ wedding. One night over Ramen Noodles and tea, Devin shook her long black hair and tears slid down her face. She said, "Our car broke down, and neither of us can get to work. Terry says the car's dead. Transmission. We couldn't even go on our honeymoon."

"I know someone with a car that needs some work, but I think it might run." Lane thought It seemed like an easy choice.

She pressed the accelerator just a bit more.

In January, over rice and

beans and coffee, Devin cheered up, revealing her amazingly wide smile, "Lane, we're moving to Florida. We'll be closer to my parents. No reason to stay near the college since we don't work there. Everyone else from our class is moving on. We are the last ones left." No I'm the last one left, Lane added silently. Terry and Devin packed the van tighter than humanly possible and drove to the panhandle in the big white van in just two days. No car troubles.

* * *

Lane rechecked her rearview mirror. No one. What was it? She felt off, but she couldn't place it. Only a few pink clouds in the sky. Not a soul on the highway. She sped up a bit more. Never any cops out here, she'd hate to get a ticket since they were broke. Nick worked part time too. Finding jobs right out of college probably would have been easier if they'd looked in another city. But Nick had wanted to stay close to their friends.

This morning like most mornings had been particularly uneventful. At the store, Lane would take overly low-cut women's clothing out of boxes, unwrap them, remove the hangers and reinsert different hangers.

"Throw all the plastic ones away in the dumpster," Lisa the manager said on the first day, tossing her long blonde hair— fried from 20 years of hair dryer. "We are out of storage," she smirked, her long fingers gesturing at the walls. She was right. The back room was the size of four racquetball courts, and every available nook was filled with clear plastic bags full of hangers. Lane could tell what decade the hangers were from by how yellow the plastic had turned.

Today, like every workday, she hung the clothes in their section by size. One side of the store held thin clothes; one side held fat clothes— so everyone could shop there. Lane shopped both sides. Working there was like being beaten to death with a boredom stick. She didn't know how much longer she could take it. Was this all she'd ever do? She wasn't allowed to dress the mannequins or make up the displays. Her degree and classes in costuming, textiles, set design didn't impress the manager. "Only managers can touch the display," the woman said smoking a cigarette in her navy-blue suit, and absolutely no makeup. Her eyes wrinkled up at the edges, and her nose turned up as if to say Lane was sure to be tempted to steal some costume jewelry while dressing the mannequins.

* * *

That afternoon had been heavenly. Lane thought she'd made a good impression in front of the directors. The tryouts were for Our Town. She'd auditioned for the part of Emily. What a wonderful play, if she ever wrote one, it would be something like Thornton Wilder's work: spare, gray and silent with the audience holding their breath on stage next to the actors serving as the silent and lost. Sometimes, she would quietly whisper, "Stage Set" when she would clean their little living room, plumping the little blue cushions on the couch, pretending that another act was about to begin.

It was her first actual audition since graduation— trying out for the Breezy Players, community theater. Sure it didn't pay, but maybe someday after Lane got to know everyone, she could direct, or teach the kids camp, the adult classes. Lane veered to the outside lane to her exit on Red Bridge Road.

Really anything would be better than what she did after work: cook and clean the apartment ... sometimes clean for a neighbor or two. On the weekends, she cleaned for the Scantons. They had six kids in a tiny townhouse. All adopted. Somehow, not able to clean up after themselves." And this is Tommy," Mrs. Scanton had said when they entered the last and bedroom. I have the kids do chores like hang up their coats and backpacks, but the kids don't have time to clean— too much homework."

Lane exited the highway and merged onto a country road that led to their house outside Breezewood. She adjusted to the new speed limit. Now she saw one or two cars. Still less than usual. She slowed a bit. Eight miles over should do it.

Through the thickets of trees growing behind each field, the sun, now sinking in a red sky, briefly blinded her. What would she serve with the noodles? Lately, eggs were often the only things in the fridge. The pantry was actually the closet space under the stairs. It was the most basement-like thing about their basement apartment. The best part of where they lived was the farm next door with its red barn and swooping arms of a cornfield. The farm felt right— like she lived in a story, even if it was more like Charlotte's Web than Thirty Shades of . . . something.

Now, focus. What was in the pantry to go with dinner? She knew there was something. Knowing there were twenty-six dollars left in their bank account, she hadn't bought anything else. She would say, dinner was vegetarian, to save money on beef. Had already used those cans of green beans, or hadn't she? Lane tried to imagine what was in the pantry. She pictured its door opening in her mind and perused the shelves.

That was easy. She often opened the pantry several times a day, staring into its dark recesses that only a closet in the basement under stairs could have. It's one bulb that hardly shone bright enough to light the razor-thin shelves. Usually, there were a few cans, a bag of cornmeal, a box of spaghetti. Her roommate in college, Milli, had taught her a few Ethiopian recipes— which she'd appreciated.

"You can make anything out of this African cookbook," Milli had said one day over a spicy bowl of wat and injera. "As long as you have an onion and cabbage on hand." Who didn't always have an onion and cabbage on hand? Well, she didn't this time.

She was sure the cupboard was bare, the only thing left in there would be the Ketchup. The Ketchup had been the first thing she bought to stock the pantry when they moved in, and it was still there.

Good ol' Ketchup. Lane's dad had been a ketchup fanatic— even more for pepper sauce. Nick didn't really eat the stuff, so she just had it for when they would make hamburgers. Course they never could afford any meat. So the Ketchup stuck around. When Lane added too much black pepper to Nick's eggs or soup, he usually said something like, "Wow, this is spicy, Lane!" Then he'd usually find an "eggshell" or "hair" in the dish so he would have a reason to make a ham sandwich. Whenever she had a fight with him over money, her cooking or getting a cat, she'd stop, open the pantry and say, "At least there's ketchup, so we will be all right." Sure it was odd. Post-college life was hard on the pocketbook, especially in this economy. So what if she talked to her Ketchup? It seemed to her that the Ketchup was her friend watching out for the pantry. The ketchup bottle would be there to welcome more food when it came.

Lane put her mind back to the road. She was driving pretty quickly around the bend by the Turner farm. She touched her ear. Had she put on earrings before she left? No. She felt naked without earrings. And she had auditioned without them! She left her pearl ones on the dresser; she'd have to remember to put them in before everyone came.

A sign after the farm read, "Entering Breezewood County." Her watch read 4:05. She was almost home! She'd take the shortcut around the back way. It was a narrow old bumpy gravely, pot-holed road covered with trees. Even in late fall, there was no visibility to the main drag. She always liked to take this little farm road before turning onto Highway 80 near their neighbors' farm. Usually, there was no one coming, and you could just merge across the two lanes of traffic from the left-hand side of the road.

She was pretty sure this was a good time— a good time not to slow down. As she approached the Y intersection, she looked south out of habit. On her left stood a small fence; a triangular-shaped pen that ran along the road. It often held little black goats. But she kept going, she hasn't seen them in a while.

Wait! Something was breaking out of the fence! Something was coming out onto the road! It was a little goat — a white one. Well, maybe a rather large goat. And it was in the middle of the road! The goats were escaping their pen. The first one jumped in front of her car with the next one on its heels. They sort of leapt like in storybooks she mused—when sheep jump over things to put little kids to sleep. Lane finally realized that it would be close. She pressed the brake hard. Her car skidded towards them. One. Two Three. Three little goats. Time seemed to stop, but her car didn't. She just kept skidding, and the goats continued to prance across the road like some strange animal farm parade. Lane didn't look at the fence or how they broke through. She just stared— worried she'd clip the last little guy because the Jeep had too much momentum. Lane floored the brake...then, in a blink of an eye, they were gone, disappearing into the forest on the other side of the little road.

Funny, how the goats had disappeared so quickly? The car had never even fully stopped—as though time had slowed down a bit. She shrugged it off: no one was hurt, the goats were gone. She headed home. This time, at a reasonable pace. Lane carefully and slowly exited the little back road and got back onto the highway only a quarter of a mile from their house. No use speeding if you ended up having an accident. Those poor goats! She might have hit them if she had been going any faster.

* * *

At home, Lane angled into the driveway to save room for the others coming for dinner and ran inside.

Nick was taking a nap. Poor thing. Work tired him out. She breathlessly called out, "Hello, Honey. I'm making pasta for dinner for the book club," as she washed her hands. She heard a murmur in reply from the bedroom. While the water was boiling, she went to tidy up the living room. Back in the kitchen, she turned the burner on to mix some sauce in a stockpot. She poured the sauce in. Oh no. There wasn't enough. Her pasta would be dry again. It looked terrible. She opened the pantry.

Nothing but the Ketchup. Shoot. Beans were out of the question. Noodles was it. Maybe Rhianna would bring a salad. Yes, she was sure of it. Lane swallowed hard and grabbed the Ketchup by the neck. It would do. Lane opened the Ketchup. The sound of the air escaping hit her in her heart. She stared at the bottle. No one would be the wiser. But why was it hard to part with it; hesitating over the pot, she let half the bottle pour out. It was just a bottle of Ketchup. Sure it had been in the pantry since they moved in. But so what? She poured in a little and put the telltale evidence in the fridge. The bottle now looking just like any other condiment in the cool light of the blue bulb.

Right after six, two other couples came over for dinner. The kitchen door served as the front door to their walk-in basement abode, so there wasn't a doorbell just a hearty knock.

"Lane! The first couple shouted in unison. Derrick and Rhianna, both robust looking, came into the kitchen wearing suit jackets and bearing a layered salad with cheese and croutons. Newlyweds and polar opposites, Lane could never get a clear answer about what they did for a living—taking the train to the city for computer engineering of some kind. She didn't ask.

"We are so sorry we were late," Derrek boomed.

"There was a big accident on the highway. Traffic backed up for miles both ways," Rhianna stated as she put the salad on the kitchen table.

"No worries, you two. Go on into the living room and relax. I'm almost done cooking." Lane hurried them out of the kitchen through the narrow hallway and into the spacious living room/dining room. Though it had low ceilings, everyone seemed to like the cozy gathering of couches by the fireplace and hence why book club was often at their place.

"I love this quilt, Lane," Rhianna yelled. Lane smiled through the doorway and then hastily back to the stove to add some butter and parsley to the dish, hoping it would help.

"You have to hear about this new pattern I found—kind of a take on the log cabin— You know, with those skinny rectangle pieces!" Rhianna said as she came back to the kitchen and began making glasses of ice. Lane pulled the tea out of the fridge and poured while making

what she thought was a non-committal, but positive sound. "Uhuh."

When the kitchen was empty, and everyone gathered in the living room, Lane added salt and some oregano to the spaghetti. Lane pulled the fridge handle to put the butter away, the Ketchup inside the fridge looked, she thought, a bit betrayed. Suddenly, the kitchen door opened without a knock. It was John, tall and skinny like an old dour farmer, with long hair and tiny square glasses.

"Hello, one and all, my favorite friends!" he said generously. Behind him came, Corinne, a recent college graduate in education back in town to visit her parents. Corinne was covered in freckles. She had pulled her hair back with a green headscarf that matched her tattered jeans.

"Hi Lane!" she squealed with a toothy smile. "Sorry we are late. Traffic. Way out here even. Some sort of back up. Thank you for going to all the trouble to cook for us! I'm so excited," she made a little jump in her tiny perfect shoes. "I want to see the kittens!"

"First, you are not late, you are on time, silly." Lane said, still stirring. "Two, this is not work, it's just dinner. And three, we haven't gotten them yet. No kittens. I'm sorry. Nick said, maybe next week when he has. We are waiting for him to have time to go with me to pick them out."

"Nick, why haven't you taken this woman to get her kittens?" yelled Corinne, her teeth white in the kitchen light. "God, Nick, you only work part time, what do you do all day that you can't go get a few kittens?"

Nick shrugged and made a face like he had it all under control as he crossed his arms. Lane wondered. It was like he had a bet with himself to get through the evening with as little words as possible. Like a mime.

"That's not nice, Corinne. He drives a long commute, and then he has to visit each store delivering vitamins, and sometimes they send the wrong ones, and he has to go all the way back to the warehouse. Takes forever. He usually doesn't get home until after me."

"Oh, sorry, Nick." Corinne patted his shoulder. "That sounds so draining. I shouldn't be so hard on you," she winked at him. While everyone sat in the living room talking, Lane busied herself setting the table

and replying to everyone's news of the week with as much exclamation of delight or despair— whichever was called for—as she could muster. But really, she was just so tired. Normally, she looked forward to this all week, but today she felt off. Like her mind was somewhere else.

Dinner was brief as it consisted of only salad and noodles. "Will you give me the recipe, Lane," said Corinne. "This pasta is so unusual." After dinner, Lane made coffee and tea. They sat again on the old sagging brown couches Nick's parents had cast off. Finally, when everyone had a drink, Lane sat on the edge the fireplace, legs crossed. It didn't have a fire, instead Lane had lit green candles in there. Some used ones she found at a garage sale. She thought it looked rather nice like a magazine she saw once.

After dinner was like always. John liked to stand and chew on a blade of grass or a toothpick. Derrick always talked loudly while waving his hands in the air. Nick usually said nothing or laughed in an exaggerated way. Lane hoped Nick had read the book this time. They usually shared the book, but Lane didn't have time to read it. It always seemed to be somewhere else when she had a moment. With his chiseled chin and hair parted down the center, Nick looked as though he should be wearing a tweed jacket and holding a cigar, she mused. More fitting maybe. Instead, he blew his nose with the handkerchief she had sewn for him for his birthday then said, "Dear, why don't you see if anyone wants more tea?"

Lane tried not to think about the rest of the inedible spaghetti congealing on the back of the stovetop or the fact that her feet hurt. So what if she didn't have time to read the book? She hated nonfiction, really. Couldn't concentrate. Plus, she intended to crash with a can of ginger beer she had hidden under the kitchen sink— after this was all over. She didn't listen all that well to the conversation —mentally calculating the minutes until everyone would leave. Finally, one question made her sit up.

"Does this book make you think about miracles?" Derrick posed, always the leader of the conversation with his deep preacher-like voice. Maybe it was his thick beard that made him seem older than the rest of them. Gosh, he was loud. She wondered if the family in the upstairs apartment was also enjoying the book discussion.

Lane scooted down to the floor. Her back hurt. Why wasn't everyone excited about this book? She loved miracles. She listened to the arguments over her head on both sides. Corinne said miracles were rare. She didn't add any real comments to make that related to the book— she mostly talked about her mother and the horrible things she always said to Corinne while she was home on summer vacation. "She says I need to change my major or marry a doctor," Corinne wiped her eyes a bit and smiled with her lips pressed firmly together.

Later, John added that miracles were something that didn't happen anymore "if they ever did."

Lane could see this conversation was not going in any direction she cared for. Miracles happen— what were they talking about?

"I think miracles happen all the time," She started out bravely, "And we don't really notice them. In fact, we might not even remember them or pay attention to them because they happen so often."

"Okay, Lane," Derrick said as though leading a class at

the college. "Do you have an example?"

"Oh, Let me think...Well, like tonight. I was driving home really quickly after the theater tryouts, and I slowed down for some goats crossing the road."

"Oh, how did the tryouts go?" asked Rhianna, "We forgot to ask!"

"That's your miracle, Lane? Goats?" Derrick demanded incredulously, his overly red lips smirking behind his beard.

"Don't tease her," said Rhianna "because maybe the goats were a sign or something. Right, Lane?"

"Goats?" said Nick uncrossing his arms and rubbing his thighs. He laughed to himself, then crossed his arms again.

"Yes, goats," said Lane

"How many?" John asked, leaning back in his chair.

"Three."

"They were just running across the road?" chimed Rhianna again.

"Yeah," Lane paused, closing her eyes to picture the drive again. "I was driving down that shortcut around the old Tuner farm, you know. I was going really... well, faster than I usually

go. They had escaped from their pen . . . You know that place next to that old carriage road. And I saw the first one come out of the fence, so I slowed down, and then I almost had to stop. Before I could, they had all run away. They were gone so quickly."

"There have never been animals there in that pen," said Nick.

"Yes, there are. Sometimes there are goats," Lane insisted.

"No, I've never seen goats there either, Lane," said Derrick.

"Me neither," added Rhianna.

"You only come that way to book club. We've lived here six months, and I've seen goats there."

"It's always been abandoned, that field," said Corrinne. "I know. I went to high school up here."

"Well, now it's not. Maybe the Turners got some livestock when you were away at school," Lane insisted. She stood up so everyone would quit looking down on her and walked toward the kitchen to get her ginger beer. She wasn't going to wait. No she didn't have any to offer the rest of them, but she was getting it anyway. It was her house, wasn't it? She turned and faced them all again, standing in the hallway by the pantry, now empty. The light of the kitchen glowing behind her. "I've seen goats there before. Little dark ones with long ears... These were different, though."

"What did these goats look like when you stopped your car? I mean, did you slow down or stop and get a good look at them?" John asked, fairly putting down his toothpick on the mantle and picking up a vase to look at the underside of it.

Lane came back to the room and sat down in one of the dining room chairs. She cracked open the beer with a bottle opener shaped like a kitten and took a drink. Five faces turned to look at her. The women stood up and came over to her. "I don't know," she answered. "It seems I didn't stop, I just slowed down But now that I think about it, I can't see how it all happened so quickly."

"Tell us what they looked like," Nick said, coming over and putting his hand on her shoulder.

"Well, they were white. They were really, really white. Almost too bright to look at now that I concentrate." Lane rubbed her head. Why was it pounding?

She realized how ridiculous she must sound. Why hadn't she talked this over with Nick before? Why hadn't she thought about it more closely? God, now she sounded like a daffy duck.

"What else?" John prodded coming closer.

"Well now I remember— they were, ah ... smiling." Why was everyone gathering around her uncomfortably close? "The first one especially... he smiled so big. Like he was so happy to be out of that pen." She knew this didn't sound right but Lane continued on. She knew this was even more dumb, but she better keep going, now she had stuck her foot in, she'd tell the truth as she remembered it. "Guys! You know me. I never lie. Nick knows me. Isn't that true? I'm not a liar. I'm not even that funny unless I have a script." Lane leaned against the mostly cleared table with glasses of iced tea and water. The funny thing was that she had never had a memory that seemed to grow clearer the more she tried to focus on it.

"Now look guys, the whole point is not if there were goats, said Lane firmly." She stared at Nick, but he was looking at his cuticles. "There were goats. The whole point is that if I hadn't stopped for them, I might have sped through that intersection, not looked where I was going and had an accident."

The words of agreement Lane expected never came. It was silent. Lane pictured the drive home again. She pictured the speedometer and her watch, the hills, the hay bales, the sunset with its pink fluffy clouds, and finally the goats. It had happened like she remembered, hadn't it?

Everyone shook their heads. John made a sound that was almost a snicker. Nick smiled out the side of his mouth a little. Rhianna's brows wrinkled in concern, while Corinne checked her purse for a mint.

"I did see them… three goats. The big one was the first. He almost looked right at me, but not quite. There were two others behind him. And they were prancing. Leaping really. All three of them. Right in front of me. I was so taken aback. It happened all so fast. I didn't even stop all the way, just slowed down for them. Then came on home. It's only a quarter of a mile from here. I pass by those goats like almost every day, especially when going to the store or back to town.

The room grew curiously silent

except for the candles burning in the fireplace. Lane felt her cheeks turn warm. She wished they had gotten the kittens yesterday. She ought to be on the floor playing with them.

"Okay, Lane." Derrick placed a fatherly hand on Lane's shoulder and gestured as though they were prancing across the room. "Even if you did see these goats, I mean, why is that a miracle? Three goats crossing the road. Sounds like a joke."

"They looked so free and happy—so full of life. It made me think twice before speeding on. I thought better to slow down and stay alive than speed through that blind turn and get hit by someone."

Lane stood up. Now she was angry. "Don't you see, just slowing down on the road— no matter the reason— could be a miracle if it saved someone's life. All I'm saying is that a simple incident like that could be a miracle, and we'd never know it. Miracles happen all the time, even and especially when they are just everyday things. I could maybe think of a better example. That's just what happened today. I mean miracles are all the time. They are."

"There never were any goats

there, Lane," said Nick quietly.

"Maybe it was a vision or something like second sight," said John. "I think I'll get out the dessert. Shoo fly pie. I left it in the car."

Lane sunk down into the chair the dining room table at her back. Everyone went into the kitchen. The sound of pie plates and silverware clattering with talk about the recipe seemed far away. Lane's head felt like it was in a vice. Dammit. Thank God John had not seen how empty the fridge was or the sorry bottle of ketchup in the door. He didn't put the pie in there, or someone would have commented.

"White, glowing goats? You really pulled our leg, Lane," said Derrick leaning against the couch later with his plate and fork. "Just because you didn't read the book this time. Good one, Lane."

"I think you imagined it," said Nick coming back to the table. He wrestled the pie with his fork and put a large piece in his mouth. He had an odd way of lifting his fork stiffly like a crane. "You always imagine or forget things. Your head is always in the clouds, Lane. You know that."

"Really? None of you believe me? Not even you, Nick? I guess it does sounds kind of silly." It was a relief to say it. Lane put down her soda. She felt light-headed.

"Just give it up. These men will keep harassing you, Lane," added Corinne bringing out more coffee from the kitchen and setting it on the table.

"Come on, let's eat, pie. Just ignore them," added Rhianna sitting down next to Corinne.

"Well, I guess I could have imagined it. It does sound awfully strange." Lane said, standing up and rubbing her throbbing temple. Her elbow also hurt. "Maybe my imagination got the best of me."

"There weren't any goats," said Nick.

"He's right, Lane, what you're saying sounds impossible," Derrick put his hand on her shoulder.

"I guess there couldn't have been three white goats. Seems impossible," said Lane.

* * *

Lane felt a stabbing pain in her back and arms. She fell to her knees and grabbed her head.

Everything went pink, yellow and red, and silent like the sound turned off on a television.

She collapsed onto her side. The floor was colder than it should have been. Damp too. Her head. Why wasn't anyone helping her? Why didn't they call 911? Were they just going to eat pie and ignore her having a seizure or something?

Lane tried to cry out for help, but she couldn't move. When she opened her eyes, she saw white stars like the ones on that night long ago in the Jeep when she had been happy. Wait. There was the little gray jeep next to her. Poor, Zen. All smashed in. Hardly recognizable. With a whoosh, the sound returned to her ears like an oncoming car. She was freezing, and she thought she saw the remnants of a faint sunset through some trees. Where was everyone? Why couldn't she move her legs? She'd been in an accident. Dried spaghetti pooled out of her purse and around her head like a halo. She closed her eyes. Just a few minutes of rest and she'd get up. She had to get home for book club.

* * *

Two months later:

"Thanks for helping me pack, guys." The whole gang gathered in the white kitchen in the basement walkout. The old door propped open with books, letting in the cold December sunlight.

"No problem, Nick," answered Derrick. "We are here if you need anything. Call me anytime night or day. We'll get through this together."

"Yeah," he muttered.

"I mean it, Nick. Come on back to our place tonight, and you can unpack tomorrow. I made my famous shoofly pie. Wait 'til morning to move into the new place."

"I can't believe she's gone. Lane was such a beautiful person," said Rhianna carrying a box to the door and turning back to look at Nick leaning against the fridge. "Did you check all the closets Nick? Do you have everything?"

"Yeah, we got it all. Lane's parents took all her stuff yesterday," he answered, quietly stooping his shoulders.

"What did your parents say?"

"Not much. Said they were sorry, and I should move closer to town so they could see me more often. The usual."

John grabbed the book off the kitchen table and held it out to Nick. The light caught his glasses. "You left this book about miracles here. Don't you want it?" The white book's large gold letters shone and flashed the word on the cover, "Miracles."

Nick put both hands palms out and backed to the door. "Keep it . . . You know that's the book we were supposed to talk about the night it happened—that night she...we never even got to discuss it. I can't believe we sat here while she was out there on the road. . ." Nick looked at his hands.

"Nick, we couldn't have known. We thought she was late from tryouts," said Derrick.

"Yeah," Corrine said. "If she had come around that bend even two seconds later. Just think . . . We'd have eaten dinner together and had book club like nothing ever happened. That truck would have never. . ." Corinne grabbed Nicks hand and pulled him toward her white Pontiac. "And you wouldn't be moving away, Nick." She wiped her eyes with the back of her hand.

Nick stared out at the open fields and the little white steeple in the distance. The old bells rang for eleven o'clock. "Well if I ever believed in Miracles," Nick answered with gravel in his voice. "I don't now. Leave it here for the next people. Maybe they

will want it. Throw it away. I don't care." And he climbed into the moving van, shut the door and started the engine.

"What should we do with it?" Rhianna asked as she held the book out for someone to take it from her.

"Leave it here for the next person. Just leave it," John said, grabbing the book and placing a hand on the book like a blessing. He tucked it inside the entryway of the apartment and pulled the door closed.

"Wait," Corinne said, turning back as John carefully pulled the door closed and locked the deadbolt knowing they might not have any new renters 'til Spring.

"Did anyone check the pantry?" Rhianna asked.

Corinne adjusted her purse, pulled out a mint, jangling her car keys, "Yeah, nothing in there. Just Ketchup."

* * *

The alarm blared. Lane sat up in bed, feet on the floor in one motion. The other side of the bed empty covers pulled loosely up. Nick was always up first, drinking his coffee. Solitude and all that.

Why did she feel that sinking

feeling in her stomach. Ah... That's right. Today was the day she was going to audition for Our Town. She hadn't had an audition since college.

She stood up and stretched. Padded across the weird retro pink carpet to the bathroom, and put toothpaste on her toothbrush. She needed a new one.

Nothing was going to ruin this day. She went back to the bedroom and put on jeans and a black shirt. No need to go into work today with its endless charade of waiting for customers to come in. She could almost hear the birds singing outside on the washline and maybe a tractor in the distance.

Out of nowhere, dizziness swept over her like a tidal wave. She dropped her toothbrush in the sink and gripped the porcelain edges while the room seemed to swivel. She remembered a glimpse of herself at book club. Everyone gathered around her convincing her something. Nick staring down disapprovingly, arms crossed. The dizziness cleared. She must be dehydrated. Having flashbacks of things she was sure never happened—that's all she needed.

She looked in the mirror, and it was grim. She needed a day off from everybody. No one to tell her what to do or what to believe, or tell she wasn't good enough. She put on her earrings fiercely.

Fuck them.

She almost wished she could cancel tonight. She wanted to drive home and see her parents and her little brothers. It had been five months too long.

In the kitchen, Nick sat nursing the last of his second cup of coffee, reading his phone.

"Don't forget we have book club tonight," he muttered.

"I know," I didn't forget."

"Well, you know how you forget things," Nick said, looking over his glasses like a little old man despite his ripe old age of twenty-two.

"You know what, honey. I have a great memory. Always have. Which reminds me, it's your turn to get the groceries."

"But I'm too busy," Nick said, draining his cup and putting on his jacket.

"You get off work at one. You've got time. 'Don't forget.'"

Nick walks over the pantry and opens it. "But I don't know

what to make. There is nothing in here, but ketchup."

"Here, let me help you."

Lane reached under his arm, grabbed the ketchup, and put it in her purse. She walked smartly to the door and opened it then turned back to explain, "My Dad loves ketchup. Oh, and don't wait for me. I have an audition this morning then I'm going home for the weekend. I don't know when I'll be back.

"But... Bookclub!" Nick cried out.

"Didn't read it," Lane answered, smiling, and the door shut.

Her car skidded towards them. One. Two Three. Three little goats. Time seemed to stop, but her car didn't. She just kept skidding. — The Ketchup

ALEXANDRA AMES

has been drawing and creating stories since she can remember.
Her illustrations are inspired by art nouveau, science fiction/
fantasy art, and music. Her stories are inspired by world
mythologies, history, and the natural world. Writing practices
include trying to write for at least an hour multiple days a week.
If she has writer's block she either listens to music to try to
visualize a scene or doodles concept art for the story. Readers can
find more of her work on her website at alexandraamesart.com.

The Widowmaker

Alexandra Ames

Storm Hollow was a little town surrounded by a dense forest and always seemed cloaked in mist. It held a charm and mystique to those who traveled through. Most of the people there were warm and kind. They lived in small homes in the valley, in the shadow of the Earl's Skylar Estate on the hill.

Yorka's mother and step-father arranged her marriage to Earl Landon Skylar for a prime piece of land on the coast. Even though she'd had no choice, Yorka vowed to make the marriage work. Landon had no real family the same as her. When she tried to be kind to him, his reception was icy. He had a kind housekeeper named Judith, who did most of the cleaning in the main parts of the house. Landon had said that he wanted Yorka to get settled in, and since she was accustomed to cleaning, he wanted her to clean their wing of the house. He also said that Judith was so busy doing the other chores, cleaning and buying food from the market. Yorka needed to make his meals for him. Yorka was so busy trying to please him, that she never left the grand estate to explore the town below. She wished to see what it was like. She had even brought it up again to Landon, asking if she could join him and see where he worked.

She knew to never ask again. The side of her face throbbed. Yorka jerked out of her daydreaming. She continued scrubbing the plates from breakfast. The side of her face was hot from where Landon hit her. He had told her it was her fault he'd been forced to hit her. That she needed to learn. She stared down at the soapy water in shame and confusion, had she done something wrong? She didn't think she had. She was just trying to show interest in him and his home.

She finished cleaning and put everything away where she had found it, nice and neat. She glanced over at the sink, a large white spider was struggling as it slipped on the edge of the wet sink and slid down near the drain. It swirled in the vortex of the water, thrashing at the side with its furry legs. Judith had said to kill any spider she saw, that most them were harmless, but there was a certain one native to the area, a Widowmaker. Judith said a bite from one of them was a fate worse than death. Yorka stared down at the spider as it began to get sucked down with the water. She felt a stab of panic. She grabbed a towel and scooped it out.

The drenched spider sprawled on the towel unmoving. Yorka moved to the door leading to the far wing of the house and to the front doors. She tried to open it but found that it was locked. Confused, she went back through the kitchen to the back servants' entrance. She tried to open the door and found it locked. The spider began to move. She spied a small green plant in the windowsill. Taking the towel, she dumped the it onto a leaf. The spider retreated under the leaves and hid. Yorka observed it for a moment then went back to try to open the front door. The bolt was on the outside of the door; she heaved and rattled the door handle. It would not budge.

A soft chirp of a cricket drew her attention. It was the spider. It crept out from under a leaf and chirped again.

"Earl Landon has locked me in." she spoke with a nervous laugh. She shrugged off the strange disquiet that fell over her. "He is probably just trying to keep me safe. He's told me that there are unsavory characters down in town, ones that wouldn't think twice about harming a lady." the spider chirped as it watched her.

"Don't be silly Yorka, everything is fine. You're the one talking to a spider." she laughed to herself.

She returned to the kitchen and opened the icebox, looking over the food that Judith had gotten for them. She walked over to the cabinets and rummaged until she found a cookbook. Judith had all the recipes that Earl Landon liked tabbed. She flipped through it until she found a recipe that matched the groceries.

Yorka did her best. She did everything to try and gain his favor, taking care of the wing of the estate as winter settled over the town. She wanted to go out among the villagers, but Landon explained that it wasn't safe for her to go wandering about by herself. He was away tending to his businesses all day, so Yorka spent a lot of her time alone reading or baking. The silly, little, white spider made its home in the kitchen and studied her from its plant or the corner of the room. Winter raged outside making other rooms in the wing, drafty and unpleasant even with a fire in the fireplace. The kitchen was small and warm, so she spent a majority of her time there.

On a snowy evening, Landon had shut himself in his study. She went down to the kitchen and baked a cake. The little spider watched her. It crept close to her while she was icing the cake. She dropped a small drop of icing on the counter as she licked the beaters herself. The fluffy white spider approached the glob and nibbled at it.

"You need a name." She pointed the beater in her hand at it, "I will name you Tiberius." The little spider rubbed its legs against its body and made a chirping sound, akin to a cricket, "How pathetic is it I am talking to a spider?" she laughed.

* * *

Judith was always kind to her. She, her husband and children kept the grounds looking neat. Her children thought Yorka was a princess because she was so pretty in her fine clothes. Judith's husband Roland seemed surprised that she was such a genteel person. As Judith and Yorka chatted, she pretended not to notice Roland whisper a snide comment towards Landon or a scowl when they mentioned his name. Despite that, Roland was polite and kind to Yorka. The estate was warm in the frigid winter. Judith and her family always joined her for lunch in the kitchen and they became fast friends. Judith and her family always left before Landon got home.

As the days grew colder, Yorka took to exploring the rooms of their wing of the home. She found secret passages that led to other parts of the house. The abandoned wing of the house held furniture draped in sheets. The ornate design was beautiful. She wrapped her shawl around her as she came upon a line of portraits. She heard a cricket chirp behind her. She looked back and saw the white spider scuttling across the cold marble floor. Yorka kneeled down, and the spider climbed into her palm. She meandered, looking at all the portraits stretching back for generations. She searched for Landon's face among them but didn't see him. She reached the end of the line of portraits. Tiberius hopped onto the canvas and scuttled across it. The young man looked nothing like Landon and had kind eyes.

"Hmm, how strange." Yorka mused, the white spider crawled down to the golden nameplate, "Adrian Eldred." She paused and looked at the plates of all the other names, "Eldred- Eldred- Eldred. No Skylar. Come along Tiberius, I need to go talk to Judith." She scooped the spider up and carried it back into their wing of the home. She left him in the plant by the windowsill in the kitchen and was bundling up when the door opened. Judith and Roland walked in carrying a container of something for lunch.

"Mrs. Skylar the door was locked. You been stuck in here all day?" Judith asked.

"Oh, I was exploring the other side of the home, so I didn't notice," Yorka spoke quickly. Judith and her husband gave each other suspicious looks. Yorka felt a wave of shame. She wanted to tell them the truth and ask them for help, but her shame wouldn't allow her to speak.

"You went to the other wing?" Judith asked.

"Yes," Yorka cleared her throat, "Yes I wanted to ask you both if you knew anything about the line of portraits in the hall. It appears to be the Eldred family. Is Landon related to them?"

"Oh well-" Judith stammered, "We didn't want to tell you, because we thought it might frighten you." She paused and looked up at Roland. He gave her a reassuring nod, "This home has been in the Eldred family since the 1500s. Their last heir Adrian Eldred lived here alone. He disappeared two years ago and has not been heard from since." Judith took a shaky breath, "The house was abandoned, and Landon happened upon the deed, so the estate fell into his hands."

"Oh, I see." Yorka mused.

"Mr. Eldred was such a sweet man. Can't bear to think of what might have happened to him. He never said a cross word to me and always greeted me every morning. 'How are you Judith?' is what he said. Very proper. Remember Roland?"

"Yes." Roland nodded with a smile.

"Everyone said that he left

because of finances, but he was always very good with money." Judith continued, "He would have never left his home of his own choosing. I fear someone must have killed him."

"Now don't jump to conclusions." Roland broke in with a comforting tone, "I'm sure he's fine. He ran away as simple as that."

"That's enough of that," Roland spoke gently.

Judith regained her composure, "Would you like some soup?"

* * *

Landon was nothing, but cold and cruel to her. He never called her by name, only 'wife' and even then, his tone filled with contempt. Yorka had no idea what she had done to make him so hateful towards her. When she tentatively brought up the subject to Judith, she learned that Landon had been cold and distant, even when Judith knew him as a child. Even though he had enough money to live comfortably until the end of his days, he entertained himself by intimidating and blackmailing the villagers. As the days grew colder, and the light dwindled, Judith and her family's visits became less frequent. Her only companion was Landon, who berated her and took any form of kindness she showed him as an insult.

As winter set in, Landon began to remain home and work in his bedroom and study. Whenever she tried to join him, she found the door locked. Yorka was losing herself to this cruel man. Afraid, she didn't want to do anything to incur his temper. After a few weeks, grogginess overwhelmed her like a fog. Soon she couldn't keep up with the cooking and cleaning. Landon, annoyed, told her to go rest. He began to prepare her food each day. He would sit at her bedside and watch her eat. Nothing tasted particularly good and had a strange taste of almond but she ate enough of it to please him. Landon shut her into her room, visiting her only to bring her meals. Yorka slept for a couple of days trying to will herself to get better.

After what seemed like weeks, Judith came and brought her food and left it by her door. Yorka ran to open the door to try to speak with her, but Landon intervened, telling Judith that Yorka had fallen ill and needed her rest. His intimidating presence forced Judith to retreat without questioning it further.

Landon opened the door to her room. Yorka pretended to be asleep. He set her food on her bedside table and left. Yorka ate the food in silence. Tiberius crawled across the wall towards her. She took a few crumbs from her meal and set it on the bedside table for him. The small spider slowly approached and ate it. Yorka smiled slightly, this strange little creature, even though she knew it was just an animal, and any connection she had towards it was emotions she projected onto it. The little white spider was just a spider, it didn't care for her at all. Even so, it was the only comfort she had now.

* * *

Yorka lay in her bed. Landon had left her earlier in the afternoon. She stared at the ceiling in silence as hot tears streaked across her temples and wet her hair. Something soft brushed her fingertips. She turned her head slowly and looked at where her hand lay on the bedside table. In the hazy dark of evening, the silver spider had crawled, in its strange disjointed manner, onto her opened fingers and rested in her palm. The spider stared at her through the dark in silence. She lowered it carefully back to the bedside table, so it wouldn't bite her. It brushed its legs against the fur of its body making a chirping sound. She rolled over on her side and huddled under the silk sheets as her tears flowed anew. The spider chirped as she wept in silence.

Landon came in with a small, bottle of dark liquid. Her medicine. He tried to feed it to her, but she refused. He shouted and cursed at her. But Yorka refused. Something was wrong, she didn't know what, because her mind was so hazy from her illness, but she knew she could not take any more medicine. In his rage, Landon pinned her down and forced her mouth open. Tiberius hopped up onto his arm and crawled up onto his shoulder. Landon glanced over and saw it. He jumped off of her and flailed in panic. The tiny white spider somehow made it to the right side of Landon's face and bit his cheek.

Landon screamed in agony, grabbing the side of his face as he tore from her room. Yorka heard him stumbling and crashing down the hall cursing and shouting in pain. She heard the water running in the bathroom. The water switched off after a while, Landon moaned in agony long into the night, until that too faded to silence.

* * *

Yorka awoke the next morning, feeling better than she had in a long time. Her illness had taken its course. She got up and gathered her clothing to go to the bathroom to bathe. The door was halfway ajar, which was strange, so she took a step in. Everything had been thrown around the room and Landon was lying asleep in the filled bathtub, shivering incessantly. The top layer of skin looked like it had melted on the side of his face around the bite.

As Yorka began to back out of the room, Landon jerked awake to her movement. The sight of her made him struggle out of the bathtub, his fine clothes dripping as he collapsed, kneeling on the floor.

"H-Help…" he whispered; his teeth were chattering. Something about him seemed different, the tone of his voice almost sounded humble. Yorka turned on her heel. She stood with her back to him, for a moment, before she could gather the courage to walk away from him.

"Please Yorka," he begged, "Don't leave me…" Yorka looked back, he sounded truly desperate. As long as she had known him, he never expressed any emotion other than hate and rage. He was so controlling that she doubted he would ever allow himself to appear weak in front of her. Yorka took a deep breath. She knew she should walk away from him. Leave him to suffer alone as he had done to her. She glared over her shoulder back at him. He looked up at her pleadingly, his eyes held no malice towards her, only desperation. He had never looked at her like that. She stepped back into the bathroom. She helped him to his feet and ushered him to his room. She helped him dress into warm clothes and put him to bed. She started a fire in the fireplace, put the grate in front of it and left.

She returned to the bathroom. As she cleaned up his mess, she found Tiberius lying waterlogged on the floor. She scooped him up in a towel and set him on the counter as she bathed. After she dressed and combed her hair, she looked around for the spider but did not see him.

She shut the door to the bathroom behind her. she stepped into the hall and looked on the floor for Tiberius. She walked down the hall she saw the door to Landon's study flung open. She cautiously approached and peaked in.

Everything was thrown about; papers and books littered the floor. She stepped in and glanced at the desk, but Landon wasn't there. She had only been in there once before and he had kept it extremely neat and clean. There were vials and plants on the desk. She wandered over to the desk curiously. A book lay open. Was he making her medicine? As she began to read through the ingredients, it dawned on her that it was a poison. She gasped in horror, the medicine he was feeding her was poison. Yorka took a deep breath. She needed to go find Judith, needed to get ahold of the authorities. She passed Landon's room but didn't check on him.

She walked down the stairs to the kitchen. To her surprise, Landon was sitting in his chair at the long table in the dining room. She froze and stared at him. He said nothing as she walked by. He had a wine glass upside-down on the grand table before him. Yorka quickly walked into the kitchen to start on his breakfast. As she was getting out the skillet and pans, he walked in. She glanced over at him as he slipped into the chair at the small table near the counter and stared her. He never did that. He always waited in the dining hall

for her to serve him.

"Are you well?" he asked.

"Yes, I believe my illness has run its course." Yorka answered. Confused and afraid she prepared a plate and silverware. She sliced a piece of bread and buttered it. She set it on the plate. She glanced back again, feeling his eyes on her. He smiled. She retrieved a skillet and two eggs from the icebox. She set them on the counter and nervously fidgeted with the stove.

"Lady Yorka!" Judith cried happily as she walked in carrying a parcel of meat from the butcher. She was setting everything on the table when she saw Landon sitting there.

"Earl Landon, s-so good to see you this morning," she recovered smiling. "It appears your wife is over her illness."

"Appears so." Landon answered.

"Are you well, Sir?" Judith asked softly.

"I am." He answered with the hint of a smile on his face, "How are you Judith?"

Judith looked back at Yorka, completely bewildered, before shrugging. "I believe I am well." She answered.

"Good." Landon smiled. He

sighed and rose to his feet a bit clumsily.

"Sir, why don't you go wait in the dining room?" Judith helped him towards the door as he staggered again. Judith watched after him as he meandered down the hall.

"Lady Yorka, is he drunk?" Judith asked.

"I do not understand what is going on." Yorka said as she looked up at her.

"I have never seen him behave so…benign since he moved here." She stared at him wide eyed. "He has never once asked me if I was well." She paused and looked over at Yorka. "You know, he did not come out of his study for days while you were sick. He was looking for a cure for your illness. He made all the meals for you. I have never seen him so devoted to someone. I believe you may have changed him." She grinned happily. "Here, I know you hate it when other people cook for you but let me help you prepare breakfast."

"Hate it?" Yorka looked over at her.

"Yes, Ma'am." Judith answered slowly, "Landon said that you preferred to do everything yourself."

"H-He told me you were too busy to help me," Yorka whispered realizing that Landon had been manipulating them both. They finished the meal and took it into the dining room.

Earl Landon sat in the chair at the head of the table. He baited Tiberius, holding a wine glass above the spider. Landon trapped the spider under the wine glass as it scuttled on the table in front of him. Judith screamed.

Yorka froze.

Judith swatted at the spider before Landon, sending it to the floor and grinding it under the heel of her boot, "My Lord that was a Widowmaker!"

"Oh? Was it?" Earl Landon asked with feigned innocence.

"Of course! WidowMakers are the only white spider in all of Storm Hollow! What were you thinking?" He gave her an indignant look.

"Forgive me, I did not mean to question you." Judith looked to the floor.

"It is forgiven," Landon spoke curtly. "You only feared for my safety."

"Yes, Sir. I will go get a rag." She looked at him strangely then curtsied and quickly bustled out of the room.

Yorka hovered holding the platter of food. She stared down at the smashed spider. Her hands were shaking, and her chest was tight. A deep sorrow came over her. Tiberius was one of those dangerous spiders but at the same time her companion. She fought down her conflicted feelings. She took a soft breath then set the food in front of him.

"Do not mourn that despicable creature," Landon spoke.

"Yes, Sir." She took a deep shaky breath. Tears welled in her eyes. She quickly pivoted so he wouldn't see her cry.

He reached out and touched her hand before she could turn completely. His hands coaxed her around, so she was facing him bewildered and afraid.

"Are you crying for this spider?"

Yorka couldn't stop the tears from falling, but she shook her head adamantly. He grinned which terrified her more.

"You are." His hands touched her face, more delicately than he ever had before. He leaned towards her. She shut her eyes and winced, but he kissed them and pulled her into a warm embrace.

Yorka, stunned, didn't quite understand what was happening.

"You have nothing to fear," Landon whispered holding her against him. How had he become so warm and gentle? He had been so cold and cruel ever since he had brought her home. He drew back looking down at her fondly. It was then that she noticed that the melted look to his cheek had faded to a red welt. "Don't worry everything is going to be better now." He whispered.

Judith returned with a rag and cleaned up the dead spider off of the polished wood floor, "It did not bite you did it Earl Landon?" she asked urgently.

"No, it didn't." Landon took a step back from Yorka.

"If you feel anything strange at all," Judith continued, "Go take a cold bath, as cold as you can bear, it should slow the poison."

"I will keep that in mind," Landon answered with a soft smile. Yorka glanced over at where the dead spider had been then back at him.

"Judith?" Yorka spoke slowly, "What does a Widowmaker's bite do?" she glanced over at Landon, ready for him to yell at her, but he merely smiled.

"It is said that the Storm

Hollow Widowmaker's spider is a supernatural being. It chooses its victims carefully..." Judith explained, "Its bite is painful and causes the skin around the bite to melt. The true terror of it is that the soul of the person goes into the spider. The spider then takes over the life of the victim. After a few days, the bite mark disappears and the skin around it is healed. The only way you can tell is that the two tiny puncture marks reflect silver in certain light. They are nasty and despicable creatures. I am truly glad you are safe, Earl Landon."

"Thank you, Judith." Landon smiled over at her.

Judith looked shocked by his shift in demeanor. She studied Yorka. Had Yorka had somehow changed Landon's icy disposition?

Yorka forced a smile as a wave of unease fell over her. She had not changed Landon, but something had.

"I should get back to my chores." Judith winked at Yorka then turned and quickly walked out of the room.

Yorka stared after her in silence. She looked over at Landon and felt her blood drain from her face. She took a step back. He reached out and lightly took her hands, so she couldn't escape. He brushed his thumbs over the back of her hands, Yorka let out a soft squeak of terror and jerked away from him and ran out of the dining room.

"No-no! Don't be scared. I won't hurt you." He called after her in a soothing voice, following at her heels. Yorka ran up the stairs and slammed the door to her room in his face and locked it.

"Please..." he whispered through the door. She heard him slide down and lean against the door, "Dear Yorka, I owe you my life. You saved me from drowning, do you remember? You let me hide in the plant on the window sill. Yorka, you spoke so sweetly to me when you fed me your crumbs. You were kind and compassionate to me when no one else would even entertain the thought. I know that you saved me out of ignorance." He paused for a moment then continued, "I did my best to watch out for you, I'm so sorry I couldn't do more- If I had still been a man-"

"What? What are you talking about?" Yorka spoke through the door.

"I thought- I thought that was why you ran."

"I ran because you were a

spider and you stole Landon's soul!" Yorka cried.

"My name is Adrian Eldred. I was bitten by a Widowmaker spider two years ago and confined to that body. The soul of the spider stole my body and left." His breath caught in his throat, "I'm sorry if you were frightened."

"How could you do that to another human being?" she screamed at him. But how could she mourn the loss of Landon when she could only be glad he was gone? This was all too much to comprehend.

"What? He deserved it. He was so cruel to you. Do you not understand that?!"

"Of course I understand it!" She shouted through the door, "All those times I let you come close to me; I held you in my hands so you wouldn't be cold when we explored the other part of the house."

"I would have never done that to you, Yorka! Never! I was never going to bite you. I wasn't even going to bite Landon either. I had accepted my life. I couldn't bring myself to make someone have the same fate as me. But when he started to poison you, I just couldn't stand to watch you suffer anymore."

He spoke earnestly, "You have to believe me! I'm not like Landon! He was in league with your step-parents to get your inheritance. I eavesdropped on their meetings. Your murder was planned all along. He'd spread rumors of you being ill around town. That medicine was just doses of poison! But you kept surviving every time he tried to poison you. He tried to kill me, whenever I managed to get close enough to bite him... Last night, you fought back and distracted him, I was able to get close enough..." He sank into a spell of silence, "And when Judith killed the Widowmaker, she unwittingly made sure that he will never hurt you again."

"W-What..." Yorka's voice cracked as she tried to find her courage, "What do you want with me?"

"What? Nothing. You are my friend-" he trailed off and sighed, "Just - thank you. And please don't be afraid of me."

"Can I leave?" Yorka asked.

"Why wouldn't you be able to?" He sounded confused.

"You wouldn't stop me if I went back home?" Yorka asked sharply, even though she knew it was an empty threat. Her step-parents would never take her back. And she'd never be safe with them. She had nowhere else to go.

"No, I would not. If that is what you wish to do, then you should." He answered, "I have no illusions about our relationship. I know that the fondness I have for you is not the way you could feel about me. I may be Landon now, but the man you married is dead. You are free of your commitment."

* * *

Earl Landon was reckless and cruel in his younger days. He married. Though he and his wife separated for some of their first year together, as time passed, she returned to him. His personality softened. Many attributed the change in his character for his love of his dear wife, Yorka. Over the years, after countless good deeds done by the Earl and his lady; the people of Storm Hollow no longer feared or reviled him. He became a pillar of the community, so trusted and revered by his people they pretended not to notice the silver scar on his cheek. ✎

Illustration by Alexandra Ames

"I will name you Tiberius." The little spider rubbed its legs against its body and made a chirping sound, akin to a cricket. — The Widowmaker

BRIAN C. E. BUHL

Hailing from sunny Sacramento, California, Brian Buhl is trying to save the world. Formerly enlisted in the U.S. Air Force, Brian now spends most of his time writing software for the solar industry. When he's not engineering technical solutions, he can sometimes be found playing saxophone with local community bands. Also, he writes science fiction and fantasy. His blog is briancebuhl.com.

Unclaimed Goods

Brian C. E. Buhl

"How many bodies do we throw in a day?" Tony asked as the chamber doors hissed open.

"That depends," Vince said as he scratched his gray bearded cheek. "If it's a holiday, there's more. If they're coming from a larger city, there's more. But it's better not to think of it as 'throwing' Tony. You wouldn't throw your mama. Don't throw the customers."

The holding chamber stretched out before the two men, a long metallic hall making up the swollen belly of a passenger ship. The two baggage men stood at the bottom of the ramp. Dim lights flickered into life along the ceiling, spreading wan illumination along the length of the vehicle's interior. Row upon row of matte black boxes lined the sides of the walkway with digital readouts offering their own green and red glow to the room.

Tony and Vince stepped up the ramp into the chamber. Automatons whirred passed, their forked arms raised as if in surrender. A scowl twisted Tony's features when one of the robots brushed passed him close enough to stir his short black hair.

"Besides," Vince said, watching the diminutive worker bots move ahead of them, "they'll be doing all the work."

"If robots do all of the lifting, what do they need us for?"

"You still don't get it." Vince gripped Tony's shoulder and turned the younger man to face him. "These are people. Not bags. They trust the company to get them from one place to another. If it was your mama in one of these boxes, wouldn't you feel better knowing that there was someone like you looking after her?"

"If you say so." Tony drew out his cell phone and pawed at the screen with disinterest.

Grinding his teeth, Vince stepped into Tony's personal space, putting his nose within inches of the younger man's. "Listen to me. I don't care who your father is. I don't care who you think you are. If you don't impress me today, you don't get the job."

Tony fumbled his phone back into his pocket. He took a step back from Vince but not before noticing a hint of garlic and alcohol on his trainer's breath. "Sorry, man. Sorry. What do we do now, sir?"

Vince took a deep breath. The creases in his brow diminished and his expression softened from anger to simple irritation. He gestured behind him towards the cargo area. "We watch. We wait. We make decisions the robots can't make. One time, a fella's mind was on its way to Orlando while his body was on a long layover bound for Titan. That was a helluva mix up, and it was all because a label got scraped passing through the Lunar colony. One little scratch and the robots couldn't read it right."

"How often does that happen?" Tony frowned as another automaton cut between him and his trainer.

"Not often." Vince didn't even blink as the robot whipped past. "But shit happens."

The baggage handlers wore gray jumpsuits. Tony's uniform still looked bright and new, with crisp, stiff lines running across the elbows and knees. Vince's jumper had faded over the years. No amount of washing would ever rid the drab material of its permanent sweat stains circling the armpits and running down the back. Each baggage handler wore a black nylon tool belt, heavy with equipment. Vince drew a scanner from a holster on his belt and shot a crimson light at one of the closest boxes. The scanner's beep echoed through the chamber as the device's display illuminated Vince's face from below.

"This is Michelle Rodriguez," Vince said, reading from the scanner. "She's headed to Atlanta. Her tag is good. Her body is quiet. She should be getting transferred to flight thirty-two forty-four. That should be the... uh... blue stripes."

Tony stepped out of the way of an automaton. The wheeled robot rolled up to the box that Vince had scanned, its arms spread wide. It descended on the box and chirped a short, shrill complaint as it slowly lifted the box. Tony examined the robot's back, noting the prominent blue stripe over its chipped white chassis. With its cargo lifted a meter off the deck, the robot turned and descended the ramp more quickly than it had approached. A moment later, the worker bot and Ms. Rodriguez were out of sight.

"So what do we do if the wrong robot grabs a body?" Tony asked.

"Just hit it with the scanner and hit override." Vince held his scanner close to the junior baggage handler before pointing towards one of the buttons.

Tony shadowed Vince as the older, heavier man walked through the holding chamber. Every few steps, Vince consulted his scanner. A chorus line of robots rolled through the storage area, dancing off with boxes both large and small. As the worker bots unpacked the cargo, Tony observed box sizes for every body type he could imagine. With each removal, Vince witnessed the efficiency with which the passengers had been packed in the cargo area. It reminded Tony of a honeycomb, with the automatons buzzing around like chirping mechanical worker bees.

"You don't scan all of them?" Tony asked.

"We don't need to." Vince pulled the trigger, aiming the red light at one of the smaller boxes. "I like to check on the kids, but that's just me. The idea of freezing people to fly them around was to make it efficient and safe. No more security lines. No more tight, uncomfortable seats. No more stale peanuts and screaming babies and over-sized carry-ons crammed up tighter than a pair of tidy-whities. If we scanned all of them manually, it'd just slow things down."

"Okay, I think I get it. I have another question."

"Let's hear it."

"Okay, but I don't want you to get mad if this was already covered in the training."

"Spit it out already!"

"Okay, okay! Uhm. So far, I've seen robots with blue stripes, red stripes, green stripes, and yellow." Tony paused, looking around at the rapidly emptying chamber. "But there are a bunch without any markings. What's with those?"

"Those are final destination. The stripes are just for transfers."

"That's a lot of people just passing through."

"It's a spoke-hub system, and this is a major hub. Some people come here from the other side of the world, only to be switched off and headed out to within a few hundred miles of where they started. It's supposed to be more efficient, but I don't get it. Any other questions, bright guy?"

"That's it for now."

Vince responded with a grunt, and both men turned to watch the continued progress of the worker bots. Vince continued to scan boxes at random. Tony drew his scanner and copied the older man.

"So when you're done today," Tony asked after a while, "will you be getting in one of these boxes yourself?"

"I'm retiring, not moving." Vince clenched his teeth and his voice came out in a growl. Tony thought he could see a vein pulse along Vince's temple. "Besides, even if I decided to go on a nice, long vacation, I don't have the holes."

Tony rubbed the back of his neck absentmindedly, his fingers tracing the data jacks hidden beneath his thick black hair. He had wondered before why training didn't take place in virtual reality.

"So how long have you been doing this?" Tony asked.

"Since the beginning." Vince scowled without looking at his apprentice.

"You don't seem old enough to be retiring."

Vince grunted and turned to scan another box. Tony shrugged and followed his teacher deeper into the chamber.

With less than twenty boxes remaining, none of the remaining worker bots whizzing around the baggage handlers bore stripes. Tony watched as a pair of robots grabbed identical boxes opposite each other on the walkway. The robots turned, mirroring each other's movements before moving down the walkway together, side by side. It made Tony think of synchronized swimming.

With less than ten boxes left, Tony asked, "So how do passengers... uh... claim themselves?"

"Have you never traveled anywhere?" Vince gave Tony a sharp look, one grizzled eyebrow raised.

"Only with my grandparents. So we have to take the train."

"Alright, it's like this." Vince turned and faced Tony. "The passenger takes a seat and plugs in. Their mind goes off into the VR of the vehicle where they do whatever it is you kids do in cyberspace. Maybe some of them work. Maybe they just eat food that won't make them fat. I don't know.

"After they get to wherever it is they're going, their bodies are picked up and made ready to wake. That's when the passengers in the VR are shown a gate. They pass through the gate, they wake up in a chair, and then they go about their lives."

Tony nodded and looked around the chamber. There were two boxes left. As he watched, an automaton rolled slowly to the longer, wider box. The whine of its servos sounded like a strained groan to Tony's ears as the robot lifted the heavy-set passenger. It turned smoothly and wheeled off. The two baggage handlers stood alone next to the last passenger.

The chamber grew silent. One of the runners of light illuminating the vehicle flickered, then steadied, banishing all shadows from the belly of vehicle. The huge craft itself purred quietly above. Tony looked towards the direction of the ramp, then back to the remaining box.

He looked again towards the ramp, expecting to see a robot trundling up to take the last passenger. No robot appeared. He cast a glance at Vince. The older man wore a puzzled frown.

"So," Tony said.

"Sometimes there are stragglers."

"What happens when there's an extra?"

"There can't be an extra." Vince ran a hand through his thin white hair and licked his lips. He shuffled up to the box and scanned it. Tony looked over Vince's shoulder to read the scanner.

"Thomas Miller," Vince whispered. "Bound for here. Kansas City."

Tony drew his own scanner and triggered it at the box. He scrolled through detail pages, reading bits of information out loud.

"Originally from Portland. Body only. No baggage. Single. No return scheduled."

"Yeah," Vince said, his eyes drinking in information from his own screen.

"So what do we do?" Tony asked as he holstered his scanner.

"I don't know. I've been doing this for twenty-five years and I've never heard of a body getting lost. There are systems in place to keep this from happening."

"But you said, 'shit happens.' What happens when a body goes to the wrong place?"

"It gets picked up and shipped off. It always goes somewhere. If Mr. Miller wasn't supposed to be in Kansas City, a stripe would have already been here to drag him off to another transport. But his ticket says Kansas City. He's not in the wrong place."

Tony drew his scanner and triggered it on the box again. He skimmed through the information, still the same from the first and second time the box was scanned. He pressed the scanner against the sticker and pulled the trigger again. The beep echoed through the empty holding chamber. The display remained unchanged.

"Do we need to get him out of here?"

"This was the last flight of the day for this ship." Vince scratched at his beard again. "If there was another flight, the robots would have already filled the belly."

"Yeah, but what do we do?"

"I don't know!" Vince's voice boomed through the nearly empty chamber, and his scowl looked like it could curdle milk. After a moment, he shook his head and took several slow breaths. "Look, kid, let me think a moment."

Tony began to pace through the cargo area, his eyes fixed on Thomas Miller's box. The flat black rectangle sat silently, offering no clues or advice. Numbers flashed in a display on one side offering information about the status of the passenger's body. Tony didn't understand any of it. They weren't all zeroes, so Tony assumed the guy was probably still alive.

The junior baggage man's pacing took him to the ramp. He looked out and up at the overcast sky. It would be dark soon, and his first shift would be over.

"Finding a left-over body is not the best way to start a new job," Tony muttered.

"Help me move him." Vince's voice echoed through the transport again, loud, but with none of the anger he'd shown before. Tony ran back into the vehicle, his boots clanging on the deck plates.

The baggage handlers each

drew a pair of lifters from their tool belts. Tony turned the tools over in his hands. They weren't much more than heavy magnets with hand grips. With Vince taking the lead, they connected the lifters to the sides of the box. Vince gestured for Tony to take the top while he squatted to grab at the bottom.

"Don't let the head slam," Vince said.

Even with the warning, Tony nearly dropped the box. The container toppled and Tony threw a leg under it to keep it from smashing against the floor. It landed hard against his knee and Tony screamed a curse. Sucking wind through his teeth, Tony lowered the box the rest of the way to the floor before straightening and rubbing his sore leg.

"You hurt?"

"I don't think so." A moment later he limped around the narrow chamber until he could walk normally. He flexed his knees with a wince and said, "I think it's just bruised. What now?"

"We open it."

"Wait." Tony stepped closer to the box. "If his mind is off in VR, won't this kill him?"

"The brain is still here." Vince tapped the black box. "I don't know from personal experience, but I know that a digital persona is just a copy. Unplug, and the meat still remembers what the meat remembers."

"But how do you know this won't hurt him?"

"Because it's been done before." Vince leaned forward with his hands against the box. His voice sounded tired. "Shit happens. Ships go down. But we haven't lost anyone in over twenty years because the bodies are preserved. They just have to be woken up."

"Have you ever woken anyone up before? Finding a body on my first day is messed up enough, but if we accidentally kill someone-"

"We're not going to kill anyone. If the body is in any kind of distress, the lid won't open. The box is smarter than most doctors."

Tony stepped back, his stomach twisting into knots. He began to pace again. "I need this job. But I'd rather get fired than go to jail. I sure hope you know what you're doing, Vince."

Vince studied the glowing indicators on the front of the

box. He opened a panel revealing a tiny control panel next to one of the displays. Vince pressed several buttons, his stubby fingers stabbing the screen with quick, confident motions. Then he sat back to watch the display. A few moments later, Vince frowned. He leaned forward, punched the same buttons he'd pressed before. He watched the display. Nothing happened.

"Well, damn."

"Is he dead?" Tony's voice was barely more than a whisper.

Vince stood and brushed dust from the front of his jumpsuit. "No. But his heart isn't speeding up. The box says he's alive. He's just not waking up."

Tony wrung his hands and began to pace again. Vince kneeled down and closed the control panel. They both stared at the box containing Thomas Miller. The box sat between them, silent and still.

"Maybe you did it wrong." Tony gestured towards the loading ramp. "Maybe the robot that was sent to pick him up is just stuck somewhere or broke down. Stuff like that has happened before, right?"

Vince was slow to answer. "Robots break down from time

to time, but there are systems in place that account for that. There are systems watching other systems. I think everything out here is working like it's supposed to. The problem is on the inside."

"What do you mean?"

"When the passenger is flagged in VR, they go through the gate. When they go through the gate, their experiences are stored while a robot comes to get their body. What they experienced while they traveled is uploaded into their brains. Then they wake up."

"So Thomas Miller never went through the gate?"

"Yeah. Maybe he was never given a gate to go through."

Tony stepped up next to Vince and stared down at the dull black box. Vince also stared down at the box, his brow furrowed. The sound of a ship landing boomed off in the distance.

"This isn't our problem," Tony said.

Vince let out a dry, coughing laugh before saying, "Not our problem? Kid, this is the job. It is why there are still humans working in baggage claim. Thomas Miller got on a ship in Portland, trusting us to take care of his body while he dreamed whatever it is you kids dream when you plug in. Well, the robots don't know what to do with him. The autopilots that fly the ships won't know where to take him. This is up to us, Tony. You're going to have to go talk to him."

"Talk to him? And tell him what? That his body won't wake up?"

"That's probably a good place to start. Find out what he wants us to do with him."

"God damn it." Tony rubbed the back of his neck, feeling the two tiny ports there again.

"This is why they're forcing me into retirement." A touch of anger harshened the older man's voice. "It's why they're bringing you in. They trusted the bodies to me for over twenty years and I didn't lose a single one. But now I'm not good enough to take care of the customers? Bah!"

Vince shuffled over to a wall and slapped a panel at waist level with more force than necessary. It slid open, revealing a coiled data cable with two prongs.

"It's up to you, now," Vince said. "The company is trusting you to take care of them. So get to it. Help Thomas Miller and let me get out of here with a little bit of dignity."

Tony limped to the open panel. His knee throbbed and his stomach rolled, threatening to bring up his lunch. With clumsy fingers, he drew out the data cable.

"I'm sorry, Vince."

"Don't worry about it, kid. I shouldn't have said anything. Let's just help this guy and get out of here."

Tony lifted the cable and inspected the prongs. They were straight and clean and compatible with the interface on the back of his neck.

"I've used virtual reality for training before. And for screwing around. But it's never been part of my job." With a sigh, he drew the cable up, closed his eyes, and plugged in.

Tony opened his digital eyes and found himself standing in an empty banquet hall. Dozens of tables stood around him, set out with hundreds of plates of food of all sorts. Enough to feed an army. Stepping up to a dessert tray, Tony fingered a dollop of chocolate mousse into his mouth.

He knew that none of it was real, but the experience seemed

real. The mousse felt right on his finger and tasted rich and sweet in his mouth. Tony swallowed. The ship sported some of the best virtual reality Tony had ever visited.

Stepping away from the dessert table, Tony jogged to the end of the banquet hall to a set of heavy white doors. Opening them revealed a broad hallway lined with a plush red carpet, the walls decorated with classic paintings. The hall stretched as far as Tony's eyes could see, the wood paneled walls on each side interrupted periodically by closed doors.

"I need to find Thomas Miller," Tony said to the air in front of him.

He blinked and found himself standing further down the hall, facing one of the closed doors. He drew a deep breath, let it out in a sigh, then knocked.

After a moment, a male voice muffled by the door said, "Come in. The door is open."

The door opened to reveal a modest apartment. A view screen covered the far wall showing an American football game in progress. A man in a bathrobe sat on a drab green couch, lounging and watching the game. Without turning away

from the screen, the man raised a hand and beckoned for Tony to enter.

Tony stepped in. He opened his mouth to say something, then stopped when he noticed the large, glowing gateway just to the man's right. It was a silver arch full of white light. Above the arch floated the words "YOU HAVE ARRIVED" in luminous green letters.

"Mister Miller?"

"Mister Miller is my dad," replied the man. He turned and gave Tony a wide smile. "I'm Tom Miller, but I usually go by Jim."

"Jim?" Tony asked, stepping around the couch.

"My middle name is James. It's a long story. Have you come to collect me?"

"Jim, I don't know any gentle way to say this. We can't seem to wake your body. Have you tried going through the gate?"

Jim didn't flinch or give any sign of being surprised. His smile faded slowly before he turned his attention back to the game. Tony followed Jim's gaze to the screen and watched as a team in a red and white tried to pass the ball. The opposing team in blue and gray mounted a defense.

"Jim, did you hear me?"

"I heard you. Have a seat for a minute."

Tony looked at the exit with its large, unmistakable letters before settling on the couch. "You never tried the gateway, did you?"

"It's my heart." Jim kept his eyes focused on the game. "The stasis pod is keeping it going as long as I'm in here. Once my body is out of the pod, it's done. My heart won't beat on its own again. I thought I could survive one more flight, but the monitors don't lie. I hoped I'd be able to catch a Chiefs game before I had to make my peace. Now, I think this is the best I'm going to manage."

A bucket of iced beers sat on the couch next to Jim. Jim pulled one out, twisted off the cap, and offered it to Tony. Tony took it and sipped while Jim took one for himself.

"Jim, I don't think you can stay here."

"Oh, I know. I meant to get up and go a few minutes ago. It's just not that easy. Self-preservation's what gets most people to get up and walk out. As real as this may feel, everyone knows it's just a dream, and nobody wants to lose their body. But I've checked my vitals and I know the score.

As soon as I step through that gate, it's game over. This is my last stop."

Tony took another sip of his beer. He knew on some level that the VR programmers had crafted the virtual beer to taste ideal. Sitting next to Jim, knowing what was in store for the other man, Tony found it impossible to enjoy the taste. He set the bottle between his legs and looked down.

"Anything I can I do for you?"

"I don't think so. Eventually, they'll pull the plug on me. I figured that I might just watch the game, enjoy my beer, and wait it out."

Tony nodded turned his yes to the game. It wasn't his sport, but it seemed the team in red and white was winning.

After a few minutes, Tony set his bottle down and stood.

"I can't stay."

"I know. This is my fantasy, not yours. What are you going to do?"

"I don't know yet."

"I didn't mean to cause any problems. I just can't... you know..."

"No, I get it. See you on the other side, Jim." Closing his eyes,

Tony reached up to the back of his neck and pulled at a plug that didn't exist in the digital world.

Tony opened his eyes and found himself leaning against one of the cold walls of the cargo bay. The data cable was in his hands. Vince stood a short way off, watching him.

"That was quick."

"Time moves differently in VR." Tony tried to get to his feet, but the pain in his knee rushed in. He fell back to the floor. He closed his eyes and took several steadying breaths, trying to shake away the post VR disorientation.

"Did you find him?"

"Yeah." Tony looked towards the flat black box; his eyes heavy. "He can't go through the gate because he knows when he does, he'll die."

Vince frowned and scratched absentmindedly at his beard. He knelt next to the box and rested a hand gently on what was effectively Thomas Miller's coffin.

"Once the box is opened," Vince said, "the brain detaches and the digital copies fade. No ghosts in the machine."

"I know. I think Jim's waiting for us to open the box."

"Jim?"

"That's what he goes by." Tony shook his head. "He said it was a long story."

Vince nodded but said nothing.

Tony pushed himself to his feet. He wound the data cable and replaced it in the panel. As he worked, he could hear another ship land somewhere in the distance. After closing the panel, Tony looked towards the ramp of the holding chamber for several moments before turning back to the passenger box. He drew his scanner, placed the reader end to the sticker, and depressed the trigger. The scanner's beep drew Vince's attention. He looked up and frowned at Tony.

"What are you doing?"

Tony depressed the OVERRIDE button as Vince had shown him. He thumbed down through the detail panes until he saw the destination field.

"I'm sending him somewhere else."

"Kid, wait. This is our problem. Do you really mean to send him out and make someone else open the box?"

"No." Tony frowned. "I mean, I guess so. That's not what I was thinking. I just think it'd be nice if Jim could sit on his couch a little longer, drinking his beer and enjoying his game."

Tony finished tapping "Titan" onto the screen of his scanner and hit the OVERRIDE button again. Tony had just enough time to release a relieved sigh before an automaton rolled up the ramp into the chamber. It descended on the black box like a protective mother.

Vince scrambled out of the way as the robot's arms settled onto the sides of the box. With a triumphant whine of servos, the robot hoisted Jim's box up over its head, turned, and moved off towards the ramp. A moment later, it was gone. The baggage handlers stood in the cargo chamber alone.

"That was a red stripe," Vince said, rubbing his beard. "Titan, I think. One of the longer layovers tonight."

"The game hasn't even reached half-time," Tony said. "Jim will get to see the final score."

Vince clapped Tony on the shoulder, and Tony could see that the older man's eyes were watering. "I think you're going to do all right, kid. You're going to do all right." ✎

"Finding a left-over body is not the best way to start a new job," Tony muttered. — Unclaimed Goods

SOFIA AGUILAR

is a sophomore at Sarah Lawrence College in Bronxville, New York. Her work has appeared in Germ Magazine, The Griffin's Inkpot, Sound Generation, and The Gateway Review. She has received the 2018 Nancy Lynn Schwartz Prize for Fiction and the Jean Goldschmidt Kempton Scholarship for Young Writers. She writes on her laptop in her dorm or obscure corner of her college library while listening to her custom Spotify playlist of indie music. Though it isn't always easy—she sometimes twiddles with a single sentence for fifteen minutes—she writes because it's the only thing she can picture herself doing for the rest of her life. You can find more of her work at sofiaaguilar.com

Never, Not Once

Sophie Aguilar

I wouldn't say Mateo and I were friends—we had grown up together but so had everyone else in this town. Before everything went down at the end of summer, before my neighbors swapped gossip about the Gonzalez family over crates of cilantro and onions in the supermarket, Mateo was just another kid. We even played on the same Little League team a few years before being in middle school made it uncool. He never said much then or now, only raising his hand in class to ask for a bathroom pass and returning hellos with a nod and a small, uncertain smile. Everyone said he got it from his abuela, a quiet if unassuming old lady who worked at the library across the street from my house. His brother Antonio was the same, though he was older than Mateo by four years and it showed. Or, I guess, it used to.

At the funeral, that's what everyone noticed the most—not the waxiness of Antonio's skin but the wrinkles in his forehead and around his mouth and his eyes even though he still had a year left before he graduated high school. I think people were almost glad his abuela had demanded an open casket so they could have something to gossip about over dinner. It was the kind of town, where things didn't really happen but when they did, the newness of it stayed in the air for years.

Afterwards at Mateo's house, kids played outside on the lawn and adults spoke to each other in low, careful voices and sipped from plastic cups, leaving fingerprints on the sides and lipstick stains on the rims.

"When are we leaving?" I whispered to my mom for the thousandth time as I pulled on the elbow of her dress.

"When I say so, Benjamín," she replied through gritted teeth. "Go talk to your father."

She smiled and continued to nod at whatever someone else's mom was saying, and I was so bored I wanted to kick a wall. I was too old to play outside but too young to be interested in anything the adults were talking about. I wished, suddenly, that I could just grow up a little faster already.

I turned and saw Mateo sitting alone on the couch near the window. With no one else to talk to, I sank into the cushions next to him and watched him kick his sneakers back and forth against the couch.

"Hey," I said.

When he nodded, his dark hair caught the light, revealing flecks of gray near his ears that looked too big for his head, as though he had yet to grow into them.

"You okay?"

He hesitated a moment then nodded again.

I pointed towards his arm. "What's that?"

Mateo had been fiddling with the cuffs of his jacket for the past minute, which I was surprised he was still wearing considering the fact that his abuela never turned the AC on. The moment before, Mateo had pulled his sleeve back far enough to reveal a large red mark on his wrist, as if someone had slapped him.

He immediately pulled his sleeve hard enough to cover his fingers. "Nothing," he said.

I shrugged. Already out of things to say, I looked around as though another question would come to me when Mateo's abuela marched up in her ratty old chanclas instead of the tiny black heels she'd been wearing at the church.

"Mateo, kitchen. Now!" she whispered so that no one but me could hear. "Lo siento, Benjamín," she apologized, giving me a warm smile I'd seen dozens of times from behind the front desk at the library. But it faded back into a frown when she turned to Mateo again. "¡Ándale, Mateo!" his abuela demanded, grabbing his wrist and pulling him to the kitchen.

I peered behind me, huffing when I saw my mom waving her hands and chatting while my dad strained against his tie and accepted another drink from the person next to him. Seeing all this, I decided to go find a bathroom to hide in until it was time to go. But as I passed the kitchen,

I caught Mateo's abuela's voice, hard and unforgiving enough to make me pause.

"—and another stain on one of my best dishes!" she snapped like a stick that had been broken in half. "What do I have to do so you clean things properly?"

"I'm sorry, Abuela," Mateo whispered, his voice trembling. I'd never heard him sound so afraid.

"It's just terrible," my mom said later as she spooned rice and beans onto my plate for dinner that night. She clucked her tongue like a mother hen and continued, "I heard his abuela didn't even recognize the body. Poor woman."

"Ay Dios mio, Olivia, can we not tonight?" My dad shook his head and picked at his plate. "We just left the boy's funeral."

"But didn't you hear what they're saying? Why he did it?"

"Mom?" I interrupted with my cheeks full of food. "Can I leave?"

"I need a drink," my dad grunted and stood up to leave the table.

My mom shook her head and continued eating as though I hadn't said anything.

Mateo didn't come back to school for a week. When he did I noticed the gray in his hair was already spreading to the back of his head like spilled water on a countertop.

"Did you dye your hair?" I whispered to him, leaning over my desk. "My mom does the same thing. Did you have to sit under one of those helmets?"

"No," Mateo muttered to the floor. "No, I didn't."

"Didn't what?" I asked, but he only shook his head.

One morning as I was walking to school, I saw him at the coin laundromat shoving clothes into a couple of the washing machines. I frowned and made my way over.

"Hey," I said as I walked in.

Mateo jumped and straightened when he saw me. "Oh," he said. "Hey."

"Aren't you gonna get in trouble?"

He shook his head and went back to work, sorting clothes by colors, snapping machine doors closed, filling plastic drawers with detergent. It was only then that I noticed his hands, curved and gnarled, his nails thickening and yellowing.

"You okay?" I asked.

"Fine," he replied.

Several days later, when I saw his veins popping out of his skin and his eyes bloodshot and rimmed with red, I decided to follow Mateo after school. I didn't know why, just that something wasn't right.

He didn't go straight home but to the grocery store. I hid behind a car in the parking lot, straightening when he emerged half an hour later weighed down with several shopping bags hanging from his skinny little arms.

I felt like I was playing a game I would've played in elementary school, like I was a detective from a cop show as I walked on the opposite side of the street from Mateo. I held my nose when I wanted to sneeze walked on my tip-toes so he couldn't hear my footsteps.

After he shuffled up the driveway, unlocked the key to his house, and went inside, I crouched and ran to hide in his abuela's flower bushes growing under the window. Even through the glass I could hear her voice.

"And where have you been?" she demanded.

I almost fell over into some thorns as I heard a loud slap. Her hand against a table, I guessed.

A pause, then Mateo's reply that pushed his words together so tightly I couldn't distinguish one from another.

"Ay, you're just like your brother!" his abuela raved. "He was lazy and stupid, too. Never came home on time, always talked back, never respected me. Me! The woman who raised and fed you both after your good-for-nothing parents dropped you on my doorstep and ran off to Mexico!"

Her voice lowered into dangerous murmur as she said, "I won't have that in this house anymore."

My skin was covered in goosebumps, my stomach tight and clenched with fear and I wondered then if his abuela was really who we all thought she was.

Now go start dinner, your abuela's starving," she said. "And you better not burn it."

When I got home, I couldn't stop shaking. I couldn't eat or say a word. But luckily my parents didn't seem to notice.

At mass the next day, I barely recognized Mateo, his head shrunk into his shoulders and his whole body bent over like the curve of the moon. He looked so strange carrying a cane and wearing his sneakers, a baseball cap, and a sweatshirt several sizes too big. I couldn't pay attention to the priest or focus on the hymns but instead hurried out of the church during prayer and vomited my lunch all over the front steps.

"You okay, mijo?" my mom said on the drive home. She asked the question the way adults did, not really meaning it, only asking out of habit.

"He's fine," my dad muttered, drifting to sleep in the passenger seat. "Probably just a little tired, eh, Benjamín?"

"Yeah," I said. I leaned my head against the window. "Yeah, just tired."

When we got home, the landline in the kitchen was ringing. It stopped, then rang again. My dad frowned. No one ever used the landline anymore.

"Hello?" he said as he picked up the receiver. A few seconds passed, then he glanced at me. "It's for you."

"Can you meet me at the park?" Mateo said before I had even pressed the receiver fully against my ear. His voice was the only thing that hadn't changed, if just a little sadder. "By the lake?"

"How'd you get my number?"

"The phone book."

"The what?"

"Benjamín?" he said, his voice insistent.

I glanced at my parents. My mom was sifting through the fridge and my dad had flopped onto the sofa in front of the TV.

"Why?" I asked.

Mateo said nothing, just breathed static into the phone.

"Okay," I finally said. I didn't want to see him again, but I also didn't have anything else to do.

Neither of my parents stopped me as I left the house. I even left the door open, thinking one of them would, if not run after me, at least call out my name. But all I heard on the way to the park was silence punctured every once in a while, by crickets.

When I found him, Mateo was sitting cross-legged on the grass growing around the lake, holding his head in his hands. He nodded as I sat a few inches away. We sat without saying a word for several minutes until my leg began to jiggle with impatience.

"It's cold," I complained.

As if in response, Mateo shuddered and took off his baseball cap with trembling, curved fingers.

I nearly vomited again at the sight of the top of his head. Instead of more hair was a bald spot the size of a tennis ball. I stood up to leave when his voice, laced with accusation, stopped me.

"You followed me home, didn't you?"

I turned and shoved my hands into my pockets. "So what?"

"You know I have no one else."

"Cuz your abuela's crazy."

"She cares," he said, his voice hardening, I knew, to hide the fact that he didn't believe it.

"She told you that?" Admittedly, I couldn't remember if my parents ever did but they didn't do a lot of things that they should've.

Mateo bit his lip and stared at the laces of his sneakers for several moments. "Never," he finally replied. "Not once."

I shivered and sat down beside him again. "Your brother, he got old, too?"

He nodded and gazed out to the lake. "He said he was sorry."

I remembered it was all over the news. The cops, the flashing lights of red and blue, the horror and fascination mixed on my mom's face as she leaned closer to the TV. The way my dad kept telling her to turn it off. "Ay Dios Mio, Olivia," he scolded but made no move to stop her. The almost-disappointment of my mom's voice several days later when they realized Antonio had gone into the lake on his own, that no one had pushed him in but himself.

"Just terrible," she'd muttered before returning to her magazine.

"You could leave," I said to Mateo now.

"And go where?"

"You could tell someone."

"Who would believe me?" he asked.

I wanted to argue but kept silent—I remembered the smile his abuela had given me before after the funeral and wondered how I hadn't known it wasn't real.

Mateo struggled to his feet, leaning his weight against his cane.

I said his name, but he didn't turn.

He slipped off his shoes and began to walk towards the lake, each step a burden and every breath a wheeze, a rattling, as if he had marbles in his chest.

I said his name again, louder this time.

"But didn't you hear what they're saying?" I remembered my mom saying, the way she leaned forward with a secret in her eyes. *"Why he did it?"*

I jumped to my feet and grabbed Mateo's arm before his bare, gnarled feet could touch the water.

He turned to stare at me. I couldn't read his face. Gratitude, maybe. But regret and anger and resentment, too, for pulling him back.

Maybe I was too young to understand it then, how terrible and strange it all really was.

"Do you miss him?" I now asked Mateo.

For the first time, he seemed to smile. Or maybe I was just seeing things.

"Wouldn't you?" he replied.

The next morning on my way to school, I spotted Mateo in the laundromat again. He moved in slow, careful movements, his back curved like a branch bent to the will of the wind and crow's feet carved into the skin outside his eyes, visible even from outside—how little I now wished I could grow up already.

* * *

Without a word, I walked in, set my backpack on the dusty tiled floor, and stood beside him in front of the wall of washing machines. We didn't speak as we sorted clothes into piles by color, filled plastic drawers with detergent, inserted quarters like we were playing an arcade game, sat in hard-backed chairs with nothing else to do but watch the clothes swirl round and round and round. ✎

R. L. ASERET
earned an MFA in Creative Writing and has published several
fiction and nonfiction pieces—including a finalist in Storm Cellar's
(US) Force Majeure Flash Contest, a piece in the Autumn 2018
issue of The Fiddlehead (Canada), and stories in Delivered (UK),
Sediments (US), HCE Review (Ireland), Soliloquies (Canada),
among others—but hasn't submitted nearly enough. She
endeavors not to let the demands of everyday life interfere with
reading, writing, doing Yoga, and playing bad tennis—but they
almost always do. Carving out time for writing is an ongoing
challenge. Some of her most productive time is as a passenger
while her husband drives. She's constantly in the middle of at
least one book, one journal, and an issue of the New Yorker, and
believes that daily reading and writing are necessary for survival.

One Way Ticket

R.L. Aseret

Much had changed since 1992 when Milena had come to the United States on a temporary visa from the Czech Republic to marry Vuong. Eight years before that, he'd come from Vietnam. He'd invited her to come to San Buenaventura for a trial marriage. The visa he'd mailed identified her as his fiancée. With the money he sent, she'd purchased a ticket from Prague to Los Angeles, a one-way ticket.

The rest of the money, combined with her savings, she'd spent on a Czech violin. Her old violin she'd given to her music teacher to pass on to another student. She'd heard that in America you could buy only violins made in a factory in China. Although Vuong had suggested she buy clothing with any money remaining after she bought her tickets, she knew she could buy clothes anywhere, and she wouldn't need a return ticket.

When Vuong had come to her guided tour of Olomouc for the second consecutive day, Milena knew it wasn't St. Wenceslas Cathedral, or the town's one thousand years of history and architecture that drew him. He didn't speak Czech or Russian or German.

The old men and boys left in the village didn't hold her interest. On the surrounding farms, the few men not conscripted into the army, wanted meaty farm wives who could raise children and vegetables, cook and tend to livestock, and keep the barn and the house clean without complaint.

The Russian they had required her to speak in school now seemed useless. No one she wanted to talk to spoke Russian. Everyone interesting spoke English. Vuong spoke Vietnamese, some French, and English. Although short and slight, he was from America.

At first, she spoke to Vuong because she took every opportunity to speak to English-speaking tourists to make use of her eight years of study. Few came to Olomouc, and fewer still to where she lived outside Ostrava, far from Prague. Only occasionally did any of them engage in conversation.

In Prague, she'd heard there were many young people, and many tourists who came to see the ancient city, home to Kafka. If she stayed on her family's farm outside the village, she would live the life of a beetle, trundling from one life-sustaining task to another. If she could go to Prague, she could teach math or physics at a university, or give private violin lessons. In the city so many things were possible.

Her father had made sure she studied hard in school, so she could pass the test and earn a place at university. Math and Science made the Soviet Union a superpower, he insisted, and will ensure your future, too. When she'd played with the University Symphony Orchestra, his proud face glowed like a shiny pink sun in the audience. He'd always pushed and challenged her, encouraged her to be independent, while her mother clung to Milena, as if without Milena her own life wouldn't be worthwhile.

With her father gone, nothing held Milena on the farm. Her mother had sold off the outer acreage. Bohdan, her mother's tenant, farmed the remaining acres behind the house. He looked Milena over as if she were a cow he considered buying. Nothing would be left for her to inherit; when her mother died, Milena would need to sell the farmhouse and outbuildings to pay the mortgage.

Bohdan would help her mother, as would Milena's cousins— Radka and Miroslava. Bohdan tried to ingratiate himself with her mother, hoping she'd grow fond enough to will the land to him. Radka and Miroslava had settled on farms farther up river and joked that now that they lived in the country, the village seemed like a big city to them. Her cousins had laughed, but looked around with greedy, curious eyes, as if Milena's family farm did lie in the middle of the city, rather than on the outskirts of a dwindling country village.

Over coffee after the second day, he came on her tour, Vuong managed to say he was an electrical engineer. She laughed in surprise when he made the sugar bowl she reached for, dance away out of reach. She didn't think Bohdan had ever heard her laugh. After a week of walks and coffee, at the train station, with a shy smile, he asked her to write to him, promising that he'd write back. That way they could get to know each other better, and she could practice her English.

He wrote that in Vietnam, people ate to live, yet in America, it was very different. Milena began eating as little as she could while still maintaining her strength and health. Her mother fretted, but Milena only looked out the window, smiling at something in the distance. Vuong's letters had been full of philosophical questions, such as what she saw as the purpose of men and women, how to raise children; and the importance of an extended family.

His own family, he wrote, had moved far away from where he lived in Central California, to a place called Seattle, which made life very different from when they all lived in a village in the northern part of Vietnam. He visited them usually only once a year. Unhappy that he didn't settle near them and marry a Vietnamese girl, they never

came south to visit him.

She wrote to him that no one in her family thought music important. So, she'd had to seek out violin lessons on her own, although her father had gone to all her concerts and spoken of her with great pride to his friends. She didn't reveal that she had never had a boyfriend, that no one in her village appreciated physics, mathematics, or violin.

After seventeen months, he came to visit Milena again. He told her the week he would arrive, but not which day.

Each day as she led the tour she knew by heart, she found herself making mistakes, repeating herself and leaving out parts, trailing off in the middle of sentences as she searched the square or the street for his slight form. She felt his visit would be an audition, just as his letters had seemed to be tests. She didn't know what would happen if she passed, but she knew she didn't want to fail.

At week's end, she felt someone staring and turned to look. Most of the tour group watched her with varying levels of interest. A boy with a yarmulke atop his cropped hair fidgeted and toed something on the ground, a stone or a stick, avoiding her eyes. A large woman with yellow hair, orangey black at the roots, smirked and looked away. An older couple attired in matching Paris is for Lovers T-shirts, khaki shorts, and running shoes looked up, smiled, and returned to their guidebook.

The skin on the back of her neck prickled again. She scanned the medieval square.

In a shadowed corner Vuong's black hair fell over his forehead as he ducked his head. He swung his head up, then dodged back and forth around a pillar.

She grinned at him.

He smiled back.

She wondered how long he'd stood there, whether this was the first day of his visit. Had he watched her all week?

They didn't speak about what they'd written to each other. His continued playfulness surprised laughter out of deep inside her—he jumped out like a frog when she came through a door, raced leaf boats bearing seed pods in the gutter overflowing with rainwater, pretended to joust with his umbrella.

She felt off balance, not rooted to the ordinary as she usually did.

He popped up with a growl, wearing a silly mask made of leaves and twigs and an expression to match.

She laughed so hard she doubled over, nearly toppling into a fountain, before she stood and straightened her clothing, relieved to see no one in the square who knew her. She didn't recognize herself with him and that stunned and excited her.

Yet, his mild demeanor revealed no secrets. He didn't answer questions. Instead, he'd address topics generally without refusing or agreeing.

When Milena asked what brought him to the Czech Republic and if he had visited Prague, Vuong said, "Prague is very old and beautiful city."

How much was due to their language difficulties? How much was his way? How could she find out? Would she be glad to have the answer?

* * *

After traveling for the better part of three days, she arrived in California. She'd left her family's farm outside the Northern Moravian village of Ostrava in Bohdan's truck. Bohdan drove in sullen silence after throwing her luggage into the loose hay in the fenced back of the truck.

She'd gone from Olomouc to the Prague airport, five hours by train, and to Frankfurt on a seventy-minute flight. After enduring a twenty-six-hour layover in the airport, she boarded the twelve-and-a-half-hour flight to Los Angeles.

Vuong met her at the airport.

For the first time, she saw the ocean. As he drove two hours up the curving rocky coast of California to his home, the horizon of the blue-green sea looked so high she almost wondered why it didn't crash on top of them, the way the waves crashed upon the rocks.

At his large, two-story suburban tract home, she felt fatigued, light-headed, and as if she'd entered a fraternity house, the sort she'd seen in an American movie on the plane.

Several men from Southeast or Southwest Asia lounged about the house—watching television, playing cards, and violent war games, or working on computers. She couldn't be sure how many men lived there or if some only visited, as they abruptly came and went. She wondered if they all lived with Vuong.

In the living room, a large hexagonal piece of glass atop a zigzag metal structure served as a table. Crumpled cans—most with unfamiliar English lettered labels, a few with Asian characters or flowing Arabic script—littered the table, along with wrappers labeled in a variety of languages unknown to her, and a large cellophane bag torn open to allow irregular reddish-brown shapes to spill out onto the table and cascade onto the carpeted floor. One area of the pale aqua carpet just under the edge of the table had a large, crusted charcoal-colored stain as if dark liquid had spilled and mixed with the contents of more than one overflowing ashtray to make mud before drying.

While he shared the house with many, the walls belonged only to Vuong. He'd decorated with some framed pictures—prints, idiosyncratic collages, and enlarged photographs—but mostly with his own artwork painted on the walls.

Although he worked as an electrical engineer for the American military, he'd spent much of his free time painting and sculpting. Women, many buxom women, were the subjects of most of the posters, collages, and framed photographs, including one of a black Olympic athlete posed in a lunge, with powerful legs, arms, and torso as well as full breasts that her stretch sports attire didn't hide. Painted nude women reclined on the walls of the master bedroom. Lush sculpted torsos topped truncated pillars painted with twisting vines in the living room, bedroom, and hall. Milena's stomach clenched at seeing the images, especially those on the master bedroom walls, but she reminded herself that he'd deemed her good enough to send for and call his fiancée.

While Vuong gave her measuring glances, the other men stared—first as if to gauge how available she was to them, then as if waiting to see how long she'd last. From their glances, she surmised she wasn't the first woman Vuong had brought to this house. That mattered not at all to her. Without doubt, she knew that she'd be the last.

Nothing that Vuong had said during his two visits or in any of his twice-weekly letters prepared her for his house full of roommates. She closed her eyes and thought about what she could make of this situation in which she found herself.

While Vuong tried to keep things neat—straightening piles of magazines or newspapers and picking up lint from the carpet—none of the men cleaned. How many years had Vuong owned the house? Likely the same number of years since the bathrooms had been clean. The house Vuong may have bought when new, so perhaps they'd never been cleaned—new, then dirtier and dirtier, until rife with filth.

Vuong brought her to a small, windowless room in the corner of the master bedroom. "You would like to put things here?"

Milena blinked, gazing about the empty room, the blank white walls of which she could almost touch with outstretched arms. She opened her mouth and closed it again, looking to Vuong for clues.

Looking at the carpet, Vuong said in a voice she might not have heard in a larger room, "Clothing? Shoes?"

Looking up, she saw the pole below the high shelf that ran around three of the walls. She nodded. "Yes. Thank you."

Vuong smiled and began to edge out the door. Before disappearing, though, he stood gazing at her with bright eyes.

Milena couldn't help grinning.

"Very glad you are here."

She nodded and bit her lip, feeling a wild urge to cry.

After hanging up her dresses and organizing her things, she closed the door to the large closet and left the room. Through an open door with a nameplate affixed to it, she saw that Ashwini, Vuong's roommate from Bangalore, India, had placed a wide desk two steps into his bedroom, with his chair on the other side, apparently to give anyone opening the door the experience of visiting the office of an executive.

Turning toward the stairs, she encountered Ashwini himself. His eyes glittering, he leaned in until his moist, rubbery lips touched her hair, and whispered in Milena's ear, "What do you think of Vuong's artwork?"

Milena squeezed her eyes shut, knowing it wouldn't do to pull back, not if she intended to stay in the house, and said, as if beginning a lecture to a classroom of students, "Art, it is important."

Vuong turned from the top of the stairs, his face alight, his expression grateful.

Frowning, Ashwini pulled back until his double chin became a triple.

That night, when she emerged from the adjoining bathroom, she found that Vuong had turned off the light. From memory, she slowly made her way across the carpet to the bed, careful not to stub her toes. Vuong's dark shape lay on the far side of the enormous bed. She slid between the cool sheets, conscious of their smooth texture, the weight of the blanket, and the ungiving firmness of the mattress. The bedding felt clean but smelled musty. He'd removed the gleaming padded bed covering. What did Vuong expect of her?

As if in response, Vuong whispered, "Goodnight."

Milena resumed breathing, realizing she'd stopped upon leaving the bathroom. She awoke to brilliant sunshine coming in a high round window. Nowhere to be seen, Vuong had left for work.

That day, she scrubbed the shower stall in the bathroom adjoining their bedroom, the one he'd used that morning before leaving for work until her back ached. The sponge in her hand had all but disintegrated, pebbles of hardened powder rattled in the can of cleanser, and layers of grime remained.

One of the roommates, Armaghan, identified by Vuong as Pakistani, stood in the doorway in his long flowing shirt and loose pants, watching her as if she were a servant. He laughed. "It is a lost cause. We will not keep it up after you leave."

She sat back on her heels and looked at him for a moment, her lips curved into a small smile. A confident man, she reflected, for one wearing what would be considered a dress in the Czech Republic.

She took some of the American money Vuong had left for her in a carved wooden box on the dresser in their room. She walked to a nearby store they'd driven by on the way to the house and bought five packs of rubber gloves, scrub brushes, sponges, cans of scouring powder, bars of lavender soap, and hand and dish towels.

In the store, the staff and the customers spoke at least three different languages, but none close to Czech. Would she ever again be able to relax and express herself without effort?

De, the roommate Vuong met in a Thai refugee camp, giggled and bit his nails, watching her empty the bag. "We will not use these things."

In response, she only smiled and nodded. She'd seen De playing video games in his off hours, but not talking on the telephone or sending email the way the others did. Did he have a family? Did they live nearby?

That night, when she clicked off the bathroom light, she again found the room in darkness. Again, Vuong whispered, "Goodnight," once she got into bed. She whispered back, closed her eyes, and slept.

The following day she found that Vuong had replenished the stack of bills in the box carved with fish, she assumed were native to Vietnam. While the sheets and towels agitated in the washing machine, she walked to the store that she'd noticed next door to where she'd gotten the cleaning supplies. She bought herself shampoo and conditioner with the fragrance of wild grass and flowers that the package promised would make her hair silky, and sandalwood-scented lotion to keep her skin soft.

In a window display, an enlarged picture caught her eye. Last year's calendar on sale, each page contained a photograph of a different rural landscape. The one on the cover reminded her of the countryside outside Ostrava. Two photographs inside had the same flowering trees, the same rolling terrain she'd seen out the window on the train from Olomouc to Prague. She bought the calendar and a roll of tape. After asking De where she could find scissors, she cut a few photos away from the calendar and taped them to the walls of her closet.

Clean sheets fresh from the dryer covered the bed. Neatly folded clean towels hung on the racks in the bathroom. The shower stall, separate tub, sink, and floor were glistening when she showered, washed her hair, and rubbed lotion into her skin. While her hair dried, she played Czech music on the violin, smiling that she'd no cows or goats to milk, no stalls, pens, or coops to muck out.

Vuong brought home bags of strange, spicy food each day. After dinner, he smiled when he came into the bedroom. Gesturing at the bathroom, he said, "When you arrived, looked very different."

She sauntered over to him and draped her arms around his shoulders. He gazed at her without blinking and said, "Smell very nice."

She gazed back at him and tilted her head to kiss his neck. His skin tightened as though an electric current ran through it. Smiling as if she had a secret that she wanted to share with him, she began to unbutton his shirt. Panting, he gently maneuvered her to the bed. His face flushed, he asked if she had birth control. She grinned and pulled him into her with her legs.

The next day, she cleaned the downstairs shower stall and sink, and scrubbed the floor of that room and the kitchen.

Ashwini shook his head. Malena wondered how he made the comb marks not show on the sides of his greased hair. Pointing upwards, as though someone up there would confirm his words, he said, "You have only made it more difficult for yourself, I think you will see. Now every bit of dirt will contrast with the rest of the floor."

She ducked her head and smiled, as if embarrassed to not know the language and went upstairs to shower and play the violin. She thought of her cousins, Radka and Miroslava. Found herself wanting to hear their astonished and giggling gossip now. What would they think of Ashwini?

A letter came from the Immigration Service. She didn't understand all of it but knew that she had sixty days to leave the country or report for a deportation hearing.

Milena withdrew money from the carved fish box and walked to the grocery store she'd visited with Vuong. She would prepare pasta in the Czech way—with wheat flour added to the tomato sauce.

She wrote an invitation to dinner for the following day and slid it under the edge of the carved wooden box on Vuong's chest of drawers. Milena started out of the room, looked back at the folded paper, retrieved it, and secreted it under his pillow instead. She plumped his pillow, then hers to eliminate the contrast, and tucked the padded synthetic bedcover, smoothing out the ripples in the fabric.

Using Vuong's computer, she found that she could teach college Mathematics online. She could earn what seemed an enormous salary without having to go to the college more than once every few months. She'd have freedom to do what she wanted, without the risk

of emptying the carved box. By lessening the burden to fill the box, she might encourage Vuong to make their relationship permanent.

When she served Vuong Czech pasta, he smiled as though he had longed for food so good. "Very special dish."

She smiled back, gazing into his eyes.

Despite continuing to eat only the necessary amount, and her morning sit-ups—she'd worked up to one hundred each day— her stomach began to expand. At their civil ceremony, she wore a flowing gown.

After the wedding, Ashwini moved out, and after the birth of each of their first two children, another roommate moved out until only their family lived in the house. Whether Vuong spoke with them, or how or if he chose which roommate would move, he didn't share with her.

One landscape photograph Milena hung to one side of the sink on a kitchen cabinet, another in the powder room where it could be seen in the mirror while standing at the sink, and a third at the base of the stairwell, near the front door. She scrubbed and coated each of the walls of the vacated bedrooms with fresh paint and vacuumed and shampooed the carpet. She bought Czech books and recorded music, children's furniture, and convertible futons for guests. When she asked him why he never complained about anything she did or didn't do, Vuong put his arms around her and said, "Because I am happy." Milena had always known she wouldn't need a return ticket. ✎

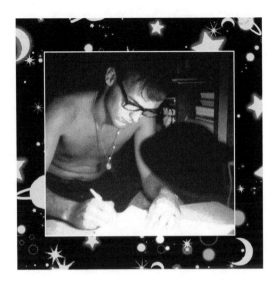

JERRY MCCANN

My life has been a wild and adventuresome ride. As a friend has said, it has been a journey without a map. Born in January 1948, despite an abortion attempt on my life, to hard-working but poor parents in Lenni, Pennsylvania. I grew up watching a TV series entitled ADVENTURES IN PARADISE. It starred Gardner McKay as an ex-GI who sailed his schooner, the TIKI, around the South Pacific. In December of 1965, as a senior in High School, I went to see where my Gardner McKay, lived. You can read about it in my short story "Pay Attention to the Signs." After High School, I wandered around eventually getting married and joining the Air Force which took me to New Mexico, sunny South Vietnam and then Florida, where I am sure God lives. I live in Pennsylvania with my wife and I have written three movie scripts, all in action adventure genre. If you know anyone in the film business who wants to make great films, have them contact me. Somehow, I have managed to accumulate three sons and six grandchildren. Thank you for reading along.

Pay Attention To Signs

Jerry McCann

In 1965, at seventeen, I had come to the island of Oahu alone on Christmas Eve. It was my senior year of high school. It had been a longtime dream to visit Hawaii.

After checking in at the hotel, I headed across the street to Waikiki Beach. I fell into a conversation with a man while soaking in the ocean. He was from British Columbia and had come on vacation with his wife, two daughters, Bonnie and Bev, and the not too favored older sister's boyfriend, Joe. He invited me to join his family for dinner. We all became immediate good friends. It was magical.

Before dinner each day, the two girls, the boyfriend and I would tour Oahu horseback riding, visiting Sea World, the Blow Hole, and more.

A few days later on December 29, we took a small plane with Aloha Airlines to the island of Kauai where South Pacific, Fantasy Island, and later Jurassic Park were filmed. It was an unspecial day in Hawaii, somewhat north of fabulous: a light breeze dispersing the aromas of miscellaneous flowers and fauna; blue friendly skies, and about 85 degrees. Who could want to be anywhere else? Not me!

We rented a VW Bug to drive us around this literal paradise. Passing a beach, we decided to do some filming with my new movie camera, a Christmas gift from my family. We staged a little animated short film. In the first scene, Joe would attack me, but I would overpower him to rescue Bonnie, with Bev filming and directing. After our movie star filming, we stopped by a picturesque beach with cliffs in the background—wonderful for photos. We did not plan to swim because we had many other sites to see, but Bonnie and Bev insisted on getting their feet wet. None of us cared about the sign proclaiming:

NO SWIMMING, DANGEROUS UNDERTOW

I began taking shots of the girls with my camera, but even only ankle deep the undertow began to take them out in the dangerous waters. Even just standing in the waves was enough for the undertow to pull the girls deeper and deeper. Despite their full-bodied resistance, they were being pulled under. They screamed for help.

Throwing my new camera to its death in the sand, I jumped in to save them. However, they were superior swimmers. The girls swam into deeper water where the "undertow" was much less and then down the beach and were able to exit this friendlier piece of ocean.

On the Other hand, while they swam to safety, I was pulled out to sea. My swimming experience had been limited to small creeks back home on hot days. A hero wannabe without the requisite skills to survive. Now, lacking even reasonable swimming talent, my body was thrown uncontrollably by the waves to the bottom, back near the top and back down again. It was a chaotic underwater ballet. Not being able to reach the surface for air, I began breathing water. I was helpless and drowning!

I hadn't breathed for two minutes; Surprisingly, I was still aware but realized that I was going to die. I would not see my parents again. They would fall into the Hell of living with the reality that their only child died in paradise but not the preferred paradise.

Suddenly, I saw a deep tunnel of warm yellow light, a man in a black suit, was waving me in. Then, just when I thought I was gone, he offered me his hand. I took it and he pulled me up. I was bashed against a rock. Grasping the rock, my finger found a hole big enough that I could pull my head up above the water. The waves were coming in cycles of two strong ones and then a softer one. Timing them, I was finally able to grab some air. It had been awhile. Regaining some alertness and strength, I jumped onto the submerged rock.

I looked toward the beach and the cliffs behind it.

VOICE FROM THE CLIFFS:

"I want you to live your life with honesty and be honest in all that you do!"

Despite the near-death experience, or maybe because of it, my senses were sharp. There was no confusion about what had happened. I know I did hear a voice, and I always felt it was the voice of God speaking to me.

My friends had been searching for me all the while I was underwater. They ran down the beach get help and found a family picnicking on the beach. When they explained the situation, the family said they happened to have a long rope in their station wagon. You can't make this stuff up! Safe on the rock, I was still about twenty feet from the beach. The first rope toss was short. The second reached me. Grabbing it with a lifesaving grip. I jumped from the rock and they towed me to the beach.

Surrounded by my friends and the picnicking family, there was much hugging and some tears. I would like to say I never made any more foolish mistakes after that and that I have always been perfect. Everyone knows that is not true. What is true is that

for the rest of my adult life, I felt that the message has never left me.

I went home to my parents. I took other adventures. Despite serving in Viet Nam, and having a long career in business, getting married, raising two sons and adopting a third, each step — I like to think — I kept up my end of the bargain in my small way: to let God work through me. To speak up honestly to my friends and my business partners. To not ignore but watch out for the signs.

Later in life, I've realized that the voice from the cliffs left me a message that was not just to tell the truth, but to be honest with myself and others. The message from God has never left me. I believe I misinterpreted it for many years. Taking it as a directive to avoid lying and any type of deceit, it was a daily goal to obey.

Some years ago, it occurred to me that the message was not to avoid lying but to be honest. I was, to be honest in my dealings. It was not okay to avoid the reality of the situation when interacting. Friends who were doing wrong, who needed guidance and direction, might need me to speak up. I would not do the confrontations in a mean-spirited way but in a manner meant to nurture and guide.

Perhaps the initial interpretation of God's message was appropriate for my early maturity levels. More years under the belt, revealed the intended meaning to me. It has been another wonderful gift from a near drowning episode long ago and far away.

* * *

What happened to the film we made? The camera never worked again. But sometimes, as I sit at my desk typing up one of my screenplays, I think back to that beautiful paradise and wish I could watch that magical vacation one more time. ✎

"I want you to live an honest life..." — Pay Attention to Signs

ASHLEY REISINGER

In true Canadian fashion, ASHLEY REISINGER spends ten months
out of the year huddled beneath a blanket while pretending she
remembers what summer feels like. She lives in Edmonton with
her husband, a dozen Marvel Pop Figures, and four thousand
empty notebooks. To fund her writing addiction, she does
reception and administration at a Swing Dance Ballroom, slipping
away from the desk to practice a little Lindy Hop whenever
possible. She can often be found reading legal transcripts,
listening to true crime podcasts, watching YouTube videos on
how to properly fire a Glock 22, and otherwise making her family
and friends nervous. Though her writing research paints a rather
questionable search history, and she spends more time staring at
a Word Document than doing anything else, she wouldn't change
a thing—unless six-million dollars, a couple book deals, and a chai
latte were to come into the picture.

One Last Goodbye

ASHLEY REISINGER

Silence stretches between them in the cab of the old pickup. She faces the passenger seat window watching the endless fields of yellow canola shimmer by. The sun bounces off the flowering heads and she squints against the blinding light but doesn't look away, as though the crops of green and yellow, painted bright against the blue sky, are her punishment.

Beside her, he shifts, hand fumbling with the position of the visor. By the crinkles around his eyes, she can tell the intensity of the sun's rays blister against his gaze too, though the rest of his expression remains stoic. He simply watches the road, his fingers back to gripping the wheel.

The engine rattles more than hums; the vents forcing lukewarm, stale air into the cab. It's the only noise, save for the rumble of the tires grating over the pavement. As they drive, an eternity down the endless highway, the truck becomes stuffy and unbearable.

She pretends she doesn't notice his dark eyes trail toward her, linger, lazily wander back to the road. Instead, she shifts against her seat, leaning closer to the cracked open window where the sweltering breeze brushes against her face. The warm wind does little to combat the beads of perspiration on her palms though, or the sweat soaked into the collar of his button-down white shirt. It's the kind of hot that reminds her of summers spent at the family cabin, catching crickets with the other lake-lot boys back when her two brothers hadn't been old enough to pester her incessantly, and her parents hadn't thought to call her in before dark.

Folding her hands over each other in her lap, she casts another wary glance in the driver's direction. He says the first words, as though he can feel her eyes on him. His voice rings too loud in the silence that's entombed them for the long hours of the impromptu trip.

"You can't say you didn't see this coming."

She flinches away from the words. Forcing a deep breath out through her nose, she blinks hard against the prickle behind her eyes and tries to ignore the way her heart pulses against her throat. Her head tips back, gaze trailing across the roof's ripped upholstery—it's something to distract her from their lapse in conversation.

As her eyes inadvertently slip back to him, she notices his fingers drumming against the steering wheel, though he seems otherwise unaffected by the silence between them. Staring at the gold band slipped on his ring finger, her stomach squirms. She tries to pry her gaze away, but he catches her, and she catches him. Their eyes meet and she wonders if he can see the panic set into her taut features.

Pressing her shoulder blades against the bench seat behind her, she has little time to steel her resolve before the words tumble out of her mouth.

"You don't have to do this." The correction follows at the glance he shoots her way. "We don't have to do this. There's another way."

With his eyes on the road, he presses his lips into a cool smile that dies before reaching his dark eyes. He doesn't have to say it, but he does anyway. "It's too late."

The words are on the tip of her tongue—it's not too late, they can keep trying, they can turn around and find a nice place to stay the night—but the sentiment sickens her and any false pretenses of courage fizzle out before they broach on fruition. She's a coward, has always been a coward—never one to broach a difficult conversation; never one to endure reprimands from parents, teachers, friends, if the only casualty was her own dignity. And she knows she'll let him end whatever charade this is the same way—in a fearful, placating silence.

"Do you know how many times I've caught you looking for a way out?" he says. His tone has become conversational, as though he's telling her a story, or reading from a teleprompter. "I could tell that you wanted to leave. Leave our life behind without even looking back.

Without saying goodbye. I'd at least grant you the courtesy of one last goodbye, you know? Do you realize how painful it was for me to watch you pull away from me? Do you know how many times you put me through that?"

"No," she says reflexively.

"Now I'm sure that's not true."

Dropping her head to stare into her lap, her eyes absently follow hands that don't feel like they belong to her, twisting about each other against her thighs. He's right. She does know.

* * *

Two years ago, nearly to the day, she tried to leave him for the first time. She sat at the foot of the bed, her shirt hanging limply off her skinny frame, her too-big leggings sagging against her hips. The pang in her stomach felt just like freshman year, trying to skip a meal or two where she could so she'd fit into a new pair of cutoffs. She'd wanted to impress a boy. How silly that all seemed now.

The industrial-style window of the apartment hung open, cool air seeping into the room like fingers wrapping around her tiny frame. Her shoulders hunched up near her ears as she suppressed a shiver, her choppy bangs falling in front of her eyes. The haircut—a shoddy hack job to be sure—didn't suit her, and neither did the from-the-box blonde that still left her scalp tingling. But he liked his handiwork, and she hadn't the heart to tell him she hated it. And it was her heart, the wild, frantic beating of some untamed animal let loose in her chest, that consumed her.

The task set before her seemed so insurmountable, every nerve beneath her skin tingling in some masochistic anticipation of what she had to do. She sat there for fifteen minutes trying to dredge up the courage to leave, trying to silence the voices of terror whispering through her mind, trying to ignore the questions of what she would do once she walked through those doors. Where she would go. What maelstrom of fire and fury she might bring down upon the people she cared about if this didn't work. If she couldn't get far enough, fast enough. If she went back to her family—the people she'd left with no word and no warning, infatuated with the subtle turn of a mysterious smile from across the dimly lit pub.

She remembered the

devastating night she met him, tears streaming unrepentant down her cheeks as she paid the bartender for whatever was cheapest on tap. The end of an era. Goodbye to her double-crossing, cheating, good-for-nothing high school sweetheart.

Then, the comforting words of a stranger with dark hair and dark eyes. The purr of his voice as he ordered her another drink. His hands on her back, him helping her into a cab when she felt sickly groggy after the Rickards Red. He'd left her with his number to text him when she made it home safely and she'd thought it was chivalrous. Classy.

She had texted him that night. And the next. They met again, multiple times, in the weeks to come.

He lay in bed on his stomach beside her, his arms crooked around his head, his face in the pillow. His bare back, muscled and strong, rose and fell with even breathing. The rest of his body lay entangled in the white duvet they had shared.

A hitch through his body sent a bolt of panic through her, and only when he settled back into a rhythmic pattern of breathing did she slide off the edge of the bed. Cringing as the springs squeaked beneath her insubstantial weight, she froze, standing motionless for a moment. She turned only her head, her deafening pulse in her ears as she looked back to him. Though she couldn't see his eyes, she told herself he was sleeping. He had to be sleeping.

Another moment without moving, then she took the first step, her socked feet silent on the concrete floor. His fingers, cold as the morning air, wrapped around her delicate wrist and squeezed enough to be possessive.

His eyes, bleary from sleep, danced up to her, his face still half buried in the feathery embrace of the pillow.

"Where are you going?" he asked.

"Nowhere," she said, though the word came out strained. She fumbled the next sentence clumsily. "Was just—was just—I'm just going to get a drink of water."

Her hand shook as she brought it to his thick forearm, but she ran her fingertips against the hairs anyway, up towards his chest.

"Come back to bed," he said,

his eyes closing and his lips turning up at the corners, reminiscent of the first smile he captured her with.

No words could come out past the lump that had formed in her throat, but she hummed an awkward affirmative as he loosened his grip on her wrist. Bile crept up her throat as she pulled back the covers on her side of the bed. Crawling underneath the warm pressure of the quilt made her shiver harder than sitting in the crisp morning air.

* * *

The second time, a year and a half into their scarred relationship, was different. Their conversation evolved into an argument of sorts, though she couldn't even remember what it was about. She had been yelling, he had been violent, and God only knew how the neighboring room of the grungy motel hadn't heard them—or maybe they just hadn't cared.

The rumpled bedspread, a ball in the middle of the mattress; the tipped over nightstand; the cup of water that had been atop it, spilled on the off-white carpet to make a gray stain in the fabric of the floor, spoke of their rift. The dark signs that no one else could see, she carried on the inside. The fading red imprint of his fingers against her throat, the gnawing hunger beneath her jutting ribcage, the goosebumps that rippled at his touch.

These thoughts she dismissed, like the television humming dimly in the background—a man on the news describing the disappearance of an Ellison Dubois and telling of the Mississauga Massacre story which was to follow at 12:00 a.m. Neither story could be heard over the sound of her voice.

"Don't touch me!" she trembled as she yelled, still fighting and swatting away his hand as he reached out towards her exposed shoulders.

Her arms wrapped around her bare midsection, as though she could hide her body from him. She wore only her matching red underwear, ones that were supposed to make her feel sexy and alluring but only made her feel defiled and unclean. She wished she could tell him not to look at her—tell him not to breathe near her, not to haunt her dreams and memories—but fear stilled her tongue.

He took a step towards her, and she took a step back—twice more until she was backed against the radiator, the hot metal against her cold legs. He touched her shoulders tenderly, running his hands down her arms, his eyes following his movement.

He made a gentle shushing noise and pulled her into his body. She shuddered and pushed pathetically back against him.

"Look at me," he said softly, taking his fingers and gently guiding her face with his hand.

His deep brown eyes bore into her, murky and dark.

"Leave me alone," she said, though the words had lost some of their conviction. Tears slipped through her eyelashes and down over her cheeks while she struggled in his arms. Her heart wrenched, and her eyes flicked to their suitcase in the corner. It sat unzipped and open, rumpled clothes haphazardly tossed half in, tiny travel bottles of shampoo resting on top of a clean but unfolded T-shirt. She hated it and everything it represented. Their transient lifestyle—constantly running and never getting anywhere. She missed home, her parents, her brothers. The creak of the porch swing in an El Niño breeze. The tang of rain and the hum of lightning lingering in the air,

despite the endless blue skies. The slam of the screen door; the babble of happy conversation and clattering dishes as a motley assortment of neighbors and family prepared food together.

"I want to go," she whispered.

"Where?" he said, the toxicity of his voice bleeding into her mind, poisoning the memories of her old life. "We can go anywhere you want. We can go right now."

She tried to picture him there, amongst the boisterous conversation and the meaningless banter. Imagined the glint of steel in his gaze if they said something he didn't like, or teased him, as they did with everyone.

"Hmm," he prompted, his arms tightening around her, the bare skin of her back meeting the bare flesh of his abdomen. "Where do you want to go, baby-doll?"

Where could she go?

Her stomach heaved. The tears came faster and harder. He held her closer, his arms over hers, pressing them against her body so she couldn't move to wipe away the tear-tracks. He brought his head against her ear, and started murmuring, his words dripping like honey.

"Don't cry. It doesn't matter where we are, I'll always be here for you, babe. I'm all you need. It'll be okay."

It was like that for a while, the two of them immersed in virtual silence with only the news whispering into the night, and his soft voice whispering into her hair.

"Don't worry, baby, don't worry."

But she worried. Ever since the glamour of the first months of their relationship had worn off, his mask chipping, revealing the quiet, fearsome secrets beneath, she learned to always be worried around him.

* * *

The next time was the last, and though it felt like forever ago, only six agonizing weeks had passed since then. Haggard and weary, she'd long since lost the will to resist him. Yellowing bruises peppered her midsection and face, deep red lines marked her wrists where the skin had been rubbed raw, scars painted her arms and legs. Her hair was once again cropped short, the same way he'd sheared it at the start to keep anyone from recognizing

her. This time, he masked her natural brown with a rusty red that bled all over her pillow. The white sheets, the pillowcase, the spotless, pristine bed, had all been sullied. Like a symbol of how his feelings had changed toward her, he lost his mind over the stained fabric. He called her filthy, he called her ungrateful and careless, he told her he didn't know why he kept her around. The crinkle of disdain over his nose, the hatred in his eyes, told her louder than his words that she was running out of time.

He still kept the ring on— the one he'd bought himself, slipped on his own finger before he started calling her missus as though they had actually made anything official—but the fear of what he would do to her if she stayed continued to grow until it became stronger than the fear of what he would do to her if she left.

And yet, the deeply ingrained anxiety about what might befall anyone connected to her still lingered. She didn't have a contingency plan for that— never had. If warning her family from a payphone once she got far enough from this place was all she could do, then it would have to be enough. She hadn't heard their voices in almost two years. Wondered if they would even want to hear hers or if they believed her dead and had already grieved the loss.

With nothing in her pockets, not so much as a bag over her shoulder, she tried, one last time. She tried to leave.

She managed to get out of their sublet apartment, the thrill and desperation in her blood fueling her farther than she'd ever gotten from him before. It propelled her forward with some false hope that she had actually done it this time.

She bolted over the pavement in bare feet, rocks digging into her delicate soles, cutting the skin open as she fled. She didn't feel it, only felt the hammering of her heart slamming against her ribs. Pain lanced through her lungs, burning in her throat. Ragged breaths tore inside, pulling at her harrowed frame, but she didn't stop. She couldn't stop.

As she cast a glance backward, her shoulder clipped a streetlight. A bolt flared through her arm from shoulder to fingertips. An inadvertent hiss of pain slid through her teeth, and her other hand instinctively grabbed for the blossoming bruise. She bit down on her lip, stifling a groan before glancing back one more time.

Before trading it in for something less conspicuous, he had driven a flaming red convertible. The top was drawn when he found her, though she hadn't yet known it—all she saw were the blazing white headlights.

The fear drove out everything else, sent her into a wild hysteria. She pressed on, faster than she knew she could run, ignoring the pain, the spots that danced before her eyes, the shape of her shrinking shadow in front of her. She ran, because she had no other choice.

The screech of the tires on the pavement sounded like all the demons she had run from for so long, laughing. The car roared around in front of her, lurching as he slammed to a stop.

She didn't even scream, she just doubled over and retched, breathing hard as she raised her head to look at him. She didn't fight the tears that time, they just came, flooding down her face as if she were a five-year-old.

"I'm sorry," she sobbed, "I'm sorry, I'm so sorry."

He reached over to the passenger seat and threw open her door. She stood there, shaking, vomit dotting the front of her shirt, heavy breathing coming through her mouth.

"Get in." His tone was clipped and short, the muscles in his jawline working as he gritted his teeth. He didn't look at her.

"Please!" she shrieked through her tears.

"Get in!" he roared, grabbing her arm and hauling her into the seat.

Neither of them closed the door, the momentum of him pulling a violent U-turn caused it to snap shut.

"I'm sorry," she cried, wrapping her arms around her knees and pulling them to her chest.

"Shut up," he said, and she flinched, hands flying up over her face. "I'm getting sick and tired of this. I saved you, remember? I looked after you. I've always looked after you."

She remembered the night they met, the drink, the cab. Back then, she'd never considered why two drinks made her stagger, why her legs gave out, spilling her into his waiting, welcoming arms when she could usually hold her alcohol. She'd never thought to pick apart the scenario he created—where she was the damsel in distress and he, the hero. Like the ring on his finger, like the tenuous illusion of their entire relationship, she never considered how he could have manipulated it all into being as, she'd begun to realize with sickening clarity, he had done before. She'd found the locket with the initials 'E.D.' etched on the back. The lady's watch that didn't belong to her. A small ring box filled with an assortment of hoops she didn't know if had belonged to one woman, or many.

She hadn't thought about it then, but it became all she could think about now.

He sped, twenty—thirty over the limit which wrenched her just-emptied stomach into a painful knot.

As always, she wanted to say something, but couldn't. Instead, her words stayed rooted firmly in her throat with her beating heart, and she lapsed into a terrified, placating silence.

The street lights flickered past them; the city loomed before them. Closer and closer it came. When buildings rose around the car, he seemed to relax, like each towering wall of metal and glass served as confirmation that he hadn't yet lost his hold on her. He inhaled deeply before letting his breath out in a steady stream.

"It's alright, my dear," he finally said. "These things will happen. We'll just make sure they don't happen again."

* * *

We'll just make sure they don't happen again. He had said that as though it were making a concession for her misdeeds, but the next weeks were strained. Sparks of anger became raging infernos that possessed him, and she never knew what would set him off.

She dried a dish before the television, a hollow shell of a person, her eyes staring blankly at the news while her hands moved mechanically. The story was of another missing woman—a thin face, high cheekbones, a smile much like her own. Her eyes had flickered, and he had noticed.

"What?" he yelled, leaping off the couch and tearing the plate from her. "Feeling sorry for yourself? Want to run away again?"

He slammed the plate against the floor, watching it shatter to pieces. She jumped, fear slithering in like a cold drug in her veins. Her eyes trained on him, watching him seethe, watching his shoulders lift and fall with uncontainable rage. She didn't know how to soothe him anymore. Feigning love didn't work, physical affection twisted her stomach into knots, and trying to avoid him always made it worse.

"I'm—I'm sorry," she tried to say, but he didn't let her finish.

The heavy smack of flesh against flesh filled her ears. A flash of pain rippled across her jaw as her head snapped to the side with the force of the blow. Tears sprung into her eyes, but she blinked them back as she licked the tang of copper from her lip. Tilting her head toward him, her fingertips lifted to lightly brush the throbbing pulse in her cheek, she watched his back while he stormed from the room. Only one harsh command trailed behind him.

"Clean that up."

* * *

Now he's asking her if she knows how many times he's had to watch her try to leave him. Yes. She knows. She sits in the passenger seat of the red pickup, both wrists handcuffed, a chain threaded through a makeshift clamp soldered to the bottom of the glove-box. Her head is dropped down, her heart racing. Every breath sends a stab of pain between her ribs.

"It was three, wasn't it?" he's saying. "I think that's very generous of me. Three times we could have parted ways, three times I could have said goodbye to you, and this wretched, ungrateful streak you have. But I didn't. Because I wanted it to work. I wanted you."

She grimaces, disgust roiling up from the pit of her stomach. He hadn't wanted her, he wanted to own her. And he had— because she let him.

She nods her head wordlessly along with his monologue, refusing to look at him.

"I've been very generous with you, numerous times. I didn't have to choose you, but I did. Now that was very kind of me, wasn't it?"

After a beat of silence where she swallows hard, he asks again. "Wasn't it?"

"Yes," she says.

They had pulled onto a gravel side road. The truck kicks up rocks which pelt the body of the vehicle in a cacophony of sound. Her head swims. She can't form a coherent thought anymore. She thinks to plead, to cry, to try to persuade him that she loves him. But she doesn't— can't bring herself to lie one more time.

When he rolls to a stop, she presses her eyes shut hard against the tears. She hears him get out, circle around to her side of the truck, each footfall grinding heavily into the dust. Her heart beats harder, louder, with each step he takes until she knows he stands beside the truck. He opens the passenger side door for her. Her eyelids flutter open and she looks into his face. He smiles, straight, white teeth; beautiful chiseled features; slightly mussed, but neatly trimmed, dark hair. The same face that drew her in those first few months, the same expression that's warped and grown to scare her.

He's gentle as he releases the cuffs from around her wrists and they fall to the floor mat with a clatter. He reaches for her hand. She doesn't look at him as she takes it, his warm palm swallowing up her small, cold one.

Like a gentleman, he helps her

out of the vehicle. Everything hits her in a wave—the smell of the canola in the breeze, the breath of the wind on her skin, the sound of the little heads of the yellow crop rubbing against each other. She breathes it in, a deep inhale of the sweet country air, and a tear shivers down her face.

He leads her down the dirt road, slow, cautious to guide her around potholes and rocks. The vehicle still lingers in her sightline, but just barely.

"I loved you like nobody else," he says.

Stopping in the road, he pulls her close. The bitter tang of his aftershave, the sweat on his body, the dust that's kicked up from the road, it all bites in her nostrils and she crinkles her nose. He draws her into him, his arm around her body. Tipping her chin up, he brings his face down to meet her, his lips on hers, his warm breath infecting the last of the sweet air in her lungs. She wants to force him away, but she has no strength. Standing passively until it's over, she can feel his displeasure as his muscles tighten beneath her.

"I thought you were different," he says as he pulls away, and she can still taste him. She can

still feel his mouth on hers as he pushes her forward, a few stumbling steps ahead.

Staring blankly at a beyond she'll never reach—the gravel road stretching into forever— she realizes she's not scared anymore.

"Turn to me, baby," he says, and she does.

He stands with both feet planted shoulder-width apart. In the background is the truck, in the foreground is his gun, extended straight in front of him, aimed directly at her heart.

He smiles at her, a dark grin that matches his eyes. She forces her shoulders back, her head high. Her gaze touches his, a shiver creeping down her spine. Though his expression demands her attention, the weapon in his hand stronger than any command he's ever given her, she lifts her eyes to the brilliant blue sky beyond. She's spent so many years looking at him, letting him dictate how she felt and when. He doesn't deserve as much, not now.

Tears pool in her eyes, warbling the images the puffy white clouds make, drawn across the azure blanket over the world. A large puff catches her attention, its crevasses and divots forming some semblance of a picture, a goat, or a sort of dog. She had a dog once.

She tips her head back to watch it gallop across the sky like the dopey dog would have done, years and years ago, careening across the yard to meet her when her bus arrived after school. Only when the wind pushes the cloud out of shape does she let her eyelids flutter lightly shut so her eyelashes brush her cheekbones. With the picturesque scenery still burned into her mind, she smiles, but not for him. She can almost hear the excited bark of the long-passed shepherd as it welcomes her home.

"Goodbye," he says.

"Goodbye," she whispers, though the word is drowned in the sound of gunfire and carried away on the wind. ✎

SOL JACOBS

Sol Jacobs is a creative nonfiction writer with work published in Meat for Tea: The Valley Review, Flint Hills Review, and other fine journals. He has also been a featured playwright/director for Emporia State University's Short Play Festival (2015), the William Allen White Festival (2016 and 2017), as well as the Valentine's Day Play Festival. Jacobs graduated from Emporia State University in 2017 (BA in English and a minor in creative writing), Sierra Nevada College in 2019 (MFA in creative writing) and is currently applying to the Institute of American Indian Arts. He is also the co-creator/editor of the Tittynope Zine and presently lives with his wife and two children at the foothills of the Rockies in Colorado.

"Sidewalk Slammer" started as a day-in-the-life story for a comp class. Though it was well-received, it had no concrete connection to society, no third rail, no thesis. The story sat on a shelf until Jacobs decided to add some skeletons from his closet: the abandonment of his oldest daughter, Tal, why he spent a decade living on the streets, and how the entire time he was trapped by a single material possession-a picture of her.

Sidewalk Slammer

Sol Jacobs

Louisiana. 2003–Since hitting the road my mornings have begun in the same manner, with regrets and yearning for enough cheap whiskey to chase them away. After taking a birdbath in the Shreveport Library's bathroom sink, I wipe my hands on my dirty overalls, cross the lobby, push open the double doors, and shield my eyes from the sun.

Against the glare, I make out two figures meandering down Texas Street. One has a spring in his step, a faded, Johnny Cash tee clings to his spindly frame, and his Carhartt cutoffs hang from a cinched-up pleather belt.

The other lumbers behind, holding a fishing pole. He towers over his companion, dressed in a tight black tee, and 501 Blues cuffed above his jump boots. His red hair sticks to his pale, freckled brow, and massive shoulders hunch forward supporting an immense REI backpack.

The smaller of the two slings his ALICE pack to the ground, nods at his handy work, and looks at me with cold blue eyes set upon a face that had yet to feel the edge of a razor. "What's up, kid? The name's Maverick." His greasy, black hair falls forward around his face as he looks from my bookbag to the bedroll I'd cinched tight with a rope fashioned into a handle, then scoffs, "You a traveler?"

I give him a sideways grin and shake my head. "I ain't your kid," I kick my bedroll, "and, no, I sport this shit as a fashion statement."

Maverick laughs and takes a step backward. "You a dick to

everyone, or should we feel privileged?"

I look towards the sky as if asking the heavens for the answer. "Let's go with privileged."

Maverick's partner, who struggles to shed his pack, says in a deep voice that vibrates my ears, "Naw, let's go with you're a dick to everyone."

After dropping his pack on the library steps, the larger of the two excuses himself as he moves his companion out of the way. He walks over like an old hound dog and offers me his hand. "I'm The Flintstone Kid."

After he lets go, I shake my hand. "Damn, you must take a lot of them vitamins or somethin'."

They sit next to me on the steps; and after Maverick bums a smoke, he goes on about sleeping in a park, spotlights, cops with guns drawn, and then pulls out a ticket. "I told him we should've squatted on a roof," he turns and starts talking at The Flintstone Kid, "but, no, he has to tote all that shit."

The Flintstone Kid gets up, never taking his eyes off his companion, "You were too drunk to climb." He excuses himself, asks me to watch his gear, and heads towards the library. Maverick looks back and forth between his partner and me, then gets up and jogs behind, halfheartedly apologizing.

I unzip the top of my bag, grab a black Sharpie and notice a picture of my daughter, Tal, lying on the sidewalk. I stare at the creased, faded image: She was jumping over a sprinkler dressed in a pink onesie, both hands in the air, eyes closed, an expression of pure joy spread across her little face. I polish off the last of my whiskey, snatch up the picture and shove it back in my bag.

I grab a pizza box leaning against a garbage can, tear it to size, and scrawl on one side, "I Bet You a Dollar," and on the other, "You Just Read My Sign." The trick to this sign is teasing people with the first side until you have their attention and have sparked their curiosity. Then look them in the eyes, flip the sign, slowly put out your hand, and stay silent until their shell-shocked expressions crumple to laughter.

I make ten dollars and some change by the time Maverick and The Flintstone Kid come strolling back. We pool our money, inquire with some locals, and start a three-mile trek through Highland-Stoner Hill to the liquor store. After six blocks of Maverick trying to sell me on how hardcore he is, I look back to see The Flintstone Kid lagging. I find a beat-up shopping cart under the Interstate 20 overpass and roll a smoke while they load their gear inside.

As soon as Maverick grabs the handle of the cart with both hands, he jumps in the air and clicks his heels. Once his feet hit the ground, he takes off in a dead sprint pushing the rickety cart down the middle of the street, hollering something about being Lightning McQueen. I feel a large hand on my shoulder and look to see The Flintstone Kid standing next to me nodding his head. "Yeah, he's a dumbass." He waves me on, and we jog behind.

Our eye-opening procession proceeds past boarded-up houses with caved-in roofs, past plastic mesh fencing surrounding crumbling foundations, and as we turn a corner, I see a group of kids playing whiffle ball in the street. Maverick jumps on the cart and looks back at us acting a fool. I motion for him to turn around, then The Flintstone Kid yells, "Look out." He whips his head around just in time to jump off and steer it towards a house.

Maverick lets go of the cart before its wheels catch the lip of the driveway, stumbles, trips over the curb, and narrowly misses a pile of scrap lumber as he tumbles onto the lawn. He quickly jumps up, tosses his hands in the air, and bows to his captivated audience. The scene erupts into laughter and exaggerated applause, and I can't help but join in, all the while admiring the kid's dedication to showmanship.

* * *

Eugene, Oregon. 2001—The early morning rush hour had traffic backed up ten deep on both sides of Roosevelt Boulevard's stoplights. A steady stream of cars whizzed back and forth on Highway 99, going about their daily business. The Ivy Minimart parking lot I was standing in was relatively deserted, and in contrast to the traffic, it seemed to be unaffected by time. I forced a smile and leaned into the backseat of a fully packed hatchback. Tal was in her car seat, chewing on a small red lollypop; her hands and face were a sticky mess, a lock of her golden hair was stuck to a flushed cheek. Even the power of sugar couldn't keep her bottom lip from quivering or mask the confusion in her wide, shell-shocked eyes. I slowly fastened the buckles around her tear-stained flower dress and kissed her forehead.

"It's okay; you're gonna to stay at Grandma's house for a while. Let Papa deal with things here, and I'll be up there before you even miss me."

In a quivering voice, Tal put me in a pickle. "Promise?"

I looked back at her mother, Yolanda, who was standing behind me, tapping her foot and staring daggers. I turned back to Tal and lied to her face, "Yeah. Sure. Papa promises."

Seemingly content with my answer, Tal went back to her lollypop as I slowly stepped back from the car. Yolanda put on her happy face and pushed by to check my handy work. Once satisfied, she perpetuated the lie in a soothing motherly voice, "Papa always keeps his word."

Yolanda's stepdad, James, was leaning on the driver's side of the car looking exhausted from the drive down from British Columbia, refusing to make eye contact, and probably wishing he was anywhere but there. Yolanda closed the car door and looked at me with confusion, a look of, what do we do next? Tal stared at us through the window. While I choked back tears, Yolanda played her part. She leaned over, never taking her eyes off Tal, embraced me, and followed it with a kiss on my cheek.

Tal and I waved at each other as the car left the parking lot and turned on Roosevelt Blvd. I could still see her arm waving as they turned on to Hwy 99 and headed out of North Eugene towards Interstate 5. I hung my head and stood motionless for what seemed like an eternity, and then slowly walked back to the Roosevelt Gardens Apartments—alone.

*   *   *

A smile creeps across my face as I see a sign looming over Kings Highway, with the words Lucky Liquor plastered across it. Maverick and the Flintstone Kid's eyes light up as I walk out of the tagged-up shack with a handle of Evan Williams Sour Mash and the components for a Sidewalk Slammer. The boys gather our gear and follow me to the rotted porch of an abandoned house.

Leaning back on my bedroll, I pull out the plastic stopper with my teeth and start on the handle of Evan Williams, all the while sizing up the two travelers.

By the holes on the soles of

Maverick's boots, I gather he'd traveled a long distance in a short time. He leans over, grabs the Mad Dog 20/20 from the bag, unfastens a Nalgene from his pack, and fills it halfway. Then he grabs the 40oz of Mickey's, uncaps it, and for some reason, tries to fill the container as fast as he can. Purple foam comes spilling out the Nalgene, covering his hands. The Flintstone Kid balls his fist, yells, "Beer abuse," and slugs his friend in the shoulder, knocking him to his hip, making him spill most of the Slammer on the porch. To square matters, I hit him in the other shoulder—for the second spill—and surprisingly, he holds on tight, refusing to spill another drop. He cusses us under his breath as he stands up, wipes his hands on his cutoffs, and then slowly fills the container.

I hand The Flintstone Kid the handle and he tips it back like a champ. His freshly shaven face, attire, and the fact that he packed everything but the kitchen sink all point to him being new on the road and attached to material possessions. Who can blame him for not wanting to get shitfaced before noon; and for thinking he needs all that plastic crap to survive in the concrete jungle when our generation was raised cross-legged, inches from the TV? Typically, after a month or so of toting around added weight—they never found an opportunity to use—new travelers downsize drastically. They realize all that's needed to survive is a tarp for keeping the rain off, a dry bedroll, food, water, and an honest hustle.

It takes half the Slammer and a couple of shots of whiskey before Maverick hangs his head and starts telling me his life story. He was born in some Podunk town called Plains, Montana. His mother was into drugs and violent men. She moved him and his younger siblings from place to place, school to school, and never had a chance to grow roots. The day he came of age, he stuck out his thumb and tried to never look back.

Maverick looks up with glossy eyes. "Yeah, Momma's whipping boy took off." He sniffles. "Yeah, I abandoned my brothers and sister, left them exposed," he shakes his head, "left them alone, alone with mother's vices, choices, and addictions."

The Flintstone Kid grabs Maverick, pulls him close, and hands him the whiskey. "What, now you're a poet?"

Maverick sheds his embrace,

takes a drink, gags, wipes the tears from his cheeks with the back of a hand, and then hands me the handle. "Yeah, we met outside Little Rock. I hustled change off him when he came out the liquor store."

The Flintstone Kid chuckles to himself, looks down and starts tightening his boots. "Then your underage ass had me buy the booze."

Maverick whips his head around, "Yeah, but remember, I'm the one helping you and your gear get to Baton Rouge."

I take a long drink and hand the whiskey to The Flintstone Kid. "What, you ridin' freight?"

The Flintstone Kid scratches his head and tips the bottle back. "I wish. We've been hitching. Well, trying. People just don't seem to want to pick up two guys with gear. Took us a week to get here from Little Rock."

Maverick nods in agreement, grabs the handle, and takes a swallow. "Yeah, we spent most of our time walking and eventually had to split up and meet in the larger towns. Shit, we met back up last night.

I grab the bottle and tilt my head to the side. "Why Baton Rouge?"

The Flintstone Kid takes a deep breath. "Well, pops passed a couple months back. Everyone in Mountain Home wouldn't stop looking at me funny, trying to tell me their sob stories, and I just had to get out, away, anywhere but there."

Maverick chimed in with, "His half-sister told him to come down; so, we're heading there."

After putting the cap on the whiskey, I stand and dust myself off. "Come on, boys; let's hit it. Train supplies ain't fixin' to drop out the sky."

We head to the southeast side of Shreveport, next to Highway 1 and the tracks, where two off-ramps are located. I jump into a dumpster, come out with two pieces of cardboard, and decide to have Maverick and The Flintstone Kid work one sign, while I showcase my hustle with the other. They fly the timeless classic, "Family Killed by Ninjas, Need $$ for Kung Fu Lessons," and on mine I scrawl, "Out of Work Supermodel." This is a very tricky sign because you must become your character. I strut off with a serious look on my face, eyes fixed on the off-ramp, shoulders back, and chin facing slightly down.

After laying my gear on the

median, I stand as straight as possible—like an invisible string is holding me from my spine to the top of my head—hold the sign high and start down the concrete runway with a look of determination. I place one foot in front of the other and walk with long strides, flirty and confident as I step to a rhythm no one else could hear. Once at the end of the runway, I wait a beat, lean on one hip with confidence and poise, whip my head around, and look at my audience.

The line of cars is at a standstill even though the light is green. As I hear a mix of honking horns and catcalls, hands reach out of windows holding cash, beckoning me to come over quickly. While I weave between cars, a man jumps from the passenger side of a truck with a six-pack of Naughty Ice under an arm. He runs over to my gear, sets the beer down, and dashes after his ride that's starting to pull away. I climb back on the median as the last driver in line drives past, honks, and then flips me off.

The next line of cars gets my Naomi Campbell strut. My legs pump up and down in deliberate steps, swinging my hips, and bouncing my body as I make my way down the median with determination and attitude—I can almost feel, hear, and see the flashbulbs popping. Forty minutes later, I've made around thirty-five dollars, so I decide it's time to check on the boys.

They're kicking back on their packs with the sign propped against Maverick's knees. If not for the whiskey bottle being passing back and forth I might have thought they were sleeping.

"This ain't how you work a sign." They both jump. "How the hell they supposed to read that shit? You think hard-working folk just gonna give you their cash? Make 'em laugh, think, or somethin'." Maverick puts his head down and hands me a dollar and some change. He grabs the sign and starts walking the line of cars. I yell over my shoulder as The Flintstone Kid and I head to the corner store to get train supplies—ramen, jerky, water, booze, and a pouch of Midnight Special rolling tobacco—"Walk that line with your pack, look 'em in the eyes, and remember you gotta work for their cash."

It wasn't all Maverick's fault. The Flintstone Kid killed the mission with his clean clothes and shaved face. He looks well off, too well off to elicit empathy from his ever-changing audience. Even if he works the sign, his muscular stature and sheer size will have people rolling up windows and locking their doors.

Upon coming back, Maverick hands me a joint, ten dollars, and some change. I wrinkle my chin, push out my bottom lip, and nod, "Now that's what I'm talkin' about. Okay. Let's hit them tracks, boys."

We find a ditch with some tall weeds next to the rails, lay back on our gear, and pass around the bottle and the joint until we hear that ol' train whistle calling.

* * *

That afternoon, I woke from my drunken stupor in an apartment littered with possessions and memories I didn't want anymore. Off-white patches of Bondo on yellow walls told tales of violence and infidelity. They reminded me of how my choices had forced Tal to live in that dysfunctional environment when her only crime was being born to a pair of selfish parents—who were still children themselves.

On those same walls hung wedding pictures that looked innocent to the passing eye, but if a person stopped and looked carefully at the downtrodden eyes, plastic smiles, physical separation, and lack of affection, they scream, "This isn't loving, it's a facade, a ploy to keep immigration off their backs." Two kittens, sleeping intertwined with each other on a flower print couch, represented failed attempts at keeping my sinking boat afloat and presented living proof that I knew it was over.

The damp musty smell of the one-bedroom apartment reminded me that no matter how many jobs I held down it was impossible to get ahead and support my family when I was the only one who could legally work; reminded me that we didn't qualify for a child tax credit, food assistance, and must pay medical out of pocket, reminded me that I was unable to buy their happiness, unable to give them the American dream.

Behind me, a baby gate stuck out from the behind the couch, a barrier used to keep Tal from digging in the cat box. In front of me was the same door she got her ring finger slammed in. I'd cradled her little body next to mine and tried to keep her from noticing the tip that was hanging on by a thread. To my right among the trails of trash and discarded possessions—things I never got around to giving away—was her red, Mickey

Mouse potty. I used to pay her quarters for using it and then walk her to the Ivy Minimart every Friday so she could buy candy. To my left, laying on its side, on the brown, linoleum kitchen floor, was a tall wooden highchair my father used to eat in, then me, and finally Tal.

My breathing became labored. Princess bed, bike, pink bunny, crayons, bursts of sunshine, and rainbows. The room started to spin, forcing me to sit down on the dingy gray carpet.

* * *

When the front end of a freight train is barreling towards you, intimidation is the natural reaction. It takes on the characteristics of an animal, a beast, an orange beast peering down through pellucid rectangular eyes set behind a protruding squared-off muzzle, its mouth agape, revealing clenched steel teeth fused together as if frozen mid gnash, and ears pinned back presenting the look of a predator in pursuit of prey. You can feel the vibration of its wheels grinding along their metal counterparts, the piercing sound of screeching brakes; even the air seems to pressurize. And then the unit blows past, bending the tall weeds to the ground,

exposing you for a moment to the engineer—if he looks down. The chaos subsides, replaced with a soothing, pulsating hiss of brakes airing down, and the hum of a diesel-electric engine.

Our train has two units, and is hauling two miles of scrap metal, lumber, oil, chemicals, corn syrup, and grain—"junk." When riding junk, make sure you're not in a rush because they stop at every little nook and cranny along the way. Another drawback to this kind of train is sometimes the car is just moving to another site, and that might be in the middle of nowhere.

Having ridden this line a month prior, I know southbound trains stop here for a crew changes, and that gives me about three minutes to direct my greenhorns towards a rideable car. I see two back-to-back rideable grainers towards the end of the train. Rideable grainers are easy to spot; they typically have gray rounded sides instead of flat, vertical, ridged walls. Grainers, like their name, are closed cars that usually hold grain; rideables have metal porches—four-feet long by eight-feet wide—split in half by two steel walls that taper to a V configuration. There's not much room to stretch out, but there's a large hole in between the walls where you can stash your gear, and even hide if you're small enough and not claustrophobic.

I decide to make the trip in a separate car when faced with the proposition of riding on a small porch packed like a sardine in-between two rookies and their gear, trapped, and at the mercy of their endless questions, nervous chitter-chatter, and heartfelt confessions.

After giving them a quick tutorial on what not to do on a train, The Flintstone Kid tugs at my pant leg as I start to turn away. "Are you going to ride with us?" he points to himself and then Maverick who's looking at his feet and twisting his hair, "People die on these trains. We'd feel less freaked out if you were within shouting distance."

Maverick looks up and chimes in, "Or at least over there," he points to the grainer coupled to theirs with an air braking system that almost spans the entire porch, "Remember, this is our first time on a train."

The Flintstone Kid looks at his partner and nods in agreement.

I shake my head, take a deep breath, and exhale through the side of my mouth. "There's no way in hell I'm gonna fit on this porch with the both of you and his gear," I say nodding at The Flintstone Kid. "I ain't ridin' dirty face. That wind will tear me up. I'll be on the other side of that grainer. It won't be hard to check on you. I'll hit the ladder, walk the top, and climb down right there." I point to the ladder on the car coupled to theirs and then hand them the rollies. "You'll be fine. I got you. Save me a smoke."

At that point, I could see in their eyes they were a little less freaked out about being left alone. Just then, I hear the sweet sound of brakes airing up and jog to my car. As the shale crunches underneath my boots a smile creeps across my face.

A world flies by, a world unaware of our existence. Shiny new cars line up at railroad crossings; rundown school buses drop off kids to awaiting mothers whose eyes never leave their cellular phones, and countless single-wide trailers flash by, all looking the same. In one blink of an eye, the people and homes are a memory, replaced by the bright yellow leaves of the poplar trees rustling in the wind. Soon this gives way to chinquapin shrubs that line the tracks and pecan trees as far as I can see.

* * *

That night, I packed our, well, my material possessions—and the memories attached—in boxes and stacked them along the walls. Once done, I sat cross-legged in the middle of the living room floor surrounded by cardboard towers, nursing a bottle of Jim Beam, a loaded shotgun lying across my lap.

The next morning, I woke to my alarm wailing just out of my reach. So, I ripped it from the wall, stomped it into a million pieces, and quit my job at the steel mill.

When I didn't have my face buried in my hands feeling sorry for myself, I would sit on the loveseat and play Tony Hawk's Pro Skater with the volume blaring to chase away the deafening silence. When I'd get enough courage to leave my apartment, I would walk with my head down to the Ivy Minimart to buy international calling cards, contemplating how to respond when the cashiers asked about my family, and all the while hoping a passerby would bump in to me or give me any reason to release the anger that was devouring me from the inside.

Eventually, my utilities were shut off, and the landlord started banging on the door threatening to call the cops and change the locks if I didn't pay the rent, but I sat there drinking in the cold darkness and pretended that no one was home.

* * *

The freight train chugs along at about sixty miles an hour, and I need a smoke something fierce. As I climb the ladder to the top of the grainer, the wind punishes my body, pushing it violently backward, and then lifts the hat off my head. I watch it get sucked down the side of the train, disappearing underneath its pulverizing metal wheels. As soon as I attempt my first step atop the grainer, we pull into Natchitoches, so I lay flat on my stomach and hope the train blows through town. Once clear of civilization, I continue my progress to the adjoining car. As soon as I see them on the porch, I know something's wrong. Climbing down the ladder, I look over a shoulder and say, "Let me get that smoke."

They both mumble something that gets lost in the wind. I finally gather that Maverick bumped The Flintstone Kid, making him drop the smokes off the train. I can feel my ears start to turn red and start contemplating kicking one of them in the face when it begins to rain. A fall Louisiana rain is very soothing and seems to cool me off. I need to get back to my gear before the rain makes it impossible. I shake the rain off like a dog, and look back before climbing the ladder, "I'm gettin' off in Natchez, need some smokes and booze. Try not to fall off the train in the meantime."

As soon as the train pulls into Natchez, I hop off and find the boys. "You both stay on the train. It'll sit for about five. Now, don't trip, I'll be back."

The Flintstone Kid leans over his partner and delivers slowly, "So you just want us to sit here and hope you come back? We don't have a clue where to get off. How do we know you're not playing us for fools? If you want me to sit tight, you're going to have to give me your word."

I shake my head, hand Maverick my gear, look The Flintstone Kid straight in his eyes, and force myself not to blink. "There, now you got all my shit, and yes, I promise. You have my word."

I turn away and head across the highway to JJ's Grocery.

* * *

About a month after Tal left, I walked to a payphone and called Debby, who came to save the day with her Ford Ranger and an eight ball of speed. We hid out in my apartment snorting lines and rolling the bowl until well after midnight and then quickly piled my boxes and loose possessions into the bed of her truck. After I tarped off the load, she drove me to my aunt's house in Sequim, Washington.

I sobered up, got a job, an apartment, and rode the ferry between Port Angeles and Vancouver Island, B.C. when picking up and dropping off Tal.

This worked for a while until Tal and I got food poisoning from a taco truck on one of our visits, so I dropped her off a day late. While Yolanda was waiting for us at the ferry's Canadian immigration checkpoint—I should have called sooner—they informed her that they had no jurisdiction in the matter and couldn't legally force a father, with joint custody, to bring his child across international lines. But they also told her the same rules apply when she's on the Canadian side.

When we showed up, Tal's face buried in my shoulder, Yolanda was surprisingly understanding, which was the farthest thing from her character. She nodded her head when I apologized and told me not to worry about it; she even smiled and laughed when I relayed the more embarrassing aspects of our ordeal. But I couldn't relax because there was something in her eyes that contradicted her kind words and actions, a coldness I had seen on many occasions, the same look she gave me through the window as James pulled his car onto Hwy 99—checkmate. As I put Tal in Yolanda's waiting arms, she turned around, her golden curls framing her lean face, and waved as her mother led her away.

Two days later, my calls started going straight to voicemail, and the week after Yolanda's number was disconnected. I heard from mutual friends that she had moved off the island and the post office claimed she left no forwarding address.

I never saw Tal again.

I was left with nothing but a single picture connecting me to the past, linking me to Tal. I thought by keeping it and forcing myself to feel the pain, I was in some way not abandoning her.

* * *

I take a drag off my cigarette and choke on the smoke. Maverick's head is poking out the side of the grainer, watching me as our freight train pulls away. Armed with a six-pack in one hand and a half-pint of Old Crow in the other, I shoot towards the train like a bull closing in on a red cape. By the time I get alongside, it's become a twenty mile an hour wall of cold steel. I was told, many times, to never "hop on the fly" if you can't count the bolts on the wheels, but I choose to throw caution to the wind. I drop the six-pack, put the half-pint in my back pocket, and focus on a ladder, three cars back. The shale crunches under my boots as I run alongside trying to time my jump. I bite my lip and hold my breath.

One hand grabs a crossbeam, and the other the side rail. As I hold on for dear life, my lower body flies back like a windsock and slams against the side of the grainer, jarring my grip on the crossbeam. At this point, I need to deal with the fact I'm hanging on by one hand, and my dangling legs are about to get sheared off by the unforgiving wheels of the train. After blindly finding a foothold on the bottom side of the grainer, I push off, hoping to clear the shale, and prepare for impact.

I try to hit the shale running, but my momentum slings me backward as soon as I touch the ground. A white light flashes before my closed eyes as I slam to the ground and skid along my side until landing in a crumpled mass amidst the tall weeds. As I pick myself off the ground, I feel a searing pain in my side, and a warm sensation dripping down my skin. I see long shallow lacerations through my shredded shirt, and a large bruise that's already taking form. Surprisingly, the half-pint survives the fiasco unscathed, so I crack it and take a shot.

I stumble up a dirt incline and onto the shoulder of Highway 1, lean to a side, grimace, and clutch what I hope are only bruised ribs. A Cadillac Deville speeds my way; I stagger out on the asphalt directly in its path and tentatively raise my hand. The car sounds its horn, fishtails as it slams on the brakes, and comes to a screeching halt five-feet in front of me. A cloud of gray smoke wafts my direction bringing with it the smell of smoldering rubber.

An elderly woman, who can barely see over the dash, white-knuckles the steering wheel and stares at me through thick-rimmed glasses. Her window buzzes as it rolls down. "Boy, if brains is leather, youse be lucky to saddle a June bug." The shiny chain dangling from her glasses shakes as she chuckles to herself. "Where dat fire at, darlin'?"

I walk over, lean on the hood, and point towards the tracks. "I gotta catch a train."

"Youse look like ten miles a bad road." She smiles, turns, and flicks the power locks. "Gets on in, we wastin' daylight."

As I hurry towards the passenger side, she leans across the leather interior, grabs her purse and Bible from the seat and places them on the lap of her Sunday's finest.

Before I'm all the way in the car, the little woman tells me to buckle up and slams down the accelerator with one of her black pumps. While being sucked back into the seat, I scramble to shut the door, and then reach for the "oh shit" bar. She leans forward and peers over the dash as we speed down the highway. We sit in silence, she preoccupied with passing a car, and me trying not to bleed on her seat.

Telephone poles fly by in a blur as we hug the tracks, for about four miles, until they veer off into the bayou. My driver, sensing worry, smiles and then assures me we'll meet up with them in a mile or so. She reaches over, turns some Zydeco music up full blast, and sings along. As we drive past Parish Road, I spot a freight train. It's blocking the road, sitting idle on the overflow tracks of a two-mile, waiting for clearance. I wave my hands to get her attention, and without a word, she decelerates and pulls a U-turn.

Before I get all the way out of the car, she taps me on the shoulder, pulls an envelope from her Bible, and puts it in my hand.

Her smile lifts her glasses, and then she yells over the blaring music, "God's good, all da time."

I put it in my pocket, then mouth, thank you, before I shut the door.

As she backs up and speeds off, the brakes hiss, and the engine takes on a strenuous tone as it prepares to depart. I quickly climb onto a porchless grainer, in the back-end of the train, about ten cars from where I think the boys are. Hand over hand, I climb the ladder, shimmy across the top, and then slide down the ladder on the other side. I repeat this until there're no cars left to check—this isn't my train. I fail at keeping my word and lost Tal's picture.

Exhausted, I flop down on my back and gaze at the darkening sky. I put the bottle to my lips, take a drink, and remember the envelope in my pocket. It contains two hundred and fifty dollars and a note that reads,

"You can only be free,

when you have nothing left to lose."

I toss the bottle off the speeding freight train and watch it shatter on the shale below. ✎

Photo credit Sol Jacobs

𝔄 wise drifter once said in a thick whiskey voice, "Not everyone starts life on the same terms, but even those handed the silver spoon will end it at the very same junction. Life is full of paths, but it's the least traveled ones that lead to adventure." — Sidewalk Slammer

GREG MORAVEC

was born and raised in Minnesota where there are lots of forests, good places for making up stories, and long winters, good for reading lots of books. Winters are also good for cultivating hobbies like cooking, drawing, and leatherworking. Finding himself in danger of being a jack-of-all-trades and a master of none, Greg took to writing with a fury, doing it every day, even on the days he didn't feel like it. Maybe especially on those days. A few years later and a couple of novel-length pieces are in the editing phase, but for now you can find some shorter pieces at gregmoravec.com

The Displaced

Greg Moravec

Two months into his stay onboard the refugee ship, Turan, Quintas was starting to get used to things, but the cafeteria would take some time — if he ever got used to it. Species from ten different worlds milled around the room, all displaced by the Ashtari Empire were being ferried to new planets. Most of them had about the same amount of arms and legs as he did, but they had little else in common. The room was a patchwork of skin colors and textures, some covered in thin wispy hair, others in scales. Quintas, with his pale gray skin and flat facial features, wouldn't have stuck out but for his tail. Try as he might, he couldn't keep it still when his mind wandered or if he was nervous, and he was one or the other most of the time. Mostly he kept to himself and tried not to stare.

Today's fare was much as it had been on other days, some nutrient rich, but bland, stew with bread to match. The only thing that brought any flavor at all to the meal was the juice and today's variety was purple and creamy with an acidic, but not entirely unpleasant, aftertaste. When he lowered his glass after a sip he found that he had company on the other side of the table. It wasn't that crowded because it was early, an intentional move on his part, but she sat at his table all the same.

Even standing crouched on the bench, she was shorter than him. Three of the seven fingers on each of her hands gripped a thick pair of blue-tinted goggles from over her eyes and raised them to rest on her forehead revealing a pair of bright green eyes hovering over a stubby nose and a wide smile.

"What's it do?" she asked.

"What's what do?"

She pointed to his tail. His cheeks warmed, and he stopped it from moving.

"Whoa, cool, you can control it. Do the holes do anything?"

He flicked the tail over his shoulder and brushed his thumb across the narrow slits she was referring to. "It helps regulate my body temperature."

"Awesome," she said and shoveled some stew into her mouth with enthusiasm, "can you grab stuff with it?"

"Not really," he said lamely, shifting in his seat.

"I've just got these." She said and stood up straight on the bench and stuck one of her feet out to one side and wiggled her toes before reaching out and using them to grab her juice glass. "Not so useful at the table, though," she said and tried to contort herself to get her mouth to the glass but came a foot short of success.

Quintas smiled despite himself and she chuckled and crouched back down. "I'm Merka," she said.

"Quintas."

"Pleased to meet you Quintas. Sorry to bother you, but there's just not that much to do around here besides meeting new people."

He didn't know what to say, so he scooped up another bite of stew to give himself a minute to think, hoping that she would fill the silence.

She didn't disappoint.

"I'm from Tovarna."

"You guys make spaceships, right?" he asked, grateful that he'd at least heard of it.

"We did, yeah, and weapons, mining equipment, pretty much anything we could make with the metal from the surrounding moons. The Ashtari decided it was critical for the war effort so they bought the satellite from us, either they didn't realize or they didn't care that it was also our home. My parents are still there working, but I took my chance and got out."

"How come?"

"They were going to make it an assembly line for weapons and I'm more interested in designing new things. Where are you from?"

"Sysquala."

"Oh, something happened with the tides there or something crazy, right?"

Quintas took a deep breath, the "something crazy" had killed his father and all but one of his brothers, but Merka couldn't have known that.

"Most of the planet is covered in water. The Ashtari space station was so large that it started altering the tides. They came higher and at odd intervals, but that wasn't the real problem."

"What was?"

"They were testing depth charges," he said softly. "For underwater warfare in an area that was uninhabited, or at least they thought it was. There were aquatic farming platforms within range of the waves they created, and they were totally wiped out. The evacuation of the major settlements happened soon after."

"That's terrible, was anyone hurt?"

Quintas dropped his eyes and stared at his plate, unable to say it aloud.

"I'm sorry," she said and squeezed his shoulder.

"That's just like them," said a new voice accompanied by the slide of a lunch tray across the plastic table. "All they care about is their wars and they'll kill anyone who stands in their way."

Quintas sat up, the discomfort of dealing with a new person quickly overshadowing his grief. Their new companion dwarfed them both and was well muscled. A pair of tusks stuck up from either side of his mouth forcing his lips to curl around them giving his speech a slight slur. Pale green skin stretched tight over the bulging muscles in his arms and shoulders and across the sharp angular features of his face.

Quintas gathered himself, "it was an accident."

The tusked alien scoffed, "always is, but they're still responsible. You don't get a pass for negligence. If you wonder what they think about it, just look at this ship," he said waving a meaty hand around. "There's guilt written all over it. People from a dozen worlds, all displaced by the Ashtari and they're trying to hide us off in some corner of the galaxy to cover their tracks."

"That's cheerful," Merka said.

"I recognize your kind, you're from Tovarna, right? You should know better than most. It wasn't even sort of accidental in your case, they just took what they wanted."

"We could have stayed," Merka said, "I just didn't want to, and they paid us for it."

"Ha, I'm sure that was a fair price, did you get a seat at the negotiating table?"

Merka said nothing, just sipped her juice.

"That's what I thought, probably wasn't even a table. That's how they do things."

"So what happened to you?" Merka asked. "What got you so pissed off?"

"Same as you, my home was taken, but I won't be here long."

"What do you mean?"

"I'm going to join up with the Naxalites."

"Who?" Quintas asked.

"They're our only chance against the Ashtari, the only ones trying to fight back." Then he puffed up his chest and sat up straighter. "They were founded on my planet. Mataram, my brother fights with them and I'm going to too."

"I thought they were from Naxal?" Merka said.

"A common misconception," he said haughtily, "the Ashtari try to cover up their origins, just like everything else. The people on Naxal resisted the Ashtari when they tried to incorporate their planet into the empire.

The Ashtari don't take kindly to resistance so they wiped them out and took the planet. Mataram is in the same system so many of my people fought back in the name of Naxal, calling themselves Naxalites, and the Ashtari attacked my planet to quell the rebellion. It didn't work, though. They may control the planet for now, but more and more people are rallying to the Naxalite cause."

"Why didn't you go with them?" Quintas asked.

"My grandparents needed looking after so I came with them on this ship a year ago, but they're dead now."

"I'm sorry," Quintas said.

"They were old anyway and now there's nothing keeping me here. When I get out of here, I'm going to join up, just like my brother."

"Nobody is going to get out of here unless the Ashtari want it to happen," Merka said. "You said it yourself, they get what they want."

He leaned forward over his tray, but it was difficult to look secretive at his size. "Have a little faith," he whispered, "I'll put in a good word for you if you want, I'm sure they could use a mechanic from Tovarna," and then to Quintas, "What can you do?"

"What do you mean?" Quintas asked, shifting in his seat.

"I mean the Naxalites stay alive because they're mobile and efficient, no room for dead weight. So what do you have to offer?"

Quintas almost asked him the same question but looked at the size of his arms again and thought better of it. "I'm a pretty good pilot," he said. It was true, but it felt odd boasting about it. This was the first time he'd left Sysquala, but the ships he'd flown in atmosphere weren't that different from what he'd seen out here so far.

"Good, good, they always need pilots, I bet they'd take you both."

"Who says I'm interested?" Merka said.

"They took your home from you and you're just going to go work for them?"

"Of course not."

"You think they're going to give you a choice? They're not just going to cut you loose with that skill set. I've been stuck here for a year and the only people I've seen them let go are those who want to work on planets in the Ashtari home system. They say they're looking for planets for the rest of us to settle on, but this ship is nothing more than a prison. They'll find nothing suitable because they're not looking for it. Anyway," he said and stood up, somehow having emptied his bowl during the conversation. "I'm Bakti and you can find me in Block A if you change your mind and want to be part of something."

* * *

Back in Block C, Quintas' brother Lucio was waiting for him.

"Where have you been?"

Lucio had never been his favorite brother, but now he was his only one. That fact hadn't helped them get along any better. It just made the pain of the other losses keener. Quintas walked past him without answering and sat on the sofa built into the wall below their only window and looked out at the stars.

"Where have you been?" Lucio repeated.

"Dinner," Quintas said, still looking out the window.

"We were going to go later, mom's been worried."

"It's always crowded later, and

I doubt she worried. You know I always go early."

"You can't just disappear like that."

"Why not. I'm not a kid anymore." Quintas snapped, turning back to face him.

"You have to tell us when you're going to leave, I'm just trying to protect you."

"What's going to happen to me here? Nobody can even sneeze without the Ashtari knowing about it. Besides, you're not responsible for me, leave me alone."

"That's not what mom told me, says you need looking after."

"Quit acting like..."

"That's enough," came their mother's voice, softly, from the doorway. It had the effect on them of shouting despite being barely more than a whisper. The brothers looked toward the floor in unison. Their mother walked past Lucio and touched him on the shoulder and Quintas scooted over without being asked to give her room on the sofa.

"Nobody is trying to replace your father," she said stroking Quintas' coarse black hair. "Nobody could." She turned to Lucio. "And nobody needs to try. I don't want to see you boys fighting. We've already lost too much."

"I'm sorry," Quintas said.

"Me too," Lucio said, but Quintas didn't believe him.

"Now let's get to dinner," their mother said. "The cafeteria will close soon."

"Quintas already ate," Lucio blurted.

"That's fine, honey, you and I can go."

They stepped into the hallway and were stopped by a tall being wearing a crimson mask with a crease down the center and diagonal black slits flanking it on either side, an Ashtari guard. Quintas had never seen one of their faces, but the mask was all too familiar. The guard had a laser rifle strapped in its collapsed form on his thigh and held a stun baton in a gloved hand.

When he spoke, the mask muffled his voice, "Curfew is in effect."

"Curfew isn't for another half an hour," Lucio said and his mother put a hand on his arm.

"There's an obstruction ahead," the guard said. "Everyone needs to stay in their cabins for the rest of the day."

Lucio was about to say something else, but his mother's hand flexed on his forearm and she said, "sir, we haven't had a chance to eat yet. Do you think we could run down to the cafeteria for a moment to grab something? We'd be happy to bring it back to our cabin and you could escort us so we don't wander off."

"Curfew is in effect; all ancillary services are closed down."

He waited until she shut the door and then strode off down the hallway, the clanking of his boots echoing behind him.

"Ughh," Lucio groaned, "I'm starving."

"It's fine," said their mother who was already opening the cupboards, "we still have a few nutrition bars left."

"I hate those things," Lucio said.

"We are lucky to have an alternative and I don't want to hear any more about it."

"But we can't just let them push us around," Quintas said. "We should do something."

"Oh yeah," Lucio sneered, "like what?"

"I don't know, fight back."

"The only thing we need to do," their mother said, "is endure this. Then we can start over on a new planet, build a life for ourselves."

"Have you heard of the Naxalites?" Quintas asked.

The cupboard door slid shut and his mother passed a bar across the counter to his brother who tore it open and took a bite. Between mouthfuls, he said, "Some fringe group that thinks they can take down the Ashtari, they need to wake up and take a look around."

"They are very dangerous, Quin," his mom said. "Who told you about them?"

"Nobody," Quintas said, "a friend."

"You don't have any friends," Lucio said. Quintas glared at him. As if he had any.

Their mother smacked the counter with an open hand, "What did I say?" Lucio rolled his eyes and went into the sleeping room attached to their main quarters. When he'd gone she relaxed and continued, "I'm glad you're making friends, Quin, but you have to be careful."

"What's wrong with someone who wants to fight the Ashtari? It's their fault we're here and look at the way they're treating us, you can't even get a meal without their permission. Why shouldn't we fight for dad and the others?"

"You know what your father would have said..."

"I know, I know, 'pick your battles,' but what could be more important than this?"

"It's not just about what's important, it's about what's possible. This isn't a fight we can win and trying would take all we have and more."

Quintas could feel his eyes filling so he looked out the window, away from her. "They've already taken everything."

Her hand rested on his arm, "Not yet and I'm not prepared to give them any more." They sat for a minute, both looking out the window, then his mother said, "There's something I want you to have."

He wiped his eyes on the heel of his hand and turned to face her. She pressed a smooth, green stone attached to a thin cord into his hand. "What is it?"

"It's a Pteriidae, they grow mostly near the ocean floor, but occasionally people find them in shallower areas. Your dad was lucky, found it on his first dive. The first time he left Sysquala,

he gave me that to remember him while he was away. Now you won't forget them, no matter what happens."

* * *

Over the next few weeks, Quintas and Merka shared meals more and more. It was good to have a friend, he hadn't needed them before, having so many brothers, but it was nice to have someone he could talk to again. She wanted to know about everything; usually more than he was comfortable sharing, but he told her what he could about Sysquala and she always listened intently and asked a million questions. The only times he could get her to talk instead of question, was when he asked about Tovarna. Once she got going, she could talk endlessly about the devices they made, weapons, ships, mining equipment, all of which were beyond anything he could have imagined. It was all new to him, and he was truly fascinated, but he still couldn't match her enthusiasm for it.

They usually didn't talk about the Naxalites, but sometimes Bakti would join them and then they talked of little else. It made Quintas uncomfortable because he knew how his mother would feel about it. But the way Bakti spoke made it sound like an inevitable, righteous mission. The longer he talked, the more Quintas had trouble denying the truth of what he said, not that he fought it that hard, he wanted it to be true. Bakti was making his rounds again, and they overheard him trying to convince a nearby group of the justice of his cause.

"I just don't know if I could leave," Quintas said to Merka, "I don't think I'm brave enough."

Merka laughed, "what, like Bakti? He's a meathead."

"What do you mean?" Quintas said and felt his cheeks flush warm with blood, "Don't you want the Ashtari to answer for what they did to your people?"

Merka smiled and put her hands up, "Easy, you're starting to sound like him."

"Is that so bad?" Quintas said more defensively than he intended.

"I didn't say he was wrong. Of course I don't want to build things for the empire, what a terrible life. All I'm saying is that you shouldn't be jealous of his 'bravery'." It's easy to go around yelling. Nobody knows what they'll do when the moment comes. I bet you'd have the courage to do what you thought was right if the situation arose."

"Do you think you would?"

Merka shrugged and stood tall on the bench, stretching her arms over her head and then crouched back down. "I don't know if I'd do anything as dramatic as what he's talking about," she hooked a thumb in Bakti's direction, "but I'm getting out of here somehow. Bakti's right about at least one thing, the Ashtari aren't doing what they claim with people on this ship. They're hiding us, not helping us."

Bakti plopped down on the bench next to Quintas and rested a heavy arm on Quintas' shoulder. "I heard my name. Did you guys miss me?"

Merka scoffed, "I was just guessing where the odor on this ship is coming from. Quintas thought it might be the hundreds of people living in closets with minimal access to proper bathing facilities, but I was sure it's just you. You opening your armpit settles that debate, careful you don't gas him out."

A wide smile crossed Bakti's face, revealing the base of his tusks where they emerged from his gums and Merka flexed her eyebrows at him. Quintas pushed the arm off of him, more for the weight than the smell, Bakti's arms were bigger than his own legs.

"So have you guys made up your minds yet?"

"About what?" Quintas asked.

"What do you think? About joining the Naxalites."

"As far as I'm aware," Merka said, "the Naxalites are a party of one and are sitting at this table. Don't talk to me about ghost stories. We're not going to have a chance to breathe, much less join up with revolutionaries until we reach a planet, this ship is untouchable."

Bakti massaged one hand with the other, "I'm just saying that you might want to start thinking about if you'd join given the opportunity. Purely hypothetical of course, like you said, the ship's untouchable. If it weren't, though, someone interested in getting out of here might go to the cargo bay on level two when the opportunity presented itself."

"What do you know?" Merka asked, studying him intently, but then waved him off before he could answer, "Never mind, there's no way you could get a message in here without them

seeing it. Not possible."

"Whatever you say."

"I've got stuff to do," she said and hopped off the bench.

"I should go too," Quintas said.

Bakti walked with Quintas through the crowd into the hallway that led to Block C. Once they were more or less alone Bakti said, "you know I'm serious, right? About all of it, if you're a good pilot you could really change things."

"I'm sure they have loads of better pilots than me."

"Not based on some of your stories from home. Flying through storms with waves all around you, I bet you've got what it takes."

They stopped a few doors short of Quintas' room and Bakti put a hand on his shoulder and looked down at him. "At least think about it, we could use you, and I think maybe you could use us."

The door opened and Lucio stepped into the hallway and saw them. "I should go," Quintas said shrugging Bakti's hand off his shoulder.

Lucio dashed to beat Quintas into their room even though he had appeared to be on his way out. "Guess who Quintas was talking to?" Lucio blurted once Quintas came through the door.

"Who?" Their mother said, not looking up from the screen she was holding.

"His Naxalite buddy, that big green thug."

That got her attention. "Quintas."

"He followed me back," Quintas blurted, "and what's the harm in talking?"

Lucio hopped up on the counter and folded his hands together, settling in for the show he'd set in motion.

"We've talked about this," his mother said, "I don't want you to get mixed up with someone who might get you into trouble."

"They're never going to let us off this ship."

"Who told you that, your... friend?"

"His name is Bakti. And yes, he said it, but what makes you think they will let us off? We've been here for months."

"They said they would, we don't have any reason to believe otherwise right now. There's nothing more that we can do."

"We can fight."

Lucio laughed, "what are you going to do? You're a shrimp, you going to have your 'friend' take care of all your fights for you?"

Lucio jumped down from the counter and took a couple of fake swings at Quintas. He couldn't help but flinch in return, which only made him angrier.

"I'm a good pilot," Quintas said and pushed his brother in the chest.

Then he was in trouble because Lucio was right, he was too small for a fight. In seconds he was in a headlock and his mom was up and yelling at them, Lucio never knew when to stop. After a few seconds of struggling, it was getting hard to breathe and Quintas flailed harder and felt his elbow connect and the grip loosened. Lucio howled and covered his nose, blood ran between the fingers. He glared over his hands as he muttered something unintelligible through them. His mother grabbed his shoulder and Quintas jerked away before he could think. She drew her hand to her chest as if she'd burned it.

"I...I'm sorry," he stammered.

As soon as the words had left his mouth, the ship slammed into emergency mode. The main lights dropped and the only remaining light came from pulsing red bulbs in the corridor. An automated message played over the ship wide comm telling everyone that they were under attack and to return to their quarters and remain calm. The door hissed shut, leaving them in darkness, but for the red light flashing intermittently through the narrow window in the door. All of it came to Quintas through a haze of frustration and confusion. The haze faded, and he grew calm staring at the left side of his mother's face as it lit red and went dark, lit red and went dark.

"I'm sorry," he repeated, barely loud enough to be heard over the alarm. He flipped the emergency toggle and the door to the main corridor hissed open.

"Quintas," she said behind him, "don't do this."

He breathed deep, trying to summon his courage. If he looked at her again, he wouldn't have the strength to go, so he called over his shoulder, "I can't sit here and do nothing."

* * *

He ran into Merka in the hallway on the way to her cabin, "Quintas, I was just coming to find you, are you ok?"

He nodded.

"Where's your family?" she asked.

"They didn't want to leave."

"I'm not sure I want to leave. We don't even know what's happening here."

"We're under attack, just like Bakti said. It has to be..."

She punched his arm and a robotic voice behind him let him know why "All passengers should return to their cabins."

He turned to find a pair of red masks looking down at him. Before they could explain themselves, the corridor shook, the red lights stopped flashing, and dim white lights replaced them, washing over the hallway.

One of the Ashtari snapped, "get down", and pushed them into the nook of a nearby doorway. The guards kneeled side by side with their rifles leveled. A sharp metal point protruded out into the hallway and the wall was bent inward where a ship had impacted from the outside. The metal of the walls whined as the probe on the front of the attacking ship split apart, peeling the metal back and creating a triangular breach in the hull of the Turan.

A ramp dropped through into the hallway and legs shot out to support it, planting themselves in the floor. The Ashtari still didn't fire, still didn't move. A door whooshed open and two canisters flew out of it. The waiting Ashtari threw small spheres that splattered into jelly, smothering the canisters. They flashed a bright light and emitted a pair of dull thuds but the jelly contained them by bubbling out and then relaxing into puddles on the floor.

Dark shapes emerged from the landing craft and fired blue lasers wildly. The Ashtari fired as one, reducing the first attackers to heaps on the floor, but there were more behind them and these had time to duck down and place bars on the ground. Thin panes of green light extended up from the bars to seal the corridor in either direction and absorbed the Ashtari lasers. They kept firing at a furious rate and the acrid smell of laser residue filled the air. The barrier closest to Quintas wore down first and the lasers started getting through, but now the attackers had numbers and returned fire.

Quintas huddled into a ball in the narrow door frame as the lasers whipped by. Two Ashtari fell and a third one stood up and Quintas saw his chance. From his curled position, he lashed out with one foot kicking the soldier's foot to the side before he could use it to support his weight. He stopped mid-fall by bracing against the wall beside Quintas, but the disruption cost him. A pair of laser bursts passed through his neck and shoulder at the joints of his armor and he slumped to the floor. The lone remaining soldier turned his rifle on Quintas.

At least he'd die knowing that he'd fought back. A green shape flew past him, taking the soldier to the ground. Bakti straddled the fallen soldier, and they struggled over the rifle between them briefly before Bakti pushed it up over the soldier's head, rendering him completely exposed, and plunged a knife savagely into the soldier's armpit and the struggle stopped.

A group of attackers, dressed in varying dark shades of utilitarian canvas suits, approached them. "Thank you brothers," the leader, whose long nose hooked out over his thin mouth, said.

"I'm Kulon's brother," Bakti said and extended a hand. The leader clasped his forearm and smacked his shoulder.

"He said you'd be here, glad to have you. Will your friends be joining us?"

There wasn't any going back from what he'd done so Quintas nodded.

"Merka?" Bakti asked.

"If somebody tells me how those energy shields work," she said pointing down the hallway at the spent bars, "I'm all yours."

The leader spared a brief smile, "you'll get all the answers you want and more later. I need to clear this block. Take this comm and meet in hangar D-3 if you don't want to get left behind."

* * *

Refuges crowded the corridor leading to Block D. A voice over the PA instructed them to proceed calmly toward hangar D-2 for evacuation. That put the thronging crowd between them and their way out and, despite the instructions, they were anything but calm.

"We're not going to make it," Merka said.

"We can get through," Bakti said, but his voice lacked its customary confidence.

"No," Merka said, "we can't. We need another way off this ship."

Bakti looked at the crowd and the Asthari soldiers shepherding them, "what did you have in mind?"

"You think you can fly a ship if we can find one?" She asked Quintas, and he felt himself nod and she nodded back and then turned to Bakti, "Can you get us to the Block B hangar?"

Bakti checked his weapon, the rifle he'd grabbed off the Ashtari soldier and strode off down the hallway they'd come from. Merka had chosen wisely and the path to the hangar was clear aside from a few stragglers. Lucio and their mother would have had plenty of time to evacuate.

Ashtari mechanics, pilots and soldiers bustled all around. Ships were taking off to join the fight and damaged ones were limping back into the landing zone on the far side. Bakti pointed out a pilot jogging toward a ship at the edge of the room and they took off after him. As they ran, more Ashtari noticed them and lasers flew over their heads and scored the ground in front of them. Bakti's rifle exploded in his hand and he clutched the damaged hand to his chest but kept running. A few more strides and they were on the pilot, he turned too late.

Bakti grabbed him by the collar with his good hand and flung him into the side of the ship. The mask cracked and separated when he hit the ground to reveal the soldier's final, fearful expression

The cockpit was less familiar than Quintas had hoped, but he began to see the shape of things and flipped what were likely the priming switches for the engines, but nothing happened.

"Hold on," Merka said and ripped a panel off the wall next to the copilot's seat. She grabbed something out of her bag, drew her goggles down over her eyes, and sparks flew over her shoulder. "Try now."

This time the engines hummed low and then caught, the roar was deafening. Merka pulled the straps over Bakti's wounded arm and he grimaced as she pulled it tight.

"Get us out of here," he said through gritted teeth.

The ship lurched forward, screeching on the ground before Quintas found the stabilizers and brought them into a smooth hover before accelerating toward the bay doors, firing at several stationary ships to reduce the coming pursuit and they sailed out into space. Once they were out in the open, the controls were more familiar, two handles that adjusted their speed and direction just like the skiffs back home. He soon had the feel for the ship and weaved comfortably in and out of the fighting staying close to the larger ship to avoid the surface cannons.

"Plug this signature into the comm," Bakti said, tossing a handheld screen to Merka which she caught deftly without leaving her chair. Naxalite communications flooded their channel after she plugged it in and a voice warned them to clear out so Quintas pulled away from the Turan. A couple of Ashtari carriers loaded with refugees had broken off also, but more remained attached to the hull of the larger ship

Once all the Naxalite ships were clear, the leader's voice came in over the radio, "Detonation in 10 seconds."

"Detonation of what?" Quintas asked in a panic.

"Of the attack probes," Bakti said, "to cover our escape."

"There are still people on that ship!" Merka cried.

"Ashtari," Bakti sneered.

Quintas felt sick.

"There are still refugees," Merka pleaded, "You'll kill them."

"They had their chance to leave. Now they're just part of

the empire," said Bakti.

Merka grabbed the comm unit.

"Abort, abort, there are civilians on that ship."

"It's too late," Bakti said pulling the comm out of her hand.

"Detonation in 3, 2, 1..." sputtered the radio.

A smattering of tiny orange bursts covered the Turan.

A second wave followed, these larger and coming from deeper inside the Ashtari ship and Quintas watched in horror as the ship tore into several pieces in the silence of space. The jagged pieces drifted apart, almost peacefully, but a closer look revealed supplies, furniture and bodies floating between them. Lights pulsed in the exposed corridors, slower and slower, and eventually stopped.

"Mission accomplished," Bakti said. "Let's go."

Tears fell softly from Quintas' eyes and drenched his cheeks.

Merka turned her chair and leveled a pistol at Bakti. "Say one more word."

Quintas dropped the controls and rubbed his thumb across the smooth Pteriidae hanging from his neck and closed his eyes, sending more tears running. His shoulders shook. His family had made it onto one of the carriers, they must have made it.

Wiping his eyes with his sleeve, to little effect, Quintas grabbed the ship's controls with shaking hands. When he spoke his voice wavered but leveled off into a robotic monotone.

"Plug in the warp coordinates. ✎

There wasn't any going back from what he'd done so Quintas nodded. — The Displaced

CLEMENTINE FRASER

lives in the City of Sails in the land of the hobbits with two boisterous sons and a ginger cat that she secretly wishes was a dog. In her day job, she teaches teenagers to love history and essays. Okay, mostly just to love history. Having worked as a professional historian before she started teaching, readers might expect her primary genre to be historical fiction- but fantasy in all its magical variations is the genre that captures her imagination and makes it sing. Writing in stolen moments at lunchtimes, after school, and in between children's bedtimes is not always easy (and requires a constant infusion of coffee) but is always worth it. When she is not writing or working, you might find her curled up in an armchair with a good book or trying not to kill the flowers in her garden.

Alia of the Rock

Clementine Fraser

The Flock would never find her out here. Icy water lapped at her bare toes and tugged at the edges of her wings. She shifted, pain slicing through her muscles as she tried to pull her sagging feathers from the waves. Her hand crept from where her knees pressed against her chest, down her torn skin to the pitted stone on which she perched. Endless horizon met her gaze, dull and fading. Such a small rock to break the surface of the ocean.

Blood flashed in her memory and she sank her head onto her knees. Echoes of accusations rang in her ears. Even half-truths stung. The ocean washed her hands clean, streams of red filtering through the currents, but the marks of that last fight marred her pale skin. If she closed her eyes, faces swam into her head, twisted with fury and contempt. The Flock Master's anger battered at her mind.

She should keep moving.

Her foot slipped into the water like an anchor and she winced as she dragged it up again.

A shrill cry ripped through the air and her head jerked, heart pounding in her throat. Tension bled out of her when a small gull flew into her line of sight. She shifted, trying to get blurry eyes to focus. Gulls that small could never have made it this far from land.

Shifting breezes brought the scent of timber, the creak of sails, and the horizon cleared. A dark smudge became a three-masted sailing ship.

Her feet scrabbled on the rock, shoulders aching as water-logged wings struggled to lift, to flap.

Light flashed as the sun reflected off a spot high on the tallest mast. Shouted words garbled by wind drifted over to her and the ship changed course.

A gust of air knocked her back, and she collapsed onto the rock, her heart sinking to her stomach. Humans would only make this worse.

The ship anchored a little way from her and she stared back at the crew hanging over the railings, pointing and exclaiming. It had been a long time since she had been this close to a human vessel. Her wings shifted, pulling at weakened muscles. A sigh escaped dried lips, snatched away by the wind.

Ropes and winches creaked as the crew lowered a small boat over the side. Oars splashed and pulled at the waves, bringing the men closer to her rock.

Their eyes raked over her and she brought her wings further around her nakedness. Humans were strange with their fixation on clothes.

"What d'you think it is?"

"A demon, surely."

"Or some monstrous beast."

"Perhaps it's like a mermaid and a symbol of good fortune?"

She glared at them with all the fire she could muster. Death might lie at her door but she was no monster.

"...I think it understands us."

Words wouldn't come so she inclined her head.

"Captain wanted to check what you were— if you needed help. D'you need help?"

Her heart stopped for a beat that lasted a lifetime. She'd sworn not to cross that line again. But her tattered skin and sagging wings battled with her honor, and pain won. She nodded again.

Strong hands reached out, took her wrists, pulled her into the boat. They stared as she wrapped tired wings around her. She kept her gaze on the water. One of the men shook his head, as if to returning from his thoughts, and gave the order to row.

Sunlight sparkled on the waves and she closed her eyes, refusing to hear the screams and wails echoing in her mind. She had no choice but to go.

When the rough wood of the deck rested under her feet and the crew crowded forward with comments and stares and shouts, she gave in to doubt for a moment. They were all ages and all colors of human. Murmurs rose and fell in an agitated buzz, 'what is she?' and 'should have left it on that rock.' Then a man stepped out of the crowd and raised his hand.

"Silence!"

The others quieted at once. She gazed at this man whose presence exuded power. He stood taller than most of the other humans on the ship, broad and long of limb. His dark hair was tied back at the nape of his neck and ruffles adorned the collar of his shirt.

He shrugged off his long great-coat and approached her, his eyes fixed on her face, a hint of red on his cheeks. "Here, you must be chilled to the bone."

She stared at the thick fabric of the coat, at the swirls of patterns and buttons, then up to his face. Small lines creased the skin by his brown eyes and he smiled. Her hands trembled, but she tucked her wings close against her back and he placed the coat over her shoulders. Warmth spread from where his hands rested on her back for a moment.

His breadth shielded her from the horde of curious eyes. "Do you have a name?"

"Alia." The word came out in a croak and the man gestured at his crew, taking a water-skin and

thrusting it at her.

Tepid water soothed the back of her throat and drinking gave her a chance to gather the thoughts that fluttered through her mind. Her hand tightened on the soft leather of the water-skin.

"I am Captain Thomas Ashem."

His voice slid over her senses like a hand stroking down her feathers. Her eyes flew to his again.

"Welcome aboard my ship, Alia of the Rock. What manner of creature are you?"

She wet her lips. Could he hear her heartbeat racing? "I am of the Flock. I do not know if there is a word in your language for what I am." Not exactly a lie. Different humans had different words. Albatross might not be one he knew.

"So, no angel then?"

His smile warmed his face but his gaze was that of a hawk. She pulled the coat closer around her, inhaling scents she couldn't recognize mixed with the ingrained smell of salt and seaweed.

"I do not know what an angel is, but I do not think I am one."

"You look too fair to be a demon. And too fragile. How came you to be on that rock?"

Thoughts of blood, of broken shrieks, filled her head. Her knees shook, and she pushed her hair back, trying to shove away memories of a fight on a cliff and her hands grasping at empty air. The youngling fell. It wasn't my fault. "There are some who would harm me. I thought no-one would find me out here."

Captain Ashem regarded her in silence, his chin resting on his hand. At last, he heaved a sigh. "Indeed the oceans bring us more mysteries than even we thought possible." He straightened, his hand sinking to rest on the hilt of his cutlass. "I will offer you safe passage to where we are headed. Maybe you can find what you are looking for there."

Grumbled protests from the crew cut through the confusion whirling inside her. She lifted her chin, the coat pulled tight around her. "I do not wish to be a burden."

His laugh soared like the chatter of a gull. "You are too small to be that big of a burden. Come, I will take you to a cabin and you can rest."

Warmth flooded her bones, and she fought not to stare at him with his open face and kind eyes.

The stares of the crew burned as she followed the Captain. Each step was another taken across a fast blurring line. Albatrosses brought ill-luck to sailors, whether they meant to or not. Squawks of the gulls perched on the mast battered her ears. Surely she had flown far enough to escape notice, but she hunched away from the beady eyes of the small birds anyway.

Beams of sunlight spilled into the cabin from the open door and small diamond-patterned windows in the walls. A bed nestled into one side of the room, with a half-pulled curtain barely concealing the mussed sheets. On brass mounts on the wall rested a curved sword. Her back tensed around her wings as unbidden memories of the execution knife glinting in the sun-flooded her mind. In the middle of the floor sat a heavy oak table, and she sank into one of the chairs the Captain pulled it out.

"Thank you, Captain."

"Please, call me Thomas."

Her eyes flicked to his and away, his smile sending her heart into unfamiliar rhythms. "Thomas, thank you for your kindness."

"Do not thank me. I could no more leave a damsel in distress than I could fly to the moon."

Her lips twisted and she shifted in the chair. "Is that how you see me?"

"Are you not in distress?"

The heavy fabric of the coat covered her twisting hands. Her fingernails remembered the tear of skin underneath them, her mind tried to shut out the sounds of the rocks falling down the cliff as the girl's body tumbled to the waves. The ringing of a bell outside saved her from answering. Thomas stood and strode to a cupboard.

"These clothes will likely be too big, but it's all I have." He turned back to her with a shirt and some breeches in his arms. "There is water in the flask by my bed and I will have someone bring you food." He placed the garments on the table and paused, his lips pursed. "What do you eat?"

"Fruit or fish is fine if you have it."

His eyes went to her back and the lump her wings made under the coat. "Of course."

He paused at the door, one hand leaning on the frame. "If you are weary, use the bed. I will take a hammock with the rest of the crew until we reach land."

The door closed behind him and her thoughts whirled in a maelstrom until exhaustion put them one by one to sleep.

She woke still nestled in his coat, curled up on the narrow bed. Someone had brought food. She grasped at the small wizened fruits. The floury flesh tasted like heaven to her starved tongue. She wiped her face and glanced at the door.

A stiff breeze caught the ends of her hair as she walked out onto the deck and she thought of the coat she'd left folded carefully at the end of the bed. The crew tried to hide their interest as she shuffled past in too big breeches and a shirt modified to fit around her wings.

She'd felt guilty ripping such great tears in the fine linen but Thomas simply raised a brow and smiled.

"It is good to see you up and rested. I have news that I hope will please you—we've spotted land. It looks to be a small island but may provide you shelter from those you flee."

A weight lifted from her and she smiled. If they could only reach the island maybe it would all be alright. She could rest, recover, fly on to a place where she could be left alone, hidden from the eyes of the Flock Master and the vengeance he sought for his daughter's death. *It wasn't my fault.* But her stomach twisted and screams rang through her head.

She leaned over the railing, her fingers catching on the wood, and gazed toward the horizon. The island rose rocky and green above the waves.

A shout rang out and she looked to where the sailor pointed.

Wings caught her eye and her blood turned to ice. Too big to be gulls. Wild thoughts of leaping overboard raced through her mind but Thomas grabbed her shoulder.

"Is this the Flock you spoke of? Are you in danger?"

"Yes." And so are you. But the words stuck in her throat and he let out a warning shout as he hustled her back toward the cabin and thrust her inside.

"Stay here."

"Why do you help me?"

"Is there a reason I shouldn't?"

Echoes of a storm whipping at torn wings, the remembered feel of fingers gripping her arms, the dread coiling in her gut. "No."

"Then stay here out of sight."

He drew his sword.

The door slammed behind him and she leaned against it, her pulse racing. Her fingers curled against the wooden panels and she listened.

Feet pounded across the deck and a great thunderous rush of air, as of many wings beating, rose above the sounds of shouting and metal clanging.

The ship shuddered with an impact and tilted to one side. Another rush of wings and a crack and the ship listed the other way. Fear rooted her to the spot and she leaned her forehead against the door. The boom of the cannons ripped into her skull and she jerked.

No. She needed to warn him. His kindness deserved as much.

Wrenching open the door, she stumbled onto the heaving deck. Feathers and gunpowder filled the air and wind whipped through tattered sails. Four of the Flock crouched at the prow of the ship, ringed by sailors with swords.

She raced toward Thomas and grasped the back of his shirt, her fingers twisting in the sweat-soaked linen.

"Do not kill them!"

He shook her off, and turned

to face her. Blood trickled from his temple and soaked the torn fabric on his chest. "Why should I be so merciful? They attacked us and sought to harm one to whom I promised safe passage."

"Great misfortune will come if you do."

A grin spread on his face, crinkling the corners of his eyes. "I have no fear of misfortune or death. Let them do their worst." He leaned forward and gripped her arm, his touch sending fire over her skin. "I will not let them have my ship or my crew." His grip softened. "Or you."

He turned from her and raised his hand. Sun sparked off swords as they sliced through wings and flesh. A sea of red flooded the deck.

Ice tore at her chest. One more step toward disaster.

The ship faltered to shore, broken sails twisting in the wind. Finally, it ran aground, wedged deep in the sand.

Those sailors who survived sank to the shore, thrusting their hands into the soil, giving thanks for being spared. The damage to the ship was extensive. It could be repaired—there was wood aplenty on the island, and flax to repair torn rigging—but it would be a long time before it was sea-worthy again.

Night covered the island like a blanket of down. The men lit a fire and curled up beside it, looking more like lost boys than burly sailors. Thomas sat close, a bulwark between her and the others. He tossed a twig onto the fire, watching it snap and burn.

"I don't regret it."

His voice was a hushed murmur, and she leaned closer, unsure she'd heard him correctly. He turned to face her and his eyes glowed warm in the firelight. His fingers reached out to trace over the marks still visible on her face. "They would have torn you apart. For everything we lost, I would do it again to spare you."

Heat filled her at his touch and breath caught in her throat. Danger lay that way—humans and albatrosses were never to mix. Heartbreak would be the only outcome. She shifted and his hand dropped.

"Sleep well, Alia."

"You also, Thomas." His name tasted like home on her lips and her chest constricted. No. It oughtn't be possible. But her fingers curled at her side to stop them reaching for him as he lay next to her and she knew it wasn't only possible she was falling for him, but it had happened already.

She fought it—being an albatross, once given, her heart would be bound forever—but every day his smile and his kindness and his laughter tore down a little more of the wall she had placed around her feelings.

"Alia."

His voice floated into her thoughts and she met his eyes with a smile. "Yes, Thomas?"

"Where do you go when you slip away from us like that?"

Thoughts of him whirled in her head and heat warmed her cheeks. "I think of someone who makes me happy."

His eyes lit up and he reached for her hand. Strong fingers wrapped around hers, tugging her closer. She bit her lip against the racing pulse in her throat, sparks running under her skin from his touch.

"Come," he said, "I want to show you somewhere magical."

Stones skittered under their feet as she followed him up a winding path around the edge of the cliff. Her eyes fixed on his back, on the muscles moving beneath his shirt. Beads of sweat slid from his hairline, down tanned skin, to duck beneath his collar. A gust of wind rippled through her wings and she pressed her lips together. She was not human. He was not for her.

Sunlight danced on the waves below as they stood on the clifftop. Salt left a tang in the breeze and the grass was lush and dense beneath her bare feet. Thomas clasped her hand, moving to stand shoulder to shoulder with her.

"See? Is it not a place of magic?"

Her gaze lit on his face and her heart thundered like the waves below. "It is a most magical view, to be sure."

He leaned down and kissed her, his mouth soft and warm. The walls in her mind shattered and her heart flooded through her lips into his body. Fear and doubt withered under the heat of her desire. Hands on her waist, he pulled her closer and she flung her arms around his neck.

Echoing over the island, the sound of the ship being rebuilt rang in her ears and sent chills over her skin. He would leave her soon. She leaned into his embrace, her mouth hungry for his and her body on fire at his touch.

She was doomed. But she no longer cared.

* * *

At last, too soon, dawn rose on his last day on the island. Gusts of wind snatched at her outspread wings as she stood sentinel, watching the sails fill. The clank of the anchor against the side of the ship as it rose drifted across the air to her spot on the hilltop.

As if he felt the heat of her gaze, he turned. After a moment he held up a hand in farewell.

Her wings pulled at her back, urging her to fly to him.

But her feet stayed rooted to the warm soil. She did not deserve a happy ending and she would not bring him anything but ill fortune.

He had said to her, in the curve of her arms in the darkest hour of the night, "It will be for the best. You will find someone of your own kind." But if she closed her eyes she could hear her heart beating in his chest. There would never be another. Not for her.

The wind picked up, whipping her hair across her face, blowing from the island out to sea. Cold spikes shot down her spine and she brushed the twisting strands from her face to see the boat tumbling in sudden waves. Timber groaned and men shouted curses at the darkening clouds.

Feathers, not rain, turned the sky black. The Flock had returned—Thomas should not have killed the albatross. She should never have run from them.

This time they did not land on the ship. They let their wings beat up the wind, tangle the sails, stir the water into great waves that tossed and tumbled the great vessel.

A great crack of wood splintering sounded over the distance and she watched, frozen, as the ship tore apart, men falling into the water like drops of rain.

Her knees gave way and she fell to the ground, her fingers grabbing at the soil. Her heart, now linked to Thomas, meant his fear flooded over her. Even from a distance, she felt the water sliding over his chest as the currents pulled him down.

The agony of his last breath stole hers from her lungs.

Grief slid over her face in unstoppable tears blurring her vision. She didn't move, even when three of the Flock landed in front of her, their great wings sending eddies of dust floating from the soil.

"It is ended, Alia."

"I never meant for any of it to happen. The girl's death was an accident. I let her go too far, and she slipped."

"You pushed her. You were charged with the care of the Flock Master's young and you let a moment of anger destroy everything."

She trembled, remembering echoed shouts and red rage. Empty grasping fingers as Gintia tumbled from the clifftop. Burning regret as the youngling's wings failed to open in time and she smashed to the rocks below. Her eyes went to the water down below. So much disaster and all from one foolish moment of anger—Gintia betrayed her trust and laughed about it but she hadn't meant to kill her. The girl's wings should have opened. But they didn't. Numbness spread through her. The girl's mockery seemed so very unimportant now.

"Killing the Flock Master's young brought his wrath upon us all." He knelt down, his hand on her shoulder. "You should not have fled, sister."

Her eyes stayed fixed on the spot where the ship had been swallowed by the waves. "Finish it now."

His grip tightened on her skin. "You wish for death?"

"I have nothing left to live for."

They huddled and whispered and she ignored them—the empty hollowness in her chest consumed her.

"There has been enough bloodshed," her brother said. "The sailors who dared to kill us have been punished. You, however, will be banished. Remain here on your island, apart always from the Flock and alone. Perhaps in your endless heartbreak, you will come to realize the extent of your crime."

Aching loneliness sliced through her. An albatross mated for life and her heart lay under the waves.

She staggered to her feet, cast a last look at the Flock, then stepped forward and off the cliff. Her wings yearned to expand, to dance in the wind, but she kept them tight at her back and arrowed into the water below, following her heart. ✎

REBECCA MAY HOPE

delights in reading and writing the well-crafted phrase. While wordsmithing is its own reward, her weekly writers' group provides the impetus to keep writing and polishing—so she has something to share with her fellow authors. Rebecca couldn't imagine a life without teaching; her middle school, high school, and college students give her a chance to share her passion for words with a new crop of young people each year. When she feels the need to follow Wordsworth's advice ("Up, up, my friend, and quit your books!"), you'll find her playing with or rocking her grandbabies; walking her rambunctious ninety-pound Labradoodle on the nature trails near her home in Champlin, Minnesota; or pampering her softer-than-air Ragdoll cat. Learn more about Rebecca's writing at www.RebeccaMayHope.com

Sir Manifred's Secret

Rebecca May Hope

Four *gray walls and four gray towers.* Like a dream springing to life, Castle Albion rose ahead, nestled among the trees of the Appalachian foothills. Crystal congratulated herself as she pulled up before its modern-medieval facade. After vowing to free her inner poet, even at work, she'd chosen this venue for an employee development retreat. *Achieve the Vision*—Castle Albion's motto— seemed possible here. Smiling, she relinquished her Pathfinder to the valet.

"We've been expecting you."

The scarlet-uniformed doorman bowed and directed her to the concierge desk.

"Eric?" Crystal blinked in surprise when she read the concierge's name badge. "I thought you were the Event Planner."

"Ms. Sutton." He extended his white-gloved hand. "Guilty as charged."

While planning her conference by phone, she and Eric had clicked. He knew exactly what she was looking for, and their ideas meshed perfectly. As the conference date neared, she'd invented excuses to call him just to hear his kind words and compliments—and to feel the little confidence boost they gave her. She'd suspected his appearance wouldn't live up to his personality. But it definitely did.

"You'll find I wear many hats around here." He nodded his full head of brownish-black hair streaked with hints of either sunlight or gray. "I'm pleased to meet you in person at last."

Crystal placed her hand in his, and he wrapped it with his other hand and squeezed, transmitting a warm tingle even through his gloves. His dazzling smile split his dark mustache and close-trimmed beard with a flash of white as his forehead wrinkled appealingly. His electric blue eyes held hers.

Such an expressive face. She felt their connection deepen and smiled back warmly. "Likewise."

"Your meeting room—the Elizabethan—is on the third floor, and your team occupies the entire South Tower." He motioned to his left without breaking eye contact. "I've upgraded you to the Rapunzel Suite on the fourth floor—with my compliments."

Her face grew warm under his attentive gaze. "Thank you."

"I have your paperwork." He placed a printout on the counter between them. "No need to go to registration. Just sign here."

Anchoring the contract with her left hand, she accepted the pen he offered. As she signed, his eyes dropped to her wedding ring. Was that disappointment that flashed across his face? Crystal's heart sank. Why hadn't she left her ring at home?

The courteous bellhop led her to the Rapunzel Suite, where he ushered her inside and deposited her bags. She surveyed its soothing yellow-gold walls, tall arched windows, and romantic canopy bed covered in maroon-and-gold fleur-de-lis.

"Perfect."

After accepting his tip, the young man exited backward—as if she were royalty.

Crystal stood before the full-length mirror, viewing herself from different angles. Had Eric found her as attractive as she'd found him? She was shapely for forty-one, but she should have updated her hairstyle before coming. It really was too thin to wear long. The brown tresses with their fading red highlights scattered forlornly onto her shoulders. She was no Rapunzel.

Smiling at that irony, she studied her face—fleshy rounded cheeks, delicate chin, narrow sloped nose. And enigmatic hazel eyes that sparkled with some hidden secret.

So Ronnie had said. That was what had snagged him twenty years ago—a secret he could spend a lifetime unraveling. But that lifetime had turned out to be only nineteen years.

She kicked off her kitten heels, threw herself onto the velvet couch, and glared at her ring. Her stubborn commitment to a meaningless bauble had given Eric the wrong idea. But maybe she'd only imagined his crestfallen expression. Her wedding wedding ring set often inspired looks and comments: the Celtic knotwork band of intertwined rose gold and palladium was unusual, and the large diamond guarded by four emeralds made it unique.

Unique but meaningless. She only kept it on because she'd promised herself to wear it until the divorce was final. Because she, unlike some people, kept her vows.

In fact, the decree was due any day now. She sat up and pulled out her phone. When she saw her lawyer's email, excitement mixed with dread rose in her chest. Holding her breath, she scanned the document. With a sigh, she twisted the ring off her finger and laid it on the mahogany coffee table. She was Crystal Beaudry again.

She cried. She hadn't expected to—she'd cried so much already. Then she dozed on the couch for a while. After waking, she quickly dressed for the kick-off dinner. She wanted to get to the dining room early to set out the name cards. For safekeeping, she zipped the ring into the inside pocket of her clutch. As she rode the elevator down to the main floor, she rubbed the naked finger.

How surreal her ringless hand felt as she arranged the placards. Her ring's intrinsic value had instantly plunged below zero. Naively she'd clung to a sliver of hope that Ronnie would abandon the young seductress he'd moved in with. Would she have taken him back if he had? She didn't know. But until the judge signed the decree, she had remained Mrs. Sutton, and the ring had meant something. What would she do with it now?

As Jenna Norton, the PR Director, arrived, Crystal switched Jenna's name card with the one to the left of her own. Jenna had divorced her husband a year ago.

During the main course, Crystal leaned toward her. Resting her palm on the table, she pointed out her bare finger. "The divorce just went through."

Jenna's eyes widened as she swallowed and dabbed her lips with her napkin. "Congratulations! I'm so happy for you!" Squeezing Crystal's hand, she tossed her long blonde hair and winked. "You go, girl! Should I announce it? A toast?"

Crystal laughed but shook her head. "No, no! I don't want to make a big deal of it," she whispered. "I was just curious. What did you do with your wedding ring?"

Jenna's grin spread mischievously as she jiggled her wrist a few inches above the table. Crystal eyed the silver charm bracelet that glittered with dangling figures. Confused, she squinted at Jenna for an explanation.

Jenna spun the bracelet around and pointed to a little diamond-studded silver donkey. "I had it melted down and recast. Best way to remember my Jack."

The two women giggled.

That was certainly one solution, but Crystal couldn't see destroying her lovely set that way.

As desserts were being served, Crystal spotted Eric signaling her from the doorway. She slipped away from the table.

"Nothing's wrong," he assured her, guiding her into the hallway with a gentle touch on her back. "I just wanted to let you know that we start the mystery off with a bang. It's coming any time—"

BANG!

A gunshot rang out, and even though she'd just been warned, Crystal jumped. Instinctively she gripped Eric's elbow with her left hand. Laughing, he patted it. Their eyes met. A question lingered in his as he settled his palm over her ring finger. He must have noticed it was bare.

With surprise, she saw for the first time the band on his left hand. Titanium etched with Celtic knots against an ebony background.

He squeezed her hand, flashing a smile. "That's my cue!"

Adopting his persona, he rushed to the stage, proclaiming that Duke McDougal had just been murdered.

Back in her chair, Crystal enjoyed Prince Eric's melodramatic spiel, but she flushed with embarrassment recalling that question in his eyes. Did he think she'd ditched her ring to signal she was ready for a fling? That she was broadcasting her availability for a one-night stand?

His own ring meant that if he was as interested in her as he seemed to be, he was a knave, just like Ronnie, and no prince. She'd better keep her distance.

She focused on Eric's final explanations to the guests.

"You're free to enjoy the rest of the evening on your own but keep your eyes open for clues.

They can be anywhere around Castle Albion." He swept the room with an expansive gesture. "Inside or out. You've got tonight, tomorrow, and Saturday morning to discover who shot the Duke."

After dinner, Crystal migrated to the lounge with a few others but soon excused herself. She needed to be alone to imagine her new future. She wandered aimlessly through the common spaces of the castle, deep in thought. First, she'd have to let her two daughters know the divorce was final. In high school now, they knew it was coming, but they'd still be upset. Changing her name on her license and accounts—all those humdrum realities—would be a headache.

When she rounded a corner into the hall behind the concierge desk, she met a six-foot knight. The full suit of armor stood beside a glass-fronted armoire displaying chrome reproductions of silver serving dishes. But the armor looked authentic. It wasn't the shiny metal she expected. The dull, burnished steel reminded her of Tik Tok from Return to Oz, a character she'd dearly loved as a child. The solid visor came to a point at the nose and down to the chin—like a heavy beak.

The suit bent forward intently, and his broad shoulder plates and earnest dark eye slits seemed to say, *I'm here for you, milady. I'll right your wrongs, defend your honor, and protect you from harm and betrayal.*

"I believe you will, Sir—"

Her eyes fell on the plaque explaining the piece.

Sir Manfred. Victorian Era replica of a sixteenth-century suit of armor. Made of heavy steel and fully articulated, this suit was created as home décor for an English country manor.

"Sir Manfred." She curtseyed as she whispered, "I accept your service."

She looked over her shoulder, hoping no one had seen or heard her interactions with the armor. It was nearly midnight, and the halls were empty. No reason not to indulge her imagination.

"I wish I could take you home. They don't make men like you anymore."

She seated herself across the narrow hallway on a tapestry bench where she could bask in Sir Manfred's reassurances. Again she recalled Eric's gentle hand on hers, his winsome smile, and his kind eyes. She sighed.

Men weren't what they seemed. She had to remember that and not let her heart run away with her.

As she studied Sir Manfred, she noticed he wasn't parallel to the wall. He stood angled toward the concierge desk with his dark eye slits transfixed on the counter where Eric's engraved nameplate rested. Was that a clue?

"Are you telling me Eric's the one?" She rose and aligned herself with Sir Manfred, matching her gaze to his. She nodded her understanding. "So Prince Eric murdered the Duke."

She moved to his side, stood on her tiptoes, and spoke toward the hinge of his visor. "Thanks for the tip."

At breakfast, Crystal found a seat next to Lara, the Purchasing Manager, who'd been divorced for a few years. When the others at their table returned to the buffet for seconds, Crystal showed Lara her bare finger. "I'm a free woman."

Lara nodded solemnly. "I'm sorry? Or congratulations? Which do you prefer?"

Crystal shrugged. "Both, I guess. Can I ask you something? What did you do with your wedding ring?"

Lara spread cream cheese on her bagel. "Sold it and donated the money to a battered women's shelter."

"Oh." Crystal's heart twisted as she grasped the situation. She'd never heard Lara discuss her marriage or divorce. She only remembered Lara's marital status changing to D on her personnel record. "That was a good idea."

"I never questioned it. It was always my plan."

Crystal appreciated Lara's generosity and the symbolism behind her choice—a bit of poetic justice. Altruism alone couldn't goad Crystal to donate the ring that had witnessed twenty years of her life, with all its joys and miseries. But poetic justice, if she could find the right gesture, might restore the ring's lost meaning. What might that gesture be? It would have to resonate with her newly awakened inner poet.

During the morning team-building session, led by a hired consultant, Crystal sat in the back of the room in case the hotel staff needed her. Since she'd previewed the curriculum, she could discreetly view her phone while monitoring the meeting.

Off and on she searched the internet for ideas for obsolete wedding rings.

Many women saved their rings for a son or daughter. Crystal's girls were furious with their father for his affair and for abandoning their family. With those negative associations, they'd never want the ring. Many women sold their rings and spent the cash on necessities, but Crystal already lived comfortably without unloading her ring for half its purchase price.

Unlike many women, she wouldn't wear it on her other hand. Its intertwined Celtic knots once stood for undying love, but now they reminded her only of Ronnie's betrayal.

After lunch, she returned to her room to dress for the ropes course outing. With a few minutes to spare, she skimmed another internet article. According to the author, many divorced women drove into the country, found an empty field, and hurled their rings into the weeds. For some, throwing the ring away meant casting off their bitterness and pain. Others hoped someone would come along with a metal detector and find the ring someday—so it would surprise and delight someone again.

The idea intrigued Crystal. Today while trekking through the hills she could fling her ring into a ravine for some lucky future hiker to find. She'd be paying it forward as a mystery benefactor. She retrieved it from her clutch and slipped it into the tiny coin pocket of her jeans. The stretchy fabric would keep it secure.

Then again, if she lost it, she could file a claim and receive its full insured value. Wouldn't that look rather suspicious? Losing her wedding ring the day after her divorce? Picturing herself behind bars for insurance fraud, she shoved the ring deeper into the pocket.

Along the wooded trail, Crystal laughed and joked with her team. As the sun with new confidence beat down on her bare arms, the spring air in her lungs felt intoxicating. Everywhere birds whistled their mating calls. A new day, a new season, had dawned.

She forgot about her ring until they reached their destination. Checking her pocket, she confirmed it was still safe.

At the sight of Eric welcoming the cluster of hikers ahead of her, her heart fluttered. She should have guessed. He ran the ropes course, too.

Crystal had no intention of strapping up herself—she was merely the organizer. But her coworkers insisted she take her turn climbing to the top of the pole.

As assistants began buckling people into their harnesses, Eric drew close. "You're afraid of heights, aren't you?"

Was it that obvious? She'd attempted a brave face, but yes, she was terrified. "A little."

To her chagrin, her voice quaked.

He placed his hand between her shoulder blades and spoke in her ear. "You can do this. I'll be here for you. You're completely safe."

Warmth spread from her chest through her whole body, and she lost herself in his blue eyes. She believed him.

Still, when it was her turn to ascend the towering pole, she shook like the quivering leaves about her. Each step required more and more will. Only by refusing to look down could she keep breathing. She focused on the stripped tree trunk before her as she grasped each new handhold. Finally, she reached the top.

Now she was supposed to stand atop the eighteen-inch disc at the pinnacle. Watching others attempt it before her, she'd pictured herself maneuvering smoothly onto the disc and rising to her feet victoriously. But now that she was here, with the world spread out twenty-five feet below and no one by her side, she froze. Her muscles refused to obey. She trembled uncontrollably, and her stomach churned.

"Crystal, look at me!" Eric called from below. He positioned himself at the side of the pole where she could meet his eyes. "Keep going! You're doing great!"

Far below, his encouraging smile gleamed through his beard. For a moment she focused only on him—his sturdy shoulders, his windblown mop of hair, his strong hands that gripped the belaying line connected to the harness that crisscrossed her heart. She moved upward.

Soon—following Eric's shouted instructions—she kneeled on the wooden disc. She wrapped her fingers over its edge and clawed the underside.

Swaying, she felt as fluid as an amoeba, her bones and muscles merely cytoplasm.

"Crystal!" Eric's voice reached her. He moved into her line of sight. "You are a strong woman! So powerful! You can achieve whatever you want to achieve. You can go as high as you want to go!"

No doubt he said those same words to every woman who made it this far. She swatted the doubts away. To succeed at this, she had to believe he meant the words just for her. She absorbed them into every pore.

"You're beautiful, Crystal! Look at you! Absolutely amazing. So courageous. So determined. Everything is possible for you. It's all there for you, and you're just the woman who can make it happen. This is your moment. This is your day to shine."

Her coworkers urged her on, too, but it was Eric's voice that gave her courage. Beautiful. Somehow, she positioned a foot under her. Then the other one. To rise felt like pushing against the hand of an invisible giant, but she strained upward, forcing her quaking knees to straighten.

She stood.

She was one with the sky and the eagles. Clouds floated within her grasp. One thing remained to seal this triumphant experience: to reach into her pocket and fling away her wedding band. She envisioned her fingers extracting the ring, then whizzing it across the treetops.

But her arms, outstretched airplane-style, maintained her precarious balance. She couldn't force her hand to her side.

A second later she zipped down to the forest floor. Whipping off her helmet, she shook her hair out. She staggered. Immediately Eric enfolded her in his arms.

"You're amazing!" he whispered. "I'm so proud of you."

Shaking against his chest, she felt his soft beard on her cheek, breathed in his piney scent, and melted into his strength. What would it be like to feel his lips on hers?

She wobbled out of his embrace. "I couldn't have done it without you. Wow. That was quite a feeling."

He drew his hand down her arm and turned to the next climber.

At dinner, everyone was relaxed and refreshed. As Crystal had hoped, the team-building routines had loosened everyone up. Showing off their deductive powers, they traded theories and clues about Duke McDougal's murder. No one suspected Eric, who had gained everyone's trust on the ropes course.

Unable to restrain the smirk that crept to her lips, Crystal insisted she had no inside information. Admitting she'd communicated with Sir Manfred might raise a few eyebrows.

She turned in early. Snuggling into the queen-sized canopy bed, she managed one more internet search on unwanted wedding rings. Up popped a story featuring a joyful couple backed by teal-blue ocean and white-sand beach. They'd brought their rings from their previous marriages on their honeymoon. On the count of three, she pitched his old ring into the waves and he pitched hers.

Crystal switched off the light. That was so sweet—her favorite idea so far—but she doubted she'd ever remarry. No real man could match the man she wished Eric was.

Hours later she punched down her pillow for the hundredth time. After a blissful series of dreams where she and Eric strolled Tahitian sands as newlyweds, she awoke and couldn't get back to sleep. He was already married, for goodness' sake, and she had no intention of being a home wrecker. She had to stop thinking

about him. She slipped on her jeans and t-shirt, pocketed her room key, and rode the elevator down to visit Sir Manfred.

In the dimly lit hallway, she sat on the tapestry bench hugging her knees. "Sir Manfred," she began, her voice barely audible, "maybe Eric's a Lancelot wannabe, but I'm no Guinevere. Anyway, I'm probably imagining it all. Could be he liked my ring because he's Irish and it matched his. Maybe he was sorry to see me without it."

Sir Manfred seemed unconvinced. He required honesty, even from lonely women at three a.m. She studied the carpet, unable to meet the knight's penetrating gaze. The truth? Eric's expressive face, electrifying touch, and intense eyes spoke volumes. He was attracted to her, too.

"After tomorrow, we'll never see each other again, and I'll put him from my mind. Still, it's been nice to imagine a romance—here in this magical place." She raised her eyes. "But I won't forget you, my friend."

Her heart warmed for the faithful knight, leaning toward her with such zealous valor, ready to spring to her aid. She crossed the hallway to his side and grasped his cold steel fingers. She lifted her hand to his cheek and ran her fingers down his resolute jawline to the noble chin beneath the visor.

In an instant, she knew what to do. With her left hand, she reached up and lifted Sir Manfred's visor, and with her right, she felt inside the helmet along the bottom of the chin. She was too short to see inside, but she felt a hollow that could cradle a jewel safely and, when the visor was lowered, invisibly. She withdrew her ring, which was still in her pocket, deposited it in the hollow, and lowered the visor.

"I charge thee, Sir Manfred," she whispered solemnly, "to guard this treasure and deliver it to the chosen one alone, whether duster-wielding parlor maid or ladder-bearing maintenance man. I hereby bequeath it to your wisdom and justice."

At the wrap-up Saturday morning, Eric joined them to announce the solution to the murder mystery. To Crystal's surprise, fully half her coworkers had accused her, the Lady of the Crystal Lagoon, of being the murderess. Eric's ruse of pulling her away from the dinner table moments before the gunshot had

convinced them. Only Crystal had correctly accused Prince Eric. He summoned her up front to claim her reward.

"A woman as brilliant as she is brave," he announced with a gallant sweep of his hands toward her. "Besides this coveted basket of goodies from our gift shop, I also present you with the keys to the kingdom—a complimentary week at Castle Albion." He pressed the gift card into her hand with a lingering two-handed shake. Meeting her eyes, he spoke only to her. "I hope to see you again soon."

As the audience applauded, she memorized his blue eyes and endearing smile for the last time.

After Castle Albion, Crystal's life returned to its new normal. Ronnie married his girlfriend a month after the divorce. With two graduations two years in a row, visiting colleges, and sending her oldest away to school, Crystal was too busy for jealousy—or a romance of her own. Her anger toward Ronnie gradually cooled, and she could speak to him civilly when necessary.

Shortly after their second daughter graduated from high school, Ronnie inexplicably turned kind and considerate. Over the summer he reconnected with his daughters, and Crystal could—at times—remember her married years fondly.

When Ronnie's small plane crashed in Labrador where he was hunting caribou, the girls were devastated. Though they'd just started fall term, they came home for two weeks. The funeral was awkwardly poignant. Making everyone cringe, Ronnie's widow attended on the arm of another man. Crystal, who wasn't the widow, grieved as if she was. Ronnie's relatives thanked her effusively for coming and reminisced with her about happier days.

The girls spent a week sorting their dad's things. Because of their prenuptial agreement, Ronnie's widow had inherited nothing. He left everything to his daughters, except for his Lexus, which, to her great surprise, he had willed to Crystal.

One day the girls came home from their dad's condo bearing a letter addressed to Crystal and dated four months previous. It was an apology of sorts he'd never had the courage to send. He confessed that when his second wife started cheating, he finally understood the pain he'd caused Crystal and the girls. Crystal had been his true love— but of course, he'd found out too late.

Crystal read the letter repeatedly and wept afresh each time. Finally, she stored it in a keepsake box in her room. Placing it there, she noticed the Castle Albion gift card. She'd never found time to go back.

She pictured steadfast Sir Manfred. Had he foreseen what was to come? Might he have saved her wedding ring for her? Suddenly she craved that memento of Ronnie. If there was any possibility of retrieving it, she had to try. The girls were heading back to college in a few days. With the recent trauma, her boss would understand if she needed a getaway.

The following weekend she drove to the hill country, now ablaze with autumn colors, and pulled her Lexus up to the gray-towered castle, which looked exactly as it had eighteen months ago. When she entered, the concierge stand was vacant, but a glance down the hall told her Sir Manfred was still on duty. At check-in, she learned she'd been upgraded to the Rapunzel suite, but no one could tell her why.

The room looked the same as it had last year, except that a handful of red-foil-wrapped chocolate hearts bound with netting and tied with a crimson ribbon rested on the pillow. She read the attached tag: Welcome back, Ms. Beaudry.—Sir Manfred.

She grinned. A clever marketing ploy—but so à propos. She ordered room service and watched a movie, biding her time until the hallways emptied.

After midnight, she slipped out of her room. On the main floor, she approached Sir Manfred from the back hallway. He still bent forward, eye slits aligned on the concierge's nameplate. Was it still Eric's name? Her heart tugged her that direction, but if she ventured farther, she'd be visible to the night clerk. Never mind. A married man wasn't her mission.

She turned to face the armored knight. "Greetings, Sir Manfred," she whispered. "Thanks for the chocolates." The same faithful rapport she'd felt from him before warmed her chest. "I've returned to claim what's mine—that is, if I'm worthy. May I?"

She felt his consent, and a thrill rose to her throat. The ring was still there. She could sense it.

After looking around to assure their privacy, she reached up and raised the visor. With her right hand, she felt into the depression behind the chin. The prongs of a set jewel met her fingers, and relief rushed over her. Carefully she slid the ring upward along the bottom of the helmet and closed her fingers around it.

She crossed to the tapestry bench and sat. With a tremor of excitement, she opened her fist.

A large diamond solitaire glittered in her hand.

She blinked twice, then raised her eyes to Sir Manfred. "You!" she scolded. "Are you in the business of bewitching women's rings from them? I thought better of you!"

Sir Manfred wouldn't dignify such an accusation with a reply. His valiant stance told her she'd falsely accused her loyal knight. She slipped the solitaire into her pocket, returned to his side, and once again raised the visor. Again she felt inside, this time sweeping her fingers over the entire area. She caught her breath as two rings clinked together in her hand.

Carefully she withdrew them, clasping them to her palm as soon as they reached the lip of the helmet. Clenching them, she returned to the bench.

She closed her eyes and whispered, "Let one of them be mine."

As she unfolded her fingers, she opened her eyes. In her palm lay her own Celtic knotwork band with its diamond and four emeralds.

"Oh!"

Nestled beside it was a titanium band etched with Celtic knots against a black background. Eric's.

She approached the armor. "What does it mean?"

Sir Manfred's lips were sealed. Whether Eric had found her ring there and added his to it after his own divorce, or whether Sir Manfred had enticed him to deposit it there as if no one had ever done so before, the knight would not divulge.

"Wait a minute." The full meaning of Sir Manfred's clue slowly dawned. "You told me Eric was the one, but not to help me solve the murder mystery. You meant he was the one. For me."

Sir Manfred seemed rather smug.

"Some wives cheat on their husbands—like Ronnie's new wife cheated on him. Maybe Eric's not a knave after all." Crystal smiled and tapped Sir Manfred's breastplate. "And the chocolates weren't from you."

She retrieved the solitaire from her pocket. Gingerly she returned all three rings to their hiding place and closed the visor.

In one glorious moment, she imagined herself in Eric's arms, his beard brushing her cheek, and his lips finding hers. She saw their rings sinking to the bottom of the sea and an ecstatic little mermaid adding them to her collection.

"Sir Manfred, the Lady of the Crystal Lagoon commends you." She curtseyed. "You have served me well."

Behind her, she heard footsteps, and a shiver of possibility rippled from her shoulders to her toes. She turned.

"Crystal." He broke into a run. "I knew you'd figure it out."

She held out her hands, and he pulled her close—close enough to find her runaway heart in his true-blue eyes. ✎

M.W. DREYGON

I am M.W. Dreygon. I was born on Mars. I grew up at the base of Olympus Mons. I have known only struggle in this life. And every step of the way I looked to the left and right of the trodden path to ask... What if? It is only after tragedy that anyone realizes the need to change. Now I live in the highlands of the Midwest. Above all else, I miss the stillness of my home world. I write stories. It is only in mystery you could see me as I truly am, a human seeking to brighten a world shadowed. Together, we will leave this world to walk among the planes of imagination.

Specimen

M.W. Dreygon

Dr. Mae Wong observed the alien world through a window as it passed below her.

Mae saw an alien planet similar to her own Earth. The dazzling, sapphire jewel shone in the freckled face of the starry cosmos. Green vegetation covered the landmasses, broken up by sporadic mountains and deserts. An elliptical orbit chained the planet-sized marble to a distant star. Together they drifted in the infinite expanse of outer space.

"M391," Dr. Wong muttered. "Just another wet stone with organisms not even worth a name."

She watched from the starship's habitat ring. The PXF Observant orbited M391 approximately every two hours. While the pressurized ring spun around a cigar-shaped, central hub. The constant velocity kept Dr. Wong's feet on the floor.

After a few minutes, the planet rotated out of sight. Without the refracted light, the window became a mirror. Dr. Wong saw an average, human woman with dark hair and fine features. She wore the ship's issued uniform. The gray, one-piece suit covered her fully. But it wasn't as somber as Dr. Wong's eyes. On the windowpane, her pupils blended with outer space, empty and alone. Movement broke the staring contest.

Other researchers traversed the ship's corridors. Most were non-human or xeno. They came in all different shapes, sizes, colors, and classes of beings. Hairless mammals walked beside fanged reptiles. Aquatic eels rode in pressurized suits. Amphibians tried and failed to keep to any mucus off the walls.

"Mae," A familiar voice spoke.

"Hello, Franklin," Mae greeted one of the few human scientists aboard. Dr. Jeron Franklin sported his typical mop of unruly, ginger hair and an easy grin.

"Thought I might find you here," Franklin said.

"No, you didn't."

"Oh? How's that?"

"Because I didn't know I would be here," Mae said with a raised eyebrow.

"Fair enough," He said with a good-natured chuckle. "Even after two years, I still get lost. But even on this huge Ferris Wheel, there are only so many labs you could be in."

"You mean the one I was assigned?" Mae asked icily.

"Yeah, I heard you were passed up for promotion."

"Again, Franklin. I was passed up, again. Me." Mae threw up her arms in disgust.

"To borrow a colloquialism, this isn't Kansas anymore."

"I don't know what that means."

"It means, oh brilliant sage, that you are no longer up against us, mortal humans," Franklin waggled his fingers. "You're in the big leagues now. You're—

We're up against the best the Pan-Xeno Federation could put aboard this hamster wheel. It isn't going to be easy, but we can beat these guys. Hey, Zoid." Franklin waved at a bipedal crustacean. The sentient pink lobster clicked their claw in salutation.

"That's not the problem," Mae countered. "I know my capabilities. But I feel like I finished my doctorate, got a job, and ended up back at elementary school. The director keeps assigning me babysitter research, underneath someone else. How am I supposed to prove myself with that? It's like, it's like I'm an ancient surveyor, mapping hills no one cares about in a century with millimeter accurate GPS."

"Practiced that line a bit?"

"Yeah, some," Mae folded her arms around her middle.

Franklin glanced down at his watch. He read a message on the interface. Then he ran his hand through his floppy locks.

"Well, I got good news," He said looking up.

"What?"

"At least, you'll be in good company for this project." Franklin gestured that Dr. Wong should follow. Then he joined the corridor's foot traffic. Mae groaned deeply before accompanying.

"I've been so frustrated. I haven't even checked the roster. Who is it?"

"First up, is me," Franklin gave a warm smile. Mae returned it with a mild lift of her lip. "Second up, and project leader, is the wonderful Dr. Curax."

"Curax, the Sol-Royten?" Dr. Wong frowned remembering the species. "The same Sol-Royten who destroyed their planet in a war. Who were almost rejected from the PXF?"

"Yeah, and so were humans. But, you guessed it."

"I don't guess." Dr. Wong declared. "I find answers. You know I've read the personnel manifest."

"And the safety manual, the engineering manual, the personal bios, the dissertations, and the emergency instructions for when someone falls into a deep fryer," Franklin trailed off, leaving the question wide open.

"Alright, what's the punchline?"

"Well," Franklin grinned from ear to ear. "You open a liter of ketchup and dig in." Dr. Wong rolled her eyes.

The duo meandered down the hall to their new assignment. They passed several doors for labs and an elevator. The elevator shafts connected the habitat ring to the vessel's bridge and engineering stations. Micro-gravity made life difficult for people living and working in outer space. So the habitat ring included a cafeteria, dorms, offices, and a gym. With a collapsible stage, the cafeteria could be converted to a lecture hall or movie theater. For the latter, artistic taste differed proportionally to the number of different species on board.

"This is it," Dr. Wong pointed at the hatch.

Franklin went by it, not realizing they arrived. He spun about to follow her into the lab. But before she could open the door, someone exited. They were startled for a moment at the unexpected. Dr. Wong stepped back, allowing the stranger to pass.

A Pan-Xeno Federation Marine stepped out. He wore a white suit with blue trim. Coincidently, the marine was a human being. A name tag boldly displayed: McClintock.

"Good day, Sir," McClintock

said with a nod to each. "Ma'am."

"Oh, a fellow human," Franklin said with excitement.

"Uh, yes, sir. I just came aboard last week with the supply run."

"Oh?" Franklin scrutinized Mae. "I thought you kept up with the personnel manifest."

"Yes, I do keep up with the personnel manifest." Dr. Wong glared at Franklin. "I simply didn't expect the PXF to ship a human soldier all the way out here. It seems wasteful."

"I'm a Space Marine." McClintock managed to keep discipline after the unintentional slight. "I'm trained for zero-g combat. But the PXF likes troops aboard animal research vessels in case of poachers or smugglers." He shrugged. "For any loose critters we got a platoon of Rhinos."

"Rhinoceros?" Dr. Wong inquired.

"Hurrins," Franklin said. "With their horns, that species looks vaguely rhino-like. Don't they?"

"Oh." Dr. Wong winced. "Uh, I see." She clasped her hands, nervously.

"So, what were you doing in the lab?" Franklin asked McClintock.

"I dropped off your specimen. She looks incredible. What are y'all thinking of naming her?"

Franklin opened his mouth to say, 'they hadn't seen their subject yet.'

"Hah!" Dr. Wong barked a humorless laugh. "Why name it?" She barged forward. Instinctively, McClintock moved aside. "We dissect the animals after we're done. No point naming it," She said.

The small, familiar lab matched its purpose. Four data processors circled a holographic projector. An emergency medical unit, sized to their specimen, hung on the wall. An airlock separated the kennel from the lab. The laboratory lacked volatile chemicals and subsequent safety equipment. As it only served to monitor the simulator. That sophisticated system enabled the researchers to simulate a host of planetary environments. It also incorporated gas lines for generating different atmospheres and pressures; automated systems handled food and waste.

"Greetings," said a tall figure in a soft, low voice. "Dr. Wong, I presume?"

"Hello," Dr. Wong responded respectfully. Franklin entered a moment later. "I am Dr. Wong, and this is Dr. Franklin. You are Dr. Curax?"

"Indeed, I am me." Curax extended a thoroughly green hand to the scientists.

The chlorophyll in Curax's skin absorbed red and blue light, leaving the surface a very strong color. Its human-like face blended into a pate shaped like a closed, flower bud. Tiny, white hairs danced around its crown from the circulating air. In all other features, the xeno appeared anthropomorphic.

"So, you both came together, excellent." Curax began. "I take it you are well acquainted?"

"We are co-workers," Dr. Wong preempted Franklin. "We studied Xenobiology together on Earth before we earned the opportunity to sail on the Observant."

"Ah, excellent. You both do good work, which is why I got you as a pair."

"Oh, we're not a couple," Dr. Wong defended. "Dr. Franklin is married."

"Yes, I reasoned that out." Curax made a soothing gesture. "And you can dispense with the honorifics in here. I am just a seeker of knowledge, not a bearer of titles."

"Whew, thank you, uh, Curax." Franklin relaxed his posture.

"That will suffice." Curax walked to a station. "We should begin the experiment today. The sooner we start, the sooner we can present."

Dr. Wong settled into a station chair. The sooner she could apply for a promotion the better. Thereafter she could research something important like genetics or terraforming.

"We were assigned the basic behavioral analysis of specimen M391X127," Curax read aloud from the terminal.

"Our purpose is to gauge the potential influence of colonization upon this species. We will ascertain the information using the standard method in three phases. Phase one: control study, how does the animal operate in its natural biome? How does the animal adapt to the different environments of M391? Phase two: urbanization study, how does the subject respond to the same? What level of security can the creature bypass? Phase three: domestication study, can this species be domesticated? And can it be trained as a security risk to a potential colony?" Curax looked up from the screen. "Any questions?"

"Yeah, can we get a look at one-twenty-seven?" Franklin asked. Dr. Wong affected interest even while bored.

"Yes, let me turn on the projector," Curax said. Lights rendered live video of the specimen from the kennel.

"Ah," Dr. Wong involuntarily gasped and leaned forward. Her jaw dropped.

Extraordinary colors captured her attention. The fur started a deep blue around the shoulders then shaded to a bold green towards the hind. The pattern made for excellent camouflage. The deep chest and thin abdomen reminded her of a terrestrial feline. Folded, iridescent webbing softly glittered from the heel up the underside of all four limbs. Two fins along the cheekbones flexed in time with the creature's breathing. A collapsed, cranial fin rested along the cap of the skull. It shaded to an even darker, bulbous tip.

Its head swiveled towards the center of the projection and froze. Mae shifted her inspection towards the eyes, meeting the image's gaze. Round pupils and iridescent irises stared back at her.

"It's beautiful," Mae said unbidden.

"Dr. Wong?" Curax's petals twitched at the outburst.

"I'm sorry, I was just observing all the webbing-" Dr. Wong cleared her throat. "Do you think it's vestigial?"

"It looks reminiscent of avian plumage," Curax suggested. "It might be a social tool for mating or claiming territory. The dermal webbing along the appendages are unusual in a creature this size. But it could be like the Vorucluck."

Dr. Wong silently mused over the theory.

"What's that?" Franklin asked.

"They are a species of mammal. They spread out their web-like skin to catch the thermals. It is not muscle-powered flight, just controlled falling."

"Gliding?" Dr. Wong clarified.

"Gliding, yes, excellent," Curax nodded in appreciation.

Franklin spoke over the data processor. "I've pulled up the initial medical files for the species. No way it could fly. The specimen has way too much mass for that, even in this planet's lower gravity. And that's because...Wow, get a load of this."

"Which part are you looking at?" Curax quickly hopped over the terminal almost bowling Franklin over.

"See. The bones," Franklin widened the x-rays. "Look at the density."

"That does seem very high," Dr. Wong manipulated the screens. "Planetary gravity is 0.87g. Those bones would be right for living on a world with at least 1.5g."

"Go back. Stop," Curax said. "Excellent, the circulatory system. See the heart is larger and so are the arteries."

"And the veins," Franklin jumped in. "There are valves everywhere, not just in the legs."

"So, it can't glide," Dr. Wong said quietly. She glanced back at the projection of the specimen.

"Well, not necessarily. High bone density generally prevents gliding or flight. However, my people have engineered our bodies to unfurl. So we can literally float on the winds." Franklin's jaw dropped open

"I didn't know the Sol-Royten could do that," Dr. Wong confessed.

"We have bio-engineered our original bodies for more versatility," Curax stated.

"Yeah, well I knew that. But I didn't know you could,–" Franklin sputtered coming to terms. "Well, on Earth we have hang gliding, but you need a large kite with a lot of surface area. The frames are typically hollow aluminum. I took the wife hang gliding for a vacation."

"Fascinating," Curax held up a hand to stop the story. "I will make a recommendation for when the subject is assigned to dissection. But we have other work to finish today." The xeno returned to its seat. "Dr. Wong, please assemble the baseline simulation. Franklin, start outlining the series of alternate biomes."

The work consumed the rest of the day, or nine hours to complete the assignment. After a short break, Dr. Wong brought up the camera. On-screen, the creature circled the kennel trying to get comfortable. Such a small behavior moved Mae. Didn't she always search for a place to belong? The creature laid down to groom.

"Dr. Wong, have you seen something of interest?" Curax noted her examination.

"Did, uh, how did it score on the sentience metric?"

"That is a strange question."

Curax's expression soured. "You know this experiment has set requirements. The Kalmarin telepaths and the Oswverelt empaths have already screened for sentience."

"Pity," Mae murmured.

"Already thinking of getting yourself a new pet?" Franklin asked good-naturedly.

"No, the regulations forbid pets on board spaceships. That's how one releases invasive species onto unsuspecting planets," Dr. Wong said brusquely.

"It is also the primary reason why we destroy the specimen after our research is complete," Curax stated levelly. "Life is the most unique phenomenon. It is our inherent responsibility to safeguard it. So that it might reach sentience in time."

"Sorry, Curax. I didn't mean it seriously," Franklin said.

"Excellent." Curax clapped. "Release the subject."

Dr. Wong activated the woodland simulation. The 3D projection realigned to show a vast, alien forest. A door lifted open revealing a worried, wild animal bunched up against the wall. When nothing deadly happened, the creature relaxed. Curious, it sniffed the air; the fins on its face rippled. It walked into the holographic woods then back into the kennel. It sprinted into the trees and back to its corner. Mae giggled at its antics.

"Sorry, the recycled air always seems very...dry," she said faking a series of coughs.

"Really? I notice no change in moisture," the sentient plant said with confidence. They watched the specimen leave the kneel and explore in earnest.

"Good work, Dr. Wong," Curax complimented her. "For the rest of phase one, I am implementing eight-hour watches in the lab, beginning now. I will take the second shift in the morning. You two decide your shifts."

"Oh, yeah." Franklin almost leaped for joy. Curax left on that note. "Damn, Mae. I heard Curax was a lot less draconian than some of the other project leaders. We only have to sit here for eight hours instead of like twelve or twenty-one hours."

"It'll work," Mae said.

"What's wrong?"

"Nothing," Dr. Wong said quickly. She grinned viciously at Franklin. "Because you have first watch." She left the lab while the other human protested comically.

For sixteen hours, Dr. Wong's time was her own. The first order of business, she wrote up a personal schedule. Then she implemented them in order: food, exercise, and hygiene. She ate a flavored meal cube, fried calamari. She imagined each bite was the Observant's director. That cephalopod denied her advancement every time. After dinner, she avoided the common area. She decided to sleep.

Mae climbed into her bunk, fully clothed. Procedure required she always wear the uniform. She would put on a fresh jumpsuit in the morning. Lying down she couldn't sleep. She activated a digital display. She scrolled through the frivolous entertainment options, but she wasn't in the mood. Instead she accessed the ship's library and perused the survey reports on M391.

After reading for two hours, Dr. Wong formulated a theory. The reports made out the alien biosphere to seem boring. Nothing rivaled Earth's exotic behemoths like the whale, bear, and elephant. It lacked the unusual environments of class D planets like rivers of liquid methane teeming with abnormal bacteria. She found a survey entry for a huge, amphibious predator. However, the assignment had gone to someone else.

Mae recognized the name of Dr. Barbra Hunt. The PXF extended her an offer to the Observant several years before Mae. She previously read Doctor Hunt's dissertation. But it wasn't anything worth reading. Just like all the work she had on the ship so far. Perhaps nothing she did aboard would be memorable. Mae dismissed the research options.

Mae opened up her personal folder. Images appeared: Mae playing soccer as a youth; her parents celebrating Mae at her high school graduation; Mae falling asleep during an undergraduate final; her walking proudly across a stage, carrying her doctorate; Mae holding her acceptance for the PXF Observant. She didn't dwell on the reason her mother didn't take the last two photos. And soon the good memories carried Mae off to sleep.

Routine made the next four weeks fly by. The specimen meandered through simulated environments. The original forest turned into a desert, a tundra, and so on. The evidence conveyed that the specimen could survive just about anywhere on M391. Once the data collection ended, the researchers met for phase two.

"I found out something important. I only just confirmed it," Franklin said rushing into the lab. "Our specimen is a boy."

"How is that important?" Dr. Wong squinted at Franklin.

"No, I mean yes. Our specimen is a child."

All three scientists expressed their discontent.

"A juvenile," Curax rumbled. "How did you discern this?" Franklin showed them the file on the growth rate. "This invalidates all of our work. I must inform the director."

"No," Mae barked suddenly. She followed quickly with an argument. "We should finish. Age isn't a significant enough factor. And, and a juvenile might respond more positively to phase two than an adult."

"Why?" Curax waited for an answer. Mae struggled to find a suitable explanation.

"A kid wouldn't have built up a large enough fear response?" Franklin added. "And kids tend to be more curious?"

"Interesting," Curax mused. After a minute, the xeno pursued

its lips. "Our subject is without parents and underdeveloped. And we have no way of measuring that effect for our analysis."

"Please," Mae appealed to Curax. "Let us finish this."

"Very well," Curax acquiesced. "We are well into the program, no need to start over. But there will be a disclaimer in the final report. Agreed?" Both humans agreed. "Excellent, I would like to run phase two with the urban introduction first before adding the maze dynamic."

They briefly discussed phase two. Most of the conversation wrestled with which environments to choose from. They settled on the criteria within an hour. Curax left them to program the simulations. Which only took until the end of Dr. Wong's scheduled watch. She rose to leave.

"Thank you," Mae said to Franklin.

"For what?" Franklin looked up from his console.

"Your help."

"With?"

"Keeping the project going."

"Oh," Franklin sounded surprised. "No problem. I didn't want to start over. That's why you wanted to keep going right?"

"Yeah, that's right."

"You don't sound too sure about that."

"It's just," Mae let the words come out. "When you said he was a kid, I realized that he's an orphan. Like me."

"Oh crap, Mae." Franklin walked over to put a consoling hand on her arm. "I had no idea. Like always?"

"No, no." She withdrew from the physical interaction. "It's been six years. But still-"

"I'm sorry, Mae."

"Don't. It was just a random car accident during a storm." Mae turned. "I should go."

"Wait, Mae. You, uh, aren't becoming attached, are you?"

"What?!" Mae recoiled. "No. Why?"

"You didn't want to stop the experiment. Now the creature gets to live for a couple of months."

"That's not what I meant! Don't put words in my mouth." She spun on her heels and stormed out.

Mae walked around the habitat ring twice to calm down. She let her emotions get the best of her. She shouldn't have just let the experiment end. Mae chided herself inwardly. It would have been an opportunity for a transfer. She could have pestered the director for a leadership role. The long walk settled her nerves. She resolved that she made the right choice. It was still too soon from the last application. This way she could apply with another completed project to my name. Satisfied, she returned to the lab and gave a brief apology to Franklin.

Instead of following her routine, she went to her bunk. Once inside, she closed up the dual-purpose bed and escape pod. She pulled up the live video for the specimen. Normally, Dr. Wong watched him from the lab while she made notes. Mae watched the animal investigate a stack of simulated hay bales. He pushed too hard and the stack collapsed. The falling bundles chased the specimen out of the fields into the forest.

"Ha-ha," Mae cackled. The camera reoriented on the creature quivering next to a tree. "Aww." She fell asleep while watching. The display shutdown automatically.

The first three weeks of phase two practically disappeared. Dr. Wong witnessed the subject meander through a holographic farm. While Mae delighted in the animal bumbling around blithely like a kitten. The creature rooted around in everything: crates, vehicles, and buildings.

In the fourth week, they used the area like a maze. They baited Junior to see just how far he could go. He opened doors, figured out basic locks, and generally entered where he sought to go. Though he couldn't operate a keypad or fingerprint lock.

Week nine started phase three. Mae and Franklin waited inside the lab. Phrase three meant the scientists would attempt to interact directly with the specimen. Mae trembled trying to suppress her anticipation. Franklin ran his fingers through his hair. When Curax entered the laboratory, Mae shot to her feet.

"Doctor Curax," Mae nearly shouted. After a breath, she started over. "Doctor Curax, if possible, I would like to begin the introductions. To the specimen."

"Oh, initiative," Curax relaxed. "Approved. I like volunteers. They deserve all the trouble they receive."

"Thank you, Curax." Mae opened the unused airlock.

She walked into the chamber, stepping into the subject's line of sight. The creature hissed in fear. He backed into the farthest corner of his kennel. He bared small teeth, still sharp enough to tear flesh. The blue-green fur stood out on end while his cranial bulb lifted slightly. Mae approached.

"I got the stun gun," Franklin said from behind Mae. "In case things go poorly."

Mae didn't spare Franklin a glance. Even as the subject yowled at her.

"Dr. Wong, the subject has had enough," Curax called over the speaker.

Mae bent down to one knee. Gingerly, she drew out a ration from her pocket. The wild animal stopped yowling. He recognized the food he had found in the simulator. He tilted his head like he often did when presented something strange. He sniffed deeply; his nostrils wiggled intently. Mae chuckled causing the specimen to retreat.

"Aww, sorry little guy," Mae cooed. "I didn't mean to scare you, boy. Here, eat up." She scooted it forward on the floor before withdrawing.

After a tense minute, the

specimen struck. He snatched the meal like a cat snagging a rat. It was gone in seconds. He groomed his greasy paw.

Mae felted elated at their progress, but she wanted to go further. She pulled another treat from a pocket. The specimen stopped and stared at it longingly. This time, Mae kept the treat in her hand. His face ran through a series of expressions. He tried to puzzle out Mae's intent. Finally, he stepped forward and gripped the food with his mouth.

Their eyes met over the piece of sustenance. The world disappeared; replaced by their connection. Mae saw someone entirely like her. They were both alone in a metal cocoon. Every day they repeated the motions, never knowing why. Mae let go, and the animal ate.

"It's okay, eat it. I got plenty more," Mae urged.

Satisfied, the specimen lay down. Mae hesitantly put her hand on his flank. His body radiated warmth through the soft fur. Mae stroked down and back, down and back. And he let her.

"Good boy, good-" Mae blinked. "Junior, good boy, Junior."

Mae left the kennel to finish the planning session for phase three. It was brief. After that display, Curax suggested Mae perform all experiments for phase three. Wholeheartedly, Mae agreed. Franklin didn't put up a fight. Meeting complete, Franklin left. Curax took over the watch.

"Junior?" Curax inquired before Mae could leave.

"Uh, ah, well I thought," Mae swallowed nervously. "I thought a nickname was easier for reporting rather than M391X127. It's less precise, but I just feel that it's simpler to compose my notes with a 'JR'."

"Hmm." Curax massaged the base of a petal. "I have been using one-twenty-seven, myself. Since we've agreed to a disclaimer, I am not opposed to some personal quirks."

"Oh, okay, good." Mae left the lab with a pep in her step.

Mae returned to the lab each day excited to make progress. Phase three meant taming and conditioning a wild animal for domestication. In practice, it meant tasks like playing fetch and learning to sit. Junior grew accustomed to her presence. Each time the airlock opened, Junior scampered over to the kennel door mewling for a treat. Junior loved playing fetch, he became enthralled with a blue, plastic-toy bone. Except, he often failed to bring it back. With patience, he learned to understand commands, even recognize Mae's name. So they repeated tests from phase two. With direction, Junior overcame obstacles he failed, previously.

For four weeks, Mae connected with Junior. She learned his little signals for hunger or sleepiness. Junior learned her moods. And he intuited when she needed a sloppy lick on the nose. But they couldn't stop time. The project ended.

"I can't believe it's over already," Franklin remarked to Dr. Wong. He sipped from a sphere of Martian beer. "Seems like we just started."

"Yes," Dr. Wong said. She held an untouched white wine. "It does seem like that." She gazed about the converted lecture hall. A host of alien sophonts chitchatted together. Their diverse voices rose and fell like the waves of an ocean. In the back, PXF marines stood at the ready to escort fractious or intoxicated scientists to their quarters.

"Mae," Franklin tried to speak.

"It's Dr. Wong, thank you," she said bitingly. Enough that she felt guilty. Mae started over. "I appreciate your concern. I'm fine. I don't want sympathy. It's been, delightful over the last few months. But I knew, it was going to end just the same."

"Nevertheless, I'm sorry. I wish I could do something. We can't just take random biological samples around the galaxy. Evolution is wonderful, beautiful, but completely, unpredictably dangerous." Franklin opened his mouth to say more.

"I know." Mae stopped him with a pat on the shoulder. She looked past Franklin. He followed her eyes. "That's Dr. Hunt, I believe."

"Oh, yes." Franklin's mood soured.

"Do you know her?"

"I worked under her, my first project aboard the Observant. She is a slave driver. I don't know why the director lets her stay." Franklin wanted to say more. Curax stepped into their small circle.

"Pardon me," Curax bowed slightly. "I hope I am not interrupting?"

"No," Franklin said becoming

cheerful. "Complaining about old stuff."

"Excellent, I wondered, Dr. Wong, if I might have a moment of your time?"

"Oh, of course. I'll just go talk to Zoid, see how the crusty crab is doing." Franklin exited.

"How may I help you, Curax?" Dr. Wong asked once they were alone.

"I wanted to congratulate you on a well-executed project, Dr. Wong." Curax produced a glass of seltzer water. They toasted. Dr. Wong barely sipped hers. "I was particularly impressed with the final reading of your report. It was unexpected." Dr. Wong waited for the alien to continue. "I thought your emotional attachment would interfere. So I read your previous articles as a control. I was quite pleased to see the opposite. For once, you seem invested in what you are writing." Dr. Wong was speechless. She pursed dry lips.

"Thank you," Mae said softly.

"No, thank you." Curax shook its leafy head. "But I have one question." The sophont took a small figurine from a pocket. "Why did you name the specimen, knowing it would die?"

"I," Mae faltered. She swallowed back tears. "I didn't want him to feel alone. And I didn't want to feel alone either. I named him so that he could know he was real. Even if he's just a smart mammal."

"I see." Curax nodded its head. The doctor offered Mae the blue toy. She took it graciously. "I should let you know about two developments. Firstly, the director received my letter of recommendation. I think you are a mature specimen of your species, and thus ready for promotion." Mae's eyelids shot up. "Secondly, specimen one-twenty-seven will remain in the lab until tomorrow morning." Curax leaned closer. "There should be time for one more round of fetch."

"Curax, I don't-"

"FELLOW SCIENTISTS,"

A loudspeaker boomed for attention. On stage, the director, a cephalopod, held a microphone in one of nine appendages. "It is time for the presentations to begin. Can everyone take their seats?" The sea of galactic curiosity settled.

"We present last," Curax reminded her. It wandered over to its seat.

Mae found a chair, but she fidgeted horribly. The researcher next to her cleared their throat, insinuating she should stop. Mae obliged, but she felt so apprehensive. Dr. Barbara Hunt took the stage, presenting her work. Mae couldn't pay attention to her.

Instead, she fiddled with the blue toy. Dwelling on it forced her to confront herself. Dr. Wong wanted to be a famous scientist. She wanted to be remembered forever, instead of forgotten like her parents. Mae wanted the same, but she didn't want to be alone. They-Dr. Mae Wong had to compromise.

Murmurs broke her concentration.

On the stage stood, Dr. Hunt next to a projection. Light rendered a horrendous beast. Below the image read: Specimen M391X013. Dr. Wong remembered the report about the predator. The one she ignored.

Over the furious mutters, the tall human doctor continued, "Specimen thirteen, she has endured some weight loss while adapting to a completely flora-based diet. But after several weeks, she lost her aggression and become more socially capable. I believe that we could eventually eradicate the carnivorous instinct entirely."

"Doctor!" yelled the director. "This is against protocol and in defiance of ethical research. I am appalled!" Tentacles gyrated with fury. Bedlam slowly brewed.

"Carnivore and Omnivore are social constructs built by wolf packs and apes. There's another way. As a demonstration I have brought Thirteen to meet you all," the doctor shouted over the din, flipping her long hair back.

The screen disappeared. A spotlight shone on the stage curtains. Dr. Hunt brushed them back to show the monstrous alien. Dark steel bars cocooned the weakened Thirteen. Panic greeted the prisoner.

Xenos abandoned their seats, moving for the exits. Marines marched to the stage from the rear. Less than a half dozen marines occupied the room, none carrying armor or heavy weapons. Panicked scientists blocked the marines' approach down the aisles.

"Calm down, this is ridiculous!" Dr. Hunt shouted to be heard.

Behind the doctor, a long, wet tongue slathered hungrily. A

great, primal roar froze everyone. All held their collective breath, except one.

"See, there is nothing to fear," Dr. Hunt said opening the cage.

Mae's composure fled.

Specimen thirteen bounded out of the cage. In an instant, the monster plowed into the crowd. Large teeth bit someone in half. Arterial blood sprayed over the bleating audience. Pandemonium broke out.

The stampede bowled Mae over. Someone stepped on her hand. Mae rolled, barely avoiding an elephantine scientist. An arm grabbed her, pulled her up from the ground. She recognized the marine's white uniform, McClintock.

"Run, Dr. Wong!" A mass of warty flesh rushed past her. McClintock screamed in agony.

Mae saw the creature up close. Six feet tall at the shoulder, it towered over her. Gray skin hung loosely over powerful muscles. She smelled the blood on its breath. Curved, symmetrical horns jutted from the brow. One lateral eye flicked back. The beast saw her.

"Thirteen! Thirteen, that's enough of that! You stop right this instance!" Dr. Hunt, her uniform stained with gore, attempted to assert her dominion over reality. The animal seemed to gawk at the scientist. Thirteen jumped the length of the cafeteria, over the disarray to fall upon its former jailer. The resounding crunch broke Mae's paralysis.

Mae sprinted into the corridor. She caught up with others in flight. Their loose herd scrambled to escape the danger. A thunderous crash spurned them on. Mae glanced back.

Thirteen galloped after them. She snatched up the slowest person, and green blood exploded out. Mae's ears filled with screams and pleas. The relentless juggernaut, one by one, ground them to silence. Mae sprinted around a corner; breaking line of sight. She recognized a familiar door.

Mae slammed the controls. The door opened, and she spilled into the lab. She lay there whimpering. Until she heard the telltale canter of Thirteen. She closed her eyes, hoping it was all a bad dream. The sound rose in tempo. Mae thought it was right on top of her. But the noise faded into the distance. Mae relaxed when she was sure.

"Mae?"

Mae jumped at her name.

"Franklin, you scared the crap out of me," she whispered. Mae crawled over next to the frightened man. "What are you doing here?"

"Hiding. You?"

"Same, but then I remembered Junior."

"My god, are you stupid? You came to rescue your little pet?"

"I didn't-"

The door slid open. Both humans flinched. Curax slunk into the lab. And they sighed in relief.

"What do you both think you are doing?"

"Hiding," they said.

"Fools, that-that thing required omega level security. Only the bulkheads are strong enough to impede its progress."

"How is Thirteen so strong?" Mae interjected. "Even after all she suffered?"

"I do not know, but the original survey teams nicknamed her the Devourer. She will kill everything in her territory, then slowly backtrack her way through the corpses."

"Why can't we hide in the simulator?" Franklin offered

"Those walls are rated for holding pressures, not impact damage." Mae ran fingers through her hair. "Crap. The omega breakout procedures."

"Yes," Curax substantiated.

"The what? What's going on?"

"Breakout procedures," Curax explained. "The captain will order up the Hurrins Marines. The ring will go into lockdown. We and the monster will be in micro-gravity."

"But...but we can still hide. We can stay here," Franklin begged.

"No," Mae cried a little. "They'll vent the atmosphere. Only safe place is the dorms."

"Too far, we are practically on the other side," Curax rejected the idea.

"So we need to run? Let's go, right now!" Franklin shouted a little.

"No, that's the direction it just went," Mae said through gritted teeth. "We should go the other way."

"We would just be going back through her territory. The Devourer would catch us."

"So, do you have a plan or not?" Franklin pleaded on his knees. "Please, I don't want to die."

"Pull yourself together, Franklin." Curax slapped the

human with both hands. The alien met Mae's eyes. "We should release a distraction."

"What? What do you mean?" Mae shook her head, but she knew. "What are you suggesting?"

"Tell Junior to run the way of the Devourer," Curax said evenly. "The monster should chase her natural prey more than us."

"No, no, no. That's, that's too much to ask."

"Do you want to live?" Curax asked.

Mae didn't answer.

"Why do you care about that stupid thing?" Franklin spat. "It's just a rat in a cage."

"We're all rats in a cage, or hadn't you noticed?"

Mae let it sink in. A reverberating thump shook the room. As their equilibrium vanished, the trio sailed off the ground. The gravity disappeared. The scientists bounced like ping pong balls. Mae stopped herself by grabbing a terminal. Her stomach swam uncomfortably, her short hair waved freely. Franklin vomited.

"No time to argue. Open the kennel!" Curax ordered.

Franklin tumbled ineptly towards a console. The stench of sick permeated the room. Some clicking later, the airlock hissed open.

Moments later, a curious muzzle sailed into view. Junior tilted his head, intrigued.

"Junior!" Mae called him to her, and Junior obeyed. He deployed his webbing fully, soaring masterfully. The ceiling lights shone on him. With the webbing extended, Junior transmuted into a glittering gliding kaleidoscope of color. He landed gracefully on Mae's chest.

"Oh my," Franklin muttered.

"Incredible," Curax agreed.

"He can fly in micro-gravity. But how? Why?" Mae said what they were thinking.

"No time. We need to wound him so the monster will chase him." Curax accelerated like a missile.

Junior saw the doctor coming. He deftly dodged the green humanoid who hit a wall. Franklin joined the party, but his late arrival spooked Junior. With a thrash of his tail, Junior sailed out of the human's path. Curax ricocheted for another catch. Junior sailed smoothly out the doctor's path. The animal returned to Mae's warm embrace.

"Hold him," Franklin shouted.

"I'm sorry," Mae said. She slapped the hatch controls.

"Wait, no!" Curax hollered.

The hatch released, and Mae threw Junior out. Franklin followed in hot pursuit. Mae attempted to follow, but Curax pulled her back in time. Not a moment too soon. As the Devourer barreled through the corridor.

Her open maw caught Franklin around the middle. The horns punctured his chest. Blood trailed from Franklin's body like a punctured bottle. Red droplets congealed like hanging raindrops.

"Franklin!" Mae scrambled out into the hallway.

"Run!" Curax fled the other way.

Thirteen crashed into the farthest curve of the corridor. And Mae stayed in the doorway.

"What have I done?" Mae wept.

The Devourer turned to the sound of Mae's crying. Thirteen strove to purge her new territory. She pushed off her kill to reach a wall. Using the solid ground, she shot from the surface like a bullet.

Junior climbed into Mae's arms. And she held him tightly to her. The beast grew larger as it drew closer. Mae shut her eyes expecting pain.

Suddenly, bright light pierced her eyelids. Mae peeked to see what changed, and she couldn't believe her eyes. Light emanated from Junior's cranial orb. With each steady pulse, Mae felt her weight return. But someone changed the direction of down. The floor and ceiling of the corridor became its walls. The hallway turned into a giant pit. Mae grabbed the side of the door to stop from tumbling down.

This small critter from M391 summoned gravity into being. Nature created what sentience couldn't command. Acceleration threw down with momentum. Initial momentum submitted, dropping to zero only a foot away from Junior. The Devourer flailed as 1g of acceleration imparted a new momentum in reverse. Thirteen crashed back from where she first come. Junior's glow faded.

Mae floated again as microgravity came back. She stared in wonder at Junior; he lay exhausted in her arms.

"Mae!" Curax said clutching the door frame.

"Curax, did you?"

"I saw. Quickly now, it's still alive." Curax scooped Mae around the waist and jumped. The alien leaped with far greater strength than a human being. In this manner, they traveled through the habitat ring. But an enraged bellow told them their troubles weren't over. Curax stopped.

"Why are you stopping?" Mae demanded.

Curax overrode the control panel. The elevator doors slide open to reveal an empty shaft with only a ladder. "Go, go now." Thousands of feet above, another set of doors opened.

"What about you?"

"No time, she will catch us." Curax whipped his head towards the encroaching noise.

"No, not you too." Mae resisted.

Curax shoved her into the shaft. "Yes, I will hold her off. You must save Junior. He could be the only one of his species. I will not jeopardize the future of all just for myself."

"But-"

"No. Junior could unlock the secret to controlling gravity. With gravity, we can do anything. We can build planets. We can breathe life into barren worlds. We can even fix the ones we broke, like my homeworld. Mae, there will be no problem we can't solve. But you have to get Junior to the central hub. Only the armored bulkheads will protect Junior, and you. Now go."

Mae stopped wasting time. She took hold of a ladder rung and pulled up. Without gravity she flew. Every successive pull added more velocity.

As Mae fled, Curax transformed. The anthropomorphic plant unwound into hundreds of green vines. Its surface area expanded into a large net. Curax settled above the elevator entrance.

When the Devourer jumped into the tunnel, Curax struck. The doctor entangled the creature. The bio-engineered body flexed like an octopus with steel tentacles. The fly-trap strangled the toad-like beast.

For a moment they seemed evenly matched.

Mae looked between her feet to see the contest. She tacked on more speed until the rushing air stung her eyes. She estimated her speed at close to thirty miles per hour. Desperately, she made a plan for breaking. She hoped that it would work.

The massive Devourer bucked in Curax's tight grip. She thrashed against the bindings. Curax held her with all its strength. Until Thirteen bumped into a wall. With a contact point, she set off like a rocket. Thirteen bashed into a wall pulping Curax's organs. The spinal column acted like a pike shaft with the reinforced skull at its top. It penetrated into the Devourer, causing it to wail from the pain, though still alive.

Mae began her breaking maneuver. She reached out to grab a speeding ladder rung. She bashed her hand, making her fingers numb. She tried again and wrenched her shoulder. She screamed out, as the joint socket burned. Squinting through the pain, she registered her speed. She hadn't slowed down enough.

Quickly, she oriented her feet towards the rushing armor-plated deck. The impact caused her legs to buckle. Junior was thrown from her grasp. Mae's world went white with agony.

The Devourer heard Mae's cries. Thirteen focused on her new target, she thirsted for vengeance. She tore away the limp vines of Curax's corpse. But the skull and spine remained embedded in Thirteen's chest. The Devourer accelerated with a roar.

The distant echo brought Mae back. She saw the Devourer hurtling towards her, faster than she believed possible. She attempted to move, but her legs protested. Mae peered down to see the bones sticking out. She wasn't getting away with one arm. Junior nudged her with his muzzle.

"Good, boy." Mae petted his head. She made a choice.

"Here, boy," she wheezed. "You want to play? Fetch." Mae lobbed Junior's favorite blue toy deeper into the command deck. She hoped the Hurrins would find him before the Devourer.

Instead, Junior watched the toy disappear. He chose not to follow.

"Junior? Junior, go get the toy. Go, boy, run, hide, live!" The tears bubbled up from Mae's eyes.

Junior's gaze settled on Mae's face. He blinked once. His round eyes looked so human, so understanding. With a hard shove, he pushed Mae away. She sailed out of the Devourer's path. Junior chose to protect Mae.

"Chase the toy, Junior. Leave, leave me!" Mae begged for Junior to obey.

Junior hovered in the open elevator shaft. He feebly hissed at the plummeting demon. His challenge sounded like a mouse's squeak. The Devourer accepted with a lion's yowl.

Junior extended his cranial fin again. The bulbous tip sputtered with a mild glow. Drained from before, he couldn't make a wide field. Defiant, he lengthened the field out to the target. Relentless, Junior commanded gravity. And gravity obeyed. In their first meeting, Junior had pushed the Devourer. This time, Junior pulled.

Thirteen's velocity increased exponentially. She realized the tactic a split second too late. She grabbed for a rung. Her foot tore off, and she went into a tailspin.

The Devourer plunged into the armored bulkhead warping the deck; her spine broke with a loud crack. Curax's final gift, a living spear, thrust deeper into the heart. Thirteen twitched twice and died.

Everything went still; it was over. Mae cleared the tears out of her eyes. Her injuries complained, but she ignored it. She saw Junior drifting in the micro-gravity. Mae's eyes widened in horror.

"Junior? No, Junior?"

Mae grasped him gently, bringing the furry body into a tender embrace. He tried to breathe; his eyes struggled with heavy lids. His heart drummed slower and slower. No great, pronounced gong signaled the end. The thrum listed into silence. Mae broke down.

* * *

Dr. Mae Wong stood on the surface of M391. Two years had changed her. She carried herself as someone more. She had needed all her fortitude to withstand the inquiries and trials. The Pan-Xeno Federation failed to appreciate losing so many people to foolish errors. However, they exonerated Mae. They offered her compensation for damages, but she asked for only one thing.

On her tablet, Mae accessed the drone footage. The original survey missed the gravitas angelus lounging in trees. Where their fur rendered the species, practically, invisible. Only the inexperienced youngsters thrashed playfully on the forest floor for all to see. Mae pulled up a video: an adult angelus falling up a self-made gravity well into the canopy; their young clinging to their parent's backs. Mae chuckled at the juvenile angelus watching Mae's drone.

"Dr. Wong?" McClintock approached cautiously. "Are you ready to return to base?"

"I told you, John, it's Mae." She said with a warm smile. "And do I have to?"

"No." McClintock scratched a bug bite with his prosthetic hand. "But I was wondering-"

"What?"

"Why? Why did you give up traveling the stars to live on this dirtball?"

"It isn't a dirtball," Mae corrected jovially. "It's a foundation for you, for me, for Junior's species, for everyone." ✎

"Blue Moon" photo Kēvin Callahan

Design

The Art Director on this book was Kēvin Callahan. Kēvin has won numerous awards for his publication designs as well as an award-winning writer, painter, photographer, poet, and sculptor. His writings include one self-published novel, *Morris' Code*, two anthologies of non-fiction short stories, *A Prairie Wind Blowing Through My Head*, a collection of stories about his youth on an Iowa farm, and *A Day Remembered*, stories of his years in the field pursuing upland game. His fictional *Chinese Checkers Run*, is an exciting adventure story of flight and pursuit. All available on Kindle. His most recent book *ROAD MAP- Poems, Paintings & Stuff* is available through Flying Ketchup Press in print and Ebook.

Callahan earned a BFA from Drake University in Des Moines, IA. Kēvin currently works and resides with his wife in Parkville, MO and both of his sons are accomplished artists.

For more info contact the designer at kevin@bsfgadv.com

About the Typeface

The typeface Kēvin choose for this book is the family Cheltenham. Cheltenham was designed in 1896 by architect Bertram Goodhue. Over the years Cheltenham's primary purpose as a text face morphed into one of the most popular "display" faces. As a publication designer, "Chelt" was Kēvin's go-to choice in magazine design for beauty, readability, and consistency. ✎

Illustrator

HAYLEY PATTERSON received her BA in Animation and Illustration from SUNY Fredonia 2018 and worked as a staff illustrator for the university newspaper. Her work has been featured in galleries in Suffolk County and Long Island, NY as well as the MoCCA Arts Festival in New York City, hosted by the Society of Illustrators. To keep up with her, you can follow her on Instagram@hapdoods.www.doodleaddicts.com/hapatterson/faves/

Editor

POLLY ALICE MCCANN founder and Managing Editor Flying Ketchup Press where she "curates" galleries of talent inside small sharable packages. She says her favorite thing is to tell stories–other people's, her own– maybe yours. Polly won the 2014 Ernest Hartmann award from the International Association for the Study of Dreams from Berkley CA for her research on self-awareness for writers and artists through dreamwork. Her meditative symbolist art has been published in US newspapers and magazines and is showing internationally. Her Studio is located at DesignWerx in North Kansas City. Visit her at pollymccann.com

MORE BOOKS BY FLYING KETCHUP PRESS

Tales from the Dream Zone 2019

Tales from the Deep– Our 2020 Short Story Winners

Poetry on the Very Edge: Al Extremo Borde/Le Bord Etroit

*The Right Accessory for Murder–*Melody Shore Mysteries by Carole Lynn Jones

Audacity: The March to Women's Rights– illustrated by Gloria Heifner

Flying Ketchup Press "A Kansas City Publisher for the epic acceleration of great literature, poetry, children's books and fine arts materials. Our mission: to discover and develop new voices in poetry, drama, fiction and non-fiction with a special emphasis in new short stories. We are a publisher made by and for creatives in the Heartland. Our dream is to salvage lost treasure troves of written and illustrated work- to create worlds of wonder and delight; to share stories. Maybe yours."

Made in the USA
Columbia, SC
22 December 2019

85674019R00130